Smile of Deceit

Keith Newman

London | New York

Published by Clink Street Publishing 2020

Copyright © 2020

First edition.

ISBN:
978-1-913568-17-7 - paperback
978-1-913568-18-4 - ebook

To my wife, Doreen,
without whose help this book
would never have been written

My grateful thanks to:
Jez Graves for his technical advice,
support and helpful range of comments.
David Arnold who provided helpful feedback
on my first draft.

Chapter 1

Philip Cassidy was certain he wouldn't be late but he knew it would be a near thing. He had agreed to meet Donald on his way to Gatwick and the diversion had taken him longer than expected. All he needed was the address in France for him to pick up the package, but Donald was reluctant to have any sort of conversation about that on the phone. It was now 7 am exactly, he had his instructions, and the APH coach was close to the South Terminal drop-off point. It didn't take him long to reach the departure lounge and from that point on everything went smoothly. He felt relaxed, confident and looking forward to a few days away.

The EasyJet flight was on time, the landing good and the passage through passport control went smoothly. Even the usual problems at the car hire desk were minimal by their standards and Philip was soon being shuttled to the area where he picked up the car and then on his way – heading for France.

He turned sharp left at the first main crossroads and then filtered into the right-hand lane, moving smoothly ahead and taking the slip road to the right. He was soon on the approach to the A40 and making towards the tunnels just ahead. He began filtering through the Swiss border control point when he saw two young women obviously thumbing a lift as he was moving slowly through the crossover sections. He thought he recognised them from his flight, but wasn't sure. "You going my way?" he called out across the passenger seat.

"Depends where you're going mate," the blonde one called back.

"Meribel," he replied.

"Yes, that's great – we're off to Annecy."

They were close by now and the blonde one had her hand on the passenger door handle. "Jump in quick then." They settled in quickly and he pulled away to keep up with the slow-moving traffic.

"Just arrived," Philip said, turning his head just a little towards the blonde one in the front with him. "Yes – the early Manchester flight – it's Tracy and Pippa by the way."

"Philip" he responded.

There was small talk and then they all fell quiet for a while. Philip had glanced across at Tracy from time to time noticing the generous swell of her breasts and the high cut hemline of the shorts she was wearing. She had nice legs he thought and her knees kept moving apart in rhythm with the movement of the car. "Another time perhaps," he thought to himself, he might have acted differently but now he was happy to keep his mind and his eyes mainly on the road ahead. He dropped them just past Annecy, by a campsite next to the lake and they thanked him profusely. The traffic was remarkably quiet for a change and very soon he had skirted the lake and was approaching Albertville. He reached the end of the dual carriageway just before the roundabout on the outskirts of the town and then took the second exit avoiding the town centre. The traffic began to build as he approached the western end of the town and most of the traffic was coming away from the centre and heading towards Moûtiers. Philip was heading in the opposite direction to the address he had been given, a route he had followed once before. He turned back towards the town centre and then first left up a steep slope, past a children's playground and a few boarded-up shops. The area had the look and feel of decay, peeling paintwork, crumbling plaster and rubbish up and down the road. There were only a few people about, most of whom seemed to be wandering about aimlessly. It wasn't long before Philip reached his destination. He parked outside one of the few shops that seemed to be open and made his way quickly inside. The man behind the counter looked at him suspiciously. "Do you have any old cassette tapes?" Philip asked in English, repeating the words Donald had instructed.

"Probably got some out back," came the reply.

"I came in two months ago. Do you remember?"

"Of course. And we were very pleased to do business."

"I'm just collecting this time. Everything has been arranged, I'm told."

"Come through. We can talk out the back."

The man gestured to Philip to follow him behind the counter. A young man appeared from a side door and there was a brief exchange in French between them. Philip could speak a little French but he wasn't able to understand what had been said. He assumed that the young man would be minding the shop for a while.

"Just a collection then," the man said as soon as they were in the back room and before Philip had adjusted his eyes to the gloomy interior of a small room.

"Yes, been asked to pick up a package for a friend."

"That would be Mr Denman, wouldn't it?"

"Yes, Denman. Have you got a package for him?"

The man did not reply at once but instead he turned and moved towards the back of the room and Philip began to follow.

"No, no. You stay there," the man said emphatically.

Philip blinked a few times as the man disappeared into the gloom and out of the back door. Philip waited patiently and the darkness around him seemed to close in and made him shudder slightly, partly because it was cold but also because he was apprehensive. Time seemed to stand still and the oppressiveness of the room to grow in intensity with each passing second. He had agreed to collect and deliver packages from various addresses in this part of France partly because he passed this way from time to time when he went skiing but he was never happy about it. He was aware of the contents of the packages but had no idea what happened to them in France.

Philip took the chair lift to the top of Altiport for his first run just to get his ski legs going. Only a few people were waiting and he soon took his place beside a very pretty teenager as the chairlift swept them up and started the short journey to the top of the nursery slope. When they had settled, skis dangling loosely in front of them the girl turned her head towards him slightly but she didn't say anything and Philip wasn't in the mood then to make conversation.

The afternoon went by in a flash. A mixture of fairly sedate skiing interspersed with delightful refreshment breaks – hot chocolate and fresh raspberry tarts proved the perfect choice on a warm and sunny afternoon. He didn't see the girl from the ski lift again but he had kept an eye out for her, remembering that she wore a lovely combination of grey and pink which was quite distinctive. Philip looked at his watch and was surprised to see that it showed a few minutes before 4 pm. He knew from experience that he should soon make his way back. The snow was beginning to turn slushy and the crowds would soon make it difficult to negotiate some of the narrow stretches towards the lower part of the ski area. There was a short steep section just ahead and Philip took the turn and gathered speed.

He plotted his route back to Rond Point in his head and started to move onto the stages that led him in that direction. From time to time he looked up into the clear blue sky – the depth of colour seemed unreal, almost merging into black and the brightness of the sun enhanced the whole effect. He decided to be lazy and took a taxi back to his hotel and as he sat watching the scenery slip by all he thought about was a pleasant evening ahead and how he could enjoy himself. Now the parcel had been collected and hidden safely he could relax and that's what he intended to do over the next few days; relax and just think about himself.

Chapter 2

Ingrid Peterson had just returned to Police Headquarters in Méribel when the first call came through from Mrs Dawson. "Keep me informed," Ingrid said as the duty officer told her that Amanda Dawson had been reported missing by her mother. The time was 8 pm exactly.

The second call came through at 8.30 pm just as Ingrid was leaving on one of her regular patrols. "I'm just going to the town centre anyway," she called back. "Tell her I will meet her in the square by the steps to the lift pass office. I'll only be five minutes or so."

It was just a short journey into town and Ingrid drove with her usual care and attention. She thought she had detected a hint of sarcasm from the duty officer as if to demonstrate that he felt it was probably a waste of time. 'Probably is' Ingrid thought but nonetheless she had nothing better to do and the parents were obviously worried.

Mrs Dawson stood out a mile as Ingrid approached the town square. She was standing by the steps in front of the café looking all around her and moving her weight from one foot to the other as if she found it impossible to stand still. Her right hand clasped her forehead in a gesture of despair and she spun round looking directly at an unaccompanied young woman approaching but almost immediately exhaled sharply and dropped her chin towards her chest when she did not recognise her. Then she saw Ingrid and rushed over to her. Words were falling from her mouth in Ingrid's direction but they made little sense.

"Calm down, calm down," Ingrid said and she put a hand on Mrs Dawson's shoulder seeking to emphasise her words. "Just take a few deep breaths. I can't help you like this."

Mrs Dawson took a deep breath as if it was her last and then bit the knuckle of her left hand so hard that her index finger soon began to turn white. But it did seem to calm her a little.

"That's better," Ingrid said and she removed her hand from Mrs Dawson's shoulder, but remained standing close to her. "When you are ready just answer my questions. We need to take one step at a time."

"I can't get hold of him."

Ingrid wasn't sure what she meant. "Get hold of who?"

"My husband Frank. I'm all alone here, it just makes it worse. I've tried ringing his mobile but he switches it off when he's driving. Oh, it's all such a mess."

"It will be ok I'm sure. Where is he?"

"He's driving back to Calais. He left about six."

"We can try him later, leave a message. He will probably pick it up when he stops for a break."

Mrs Dawson looked at Ingrid and nodded a few times. She was calmer now and Ingrid decided to press on. "When did you last see Amanda?"

"Went skiing with her just after lunch, until about…" Mrs Dawson paused for a while looking into the distance but not focussing on anything in particular. "Until about 3-ish," she said nodding to herself as if to confirm that she had remembered the time accurately. "Amanda met up with some friends and my husband and I went back to the Orion Hotel and then down the hill to Brides-les-Bains for an hour or so."

"And had you arranged to meet up with Amanda later?"

"Yes, I said I would meet her in the Refuge for a pizza, just down the road there, at 7 pm. I've tried phoning her loads of times – always get straight through to an answerphone, that's not like her."

"What about those friends of her. What have they told you?"

"I haven't been able to find them either. I don't really know them. It was Amanda who saw them and told us they were friends of hers."

A small crowd had gathered round them and there was a bit of pushing and shoving. "Like to get you in handcuffs," one young man called out in Ingrid's direction.

"You'd be too pissed to do anything about it," one of his friends added as he pushed him in the back and the pair of them fell onto the pavement at Ingrid's feet.

"If you're not careful you will be the ones to end up in handcuffs," Ingrid said and she started to usher people away, but soon realised it was an impossible task. Alcohol and high spirits got in the way of sensible actions and the crowd around them grew larger and more vocal.

"Get in the car," Ingrid said and Mrs Dawson who was by now just as keen as Ingrid to move to a quieter area responded immediately. Both of them were soon sitting in the car and Ingrid pulled away from the kerb carefully and moved off down the hill. Ingrid paused at the junction ahead. She turned sharp left, almost turning back on herself, and then down the hill towards the swimming pool and ice rink where she found a parking spot. "Come on," she called over her shoulder, "we can find a place to sit and talk quietly."

Mrs Dawson explained carefully all that she had done in her search for Amanda. She had not been very successful. She had established that Amanda had returned to the Orion Hotel, at least the receptionist had told her that she had seen her about 5.30 pm. But that was the only time that anyone had any recollection of seeing her. Ingrid made careful notes as Mrs Dawson explained everything. When she looked at her watch it told her that it was 9.10 pm and she knew that the Commander would not authorise a 'missing person' category at such an early stage. Ingrid offered to give Mrs Dawson a lift up to the Orion Hotel and she was surprised that she accepted, not just because it was only a ten-minute walk back into town but also because she expected that she would want to continue her own search.

When they arrived Mrs Dawson said that she would go up to her room which had an adjoining door to Room 214, the room Amanda had occupied and have a good look around. This gave Ingrid the opportunity to talk with Chantelle Pemberton, the receptionist, and very soon Chantelle was chatting away and Ingrid was making a note as fast as she could. Chantelle was either a very observant person or a busy-body wanting to know everyone's business. Or perhaps it was just that she got very bored when there wasn't much to do. In any case she certainly knew about all the comings and goings. At long last Ingrid put down her notepad where she had recorded some very interesting details about Amanda and another guest, Philip Cassidy.

At about the same time Mrs Dawson appeared as if from nowhere. "Didn't find anything that might help," she said as she approached. It was now 9.40 pm.

About 15 minutes later Ingrid was back at Headquarters and in conference with Commander Patrick Bouchard, her boss. "Ok then," he said, "tell me about this bloke, Philip Cassidy."

Ingrid paused for a moment seeking to decide exactly where to start. Chantelle had given her so much information, some of it more relevant than others, but all muddled up and somewhat confusing. In the end she decided to ignore Patrick's specific request. She took a deep breath, tapped on the desk in front of her with the palm of her hand a few times as if to attract his attention and then began. "Amanda Dawson and Philip Cassidy were seen together at least a couple of times on Tuesday evening, the same day they arrived. Chantelle wasn't sure whether they knew each other before arriving at the hotel but she thought not. They went swimming together in the hotel pool apparently. And then earlier today she saw them together just after breakfast. She said she spotted them having a quiet word together as if they were having some sort of secret conversation. She described this Philip Cassidy as a man with his tongue hanging out."

"Just keep it factual," Patrick said pointing his pen towards Ingrid as if to emphasise his point.

"OK, but it's just what she said, and, you know it does help paint a picture. Anyway she told me lots of interesting stuff about today – facts that is," Ingrid added with just a hint of sarcasm. "Right, I need to get this straight and in chronological order – it was a bit jumbled when Chantelle spoke to me."

"Yes – keep it simple. You know what I'm like. Start at the beginning and take me through it stage by stage."

"Ok then, simple it is. Mr and Mrs Dawson came back to the hotel briefly at about 3 pm and went out again soon after that. Chantelle said that she didn't see Mr Dawson again but Mrs Dawson spoke to her later, made a point of it apparently."

"And what did she say?"

"General chitchat but she also mentioned that Mr Dawson, Frank that is, had just left and was driving back to Calais that evening."

"What time was that?"

"About 6.15 or just before."

"What about…" Patrick began as his mind began to run through options, "… what about if the daughter wants to go home for some reason and right now she is travelling back with her dad all safe and well."

"Unlikely I'd say – bit of a long shot. It's not as if there was any sort of family argument or anything. Mum would know, I'm sure."

"Doesn't take much – teenage girls and all that. Can be a bit unpredictable."

"I'm not convinced, doesn't add up for me. But keep it on the list as an option if you like."

"What else did Chantelle have to say? Does any of that tie in at all timewise."

"Yes, it would fit I suppose. Chantelle says that Amanda came back late afternoon and went up to her room. She wasn't sure if the Dawsons were back by then but she thought they probably were."

"And this guy Philip Cassidy. Did she see him as well?"

"She wasn't sure about him. She says she saw him earlier, about 4-ish – he went out for a walk apparently but she wasn't sure when he came back. She was in and out, so wasn't on the desk all the time."

"Didn't miss much though!"

"No, definitely a bit of a nosy parker – lucky for us!"

"So let's assume that they are all back in the hotel by… what 5.30 or just before," Patrick paused again, eyes darting from side to side as if deep in thought. Ingrid could see the pulse in his temple ticking rhythmically. He took in a sniff of air and blew it out though his mouth as if exhaling smoke from a fine cigar. "And then by 6 pm three of them have vanished."

"That's about it, but there's more. The odd thing is there was an envelope left at reception with cash and a note. Cassidy checked out early, he wasn't due to leave until the day after tomorrow – Friday. Bill paid in full and you know what, they checked his room and everything gone – all left neat and tidy."

"Right, that's it – you've convinced me. Get the word out, all the piste bashers on the lookout. All patrols notified and you can have four to do the foot patrol – you choose them but make it quick. I'll check out the Orion – report back in one hour – no later you understand."

"Wow, that's what I call decision making."

"You know me, don't let grass grow under my feet."

"We need to follow up on Philip Cassidy, find out more about him," Ingrid said as she turned to go. She paused just before opening the door and looked back in Patrick's direction. "Do you want me to do that, or will you?"

Patrick thought for a while. He knew that Ingrid was on duty until the early hours of the morning and would have more time. "Could you?" he said. "I'll be off duty before you."

"No problem."

Ingrid made her exit before Patrick could allocate any more tasks. She already had a copy of Philip Cassidy's passport kindly provided by Chantelle plus his home address. She decided to do a quick email to the Broughton Police HQ straight away and very soon that task was completed. It was 10.21 pm French time on Wednesday 16 March when the email was despatched.

Chapter 3

Peter Lord was not in a good mood. He had slept badly and woke frequently throughout the night. He got up early and when he drew the curtains the dark clouds that greeted him were chasing across the sky and joining in clusters on the hill just a few hundred yards away adding to the gloom all around him. None of these things were the main cause of his mood, however, but they didn't help in any way. He had quarrelled with his wife the night before about all the usual things, just about holding on to his temper, but this wasn't the main reason for his mood either. It was a simple matter of the date. The day every year when it all came back to him, every last detail, every regret both personal and professional and he could never decide which of these two levels caused him the most pain. It wasn't just on this day of the year, this usually cold, dark, gloomy day in mid-March, because the feelings of failure and regret never really left him completely. But this was the anniversary and that brought with it a special sort of pain rising from the pit of his stomach and chasing through him, leaving behind an emptiness which often stayed with him long after the day had passed. It was the 17 March and the name Philip Cassidy was never far away on this of all days. He decided to leave for work early and after taking just a few sips of the tea he had made for himself he called out goodbye to his wife Kim.

"Have a nice day," his wife had called back to him. "I will see you about six." She didn't expect him either to have a good day or be home by six but she said it anyway.

Peter didn't say anything in response but simply walked somewhat stiffly out of the house closing the door quietly behind him. It seemed almost like ending a chapter in his life, but he had that feeling on so many mornings that he was used to it by now. Peter Lord started his car and when the road was clear moved away, taking his place in the slow-moving line of traffic. It would take him about 40 minutes to reach the police station and he knew that, as usual, he would be irritable when he got there. The journey seemed to get more difficult every day. All he was really looking forward to now was retirement and it couldn't come quickly enough. This thought lifted his mood just a little, but what he didn't know was that this would be no ordinary day to be ticked off on route to his pension. Peter was an old-fashioned copper if there was such a thing these days and was proud of it but he was now just marking time. He had risen to the rank of sergeant and that was good enough for him right now and had in fact been good enough for the past 16 years.

When he arrived at the police station the first thing he saw when he sat down at his desk was a card and gift box for one of his colleagues who was due to retire before him. Peter dealt with the card and gift box then pushed them to one side together with a huge sigh. That sigh was followed by another as he started the task of going through the emails he had received. Then there was silence, a long period of silence as the information he had just read hit the back of his brain and ricocheted in all directions within it, and he couldn't help calling out "Eureka."

"What's up?" one of his colleagues sitting nearby called out.

"That name at last – Philip Cassidy – it's been so long. I knew, I just knew it would turn up again one day." He sat almost in a daze as the visions from the past jumped erratically across his mind. Some were clearer than others, some were real and some imagined and it was often the ones his own mind created that were the ones he feared the most. He shook his head from side to side trying to erase the images and he was partly successful. He wanted to concentrate, to be focussed and not to be dragged down by his personal demons. He had often wondered if he would ever have the chance to look at all the evidence afresh, to sift through all the details, taking everything apart and putting it back together again and now there was a chance, perhaps just a glimmer but at least a lever of sorts. He had spoken to his DI a few times over the years about just that possibility and had always got the same answer. When Helen Grant disappeared 16 years ago it had eventually, after much anguish and with regret on everyone's part, been put down as a missing person and as such was not subject to periodic review in the way in which major crimes would be scrutinised on a regular basis. There was no real evidence of abduction, injury or a struggle even. All they really had was Helen's nearly new brown coat discarded in a remote area of the park and a disappearance which everyone said could definitely not be explained by any rational analysis. It was out of character, unplanned and it left behind an absolute mess. There was no blood on the coat, it wasn't ripped or dirty even and the only DNA they could find belonged to family members plus her own.

Peter knew that he just had to do something but he wasn't sure what, or how he could explain his actions. The email that had started it all off was from the police in Méribel and it notified them that a 15-year-old girl had been reported missing in the ski resort and that they were keen to interview Philip Cassidy in connection with her disappearance, but that he had disappeared as well.

Peter needed time to decide what to do but his mind was in too much of a jumble to make any rational plans. He was scheduled to take statements from two witnesses that morning and in a flash he decided to leave early and get them out of the way as quickly as possible. His pulse was racing and he knew he needed to settle down. He took a few deep breaths through his nose and let the air out slowly through his mouth with his eyes held tightly closed.

He relaxed slightly, his pulse rate lowered a fraction, and he felt more in control.

Peter was sure he knew more about Philip Cassidy than any of his colleagues. He had met Philip's father, Spencer, a few months before Helen disappeared and they had spoken a few times about their respective families, just the normal chit chat, but at least some background information, so he had a head start when Philip Cassidy's name came up when the initial investigation began.

Although his mind was partly elsewhere, he went through the motions that morning. He left the station promptly after reading the email knowing that he needed to keep focussed on his schedule. He arrived at the witnesses' address promptly, took the statements perhaps more carefully than usual, said all the right things and appeared to be the perfect professional. But all he was really interested in was the chance to gain some time so that he could sit and think and he wanted to do that in the park where it all happened.

He wanted to refresh his memory again and to do that properly he knew he needed to be close to the area where Helen disappeared, to take in the sights and sounds of the place where it happened and just allow his mind to lead him in different directions. He had done this so many times when he and Jim Packer were investigating, looking for signs, hoping for inspiration. Occasionally over the following months he had visited the scene alone but it had only made him feel useless and frustrated.

He had been close to Jim, very close, and he trusted him. They had worked together, got drunk together and had walked through the park side-by-side so many times in a vain attempt to make some sense of it all, but their shared endeavours had come up with absolutely nothing. Jim Packer had moved away from the area a few months after Helen went missing and they had spent a pleasant evening together the night before he left and then they had lost touch. Now Peter wished he could rekindle their lost friendship, perhaps just for a fleeting moment or two, so that he could share the latest information and work on a way forward together.

The short journey by car had passed without him really noticing. He switched off the engine, took his warm coat from the back seat and stepped out on the relatively dry ground in the car park. It had stopped raining but he knew the ground would be wet and soggy. He went to the boot of his car taking out his wellingtons and gloves. Within a matter of minutes, he was striding towards the little cottage standing alone, just off the main road on the outskirts of Broughton. He wanted to start at the beginning and he was sure that Lilac Cottage was the starting point for events that evening in March 2003. He took the circular route partly in woodland and partly in open ground. He walked past the main car park to his left and he could just about see the millpond nearby tucked away in a more secluded area. He needed to keep a clear head and not be disturbed by the personal demons which the scene rekindled. He shook his head as if to clear the memory and picked up his pace leaving the scene but not his memories behind. He checked his watch – it had taken 25 minutes to reach the Parkside Pub and he sat for a short while in the summerhouse. He knew there was a shortcut running north to south and he took that route back to his car. That path had been relatively clear in 2003 but not as well used as the circular path. He noticed that some of the larger trees had fallen. The grass was long and wet in places and bramble, bracken and sycamore trees had taken hold in areas where large canopies previously kept the ground relatively clear of any significant growth.

The sun was beginning to twinkle between some of the branches. Every 50 yards or so he stopped and looked around taking in sights and sounds around him. He thought he heard blackbirds singing in the trees above him but he wasn't sure that he could identify the species correctly and he wondered if Helen had heard the same songs the night she disappeared.

Nothing much caught his eye on the remainder of his journey back to his car. He didn't pass anyone and he was left with just his own memories. He had prepared a summary of the investigation for his DI at the end of the second day and he recalled that information now. The names of possible suspects jumped at him haphazardly and he began to feel swamped by the confusion of all the details. Then he just thought about the one simple truth of it all because he knew he needed to start at the most basic level. The fact of the matter was that five teenagers had agreed to meet at the summerhouse behind the Parkside Pub on 17 March 2003 and by 7.45 four of them, including Philip Cassidy, had arrived. Helen Grant was expected but she never turned up and as far as anyone knew she had never been seen alive again.

Chapter 4

When Peter got back to the office he waited patiently but the time ticked away slowly. He had completed his work schedules for the afternoon taking great care to do everything by the book. He didn't want his DI to be able to criticise him in any way about being distracted by the news from France, because he knew that George Baker would immediately have that in mind. There were likely to be enough obstacles in the way without creating any more unnecessarily. The clock on the wall seemed to stand still at times but he couldn't resist glancing up at it more frequently than was reasonable and he did so again now, waiting for the minute hand to click forward to the next notch. He was on the fourth cup of coffee from the machine down the corridor and he felt a bit nauseous. He was on tenterhooks and couldn't concentrate properly. The email he had sent in response to the communication from the police in Méribel had said that he would appreciate being kept informed of developments and offering any assistance they required. He knew that he needed to speak to George Baker, his DI, before providing any more information and by then he hoped to have received more details. Now all he could do was to wait and that was proving to be difficult for him. There were two parts to his anxieties, one of which was more personal, and he fought an inward battle to push that part aside. It was only his absolute conviction that it had no bearing on the case which assisted that resolve, but it still remained, nagging away, like a persistent itch. He found himself gazing up at the small windows outside taking in the angles of the building opposite, and he wondered where Philip Cassidy was at this time and what he was looking at. Nothing could be further from his own gloomy outlook lit now by amber neon lights but still taking on shades of grey, dark shadows and bleakness. He hated this time of year and he hated himself.

The ringing of the telephone startled him and he picked up the handset quickly. "Hello," he said, "DS Lord."

"Good afternoon Sergeant, it's Ingrid Peterson here – thanks for your email and for your offer of assistance."

"That's ok. Is there any further news yet?"

"Not really. We've just finished our briefing and we're due to meet again later this evening. I just thought I'd telephone to let you know that we may not have any further information for you until later tonight. I'm working now until midnight and I will send a summary of our conclusions before I go off duty and of course clarify what assistance we might require."

"I'm sure we will help in any way we can. What have you got in mind?"

"Can't say for sure yet, but probably anything you might have on Philip Cassidy. He's still missing as far as we know and his disappearance looks suspicious. Then of course the missing girl's family – that's Janet and Frank Dawson. I don't know if it's just me but something about them seems odd, can't put my finger on it exactly. They live in Gravesend, and Frank's on his way home at the moment. He doesn't know about his daughter yet because as far as we understand his wife can't get him on the phone, but I'm sure she will speak with him soon and then of course he might need a contact your end."

On the surface they were having a straightforward conversation, albeit with Ingrid doing most of the talking and Peter making the right noises in response from time to time. But below that superficial level their minds were focussing in two different directions and Peter's thoughts were never far away from a conviction that Helen had been taken, used and then discarded. Even in the very beginning he could never convince himself that they would find her safe and well, but that was what Ingrid hoped for and expected in her search for Amanda Dawson. By the time their conversation was coming to an end Ingrid had outlined everything she knew about Amanda's disappearance. She had a checklist in her mind of all the key points she needed to explain and she had come to the end of that now. She paused slightly and a question began to form in her mind. She wasn't sure, but she thought she could sense some sort of hesitancy in Peter's responses as if he was holding something back but wanting to say something. Peter had, in fact, been on the point a number of times when he almost started to tell her about Helen Grant's disappearance and Ingrid had picked up on that. Then she made up her mind. "Is there anything you can tell us now about Philip Cassidy?" she asked. "Any police intelligence that might be relevant. I understand your child protection procedures allow that sort of information to be shared."

The question raised Peter's blood pressure a notch or two and his first words in response got caught in the back of his throat momentarily. "There, there is something. We do have some information that we need to share with you. All I can say now is that his name has come up before in similar circumstances. We will share the details about that with you, but I need to get authorisation from my DI before I can say any more. I hope you understand."

"Understand, perhaps, but a bit disappointed. How soon will you get back to us?"

"First thing tomorrow I'm sure. I'll keep on top of it this end." Peter was aware of some of the regulations relating to the sharing of information between European countries, but it was complicated and he wasn't confident enough about the details to make the decision himself. He knew that one slip, one small error in following procedures could create difficulties later on and he was determined to avoid that. He was expecting further protest from Ingrid but all he heard in response was one small sniff of frustration and she didn't seek to hide it in any way. "I know how you feel," he said, "and I promise I won't let you down."

Ingrid thought for a short while. She believed that Peter Lord was sincere and that his caution was probably justified but she was impatient. The more she thought however, the more she realised that she should not let that impatience cloud her judgement. "I do believe you and thanks. But is there anything we can do to speed up the process or make it more straightforward for you?"

"Send a Request for Information through the proper channels straight away. That will help no end," Peter responded, as he recalled some more of the details about working cooperatively with Europe.

"I'll speak to colleagues this end and make sure we deal with that straight away. And thanks Peter. I'm sorry if I sounded a bit…" Ingrid didn't finish the sentence but left it hanging in the air.

"Don't worry, I know what you mean," Peter responded quickly sensing that Ingrid was struggling with the language. They both realised that they had come to the end of the professional side of the conversation and a short period of silence pushed its way between them. Peter noticed it first. "Better let you get on then," he said.

"Yes, still a lot to do and as always, it's the first 24 hours that are the most important."

Peter decided to give his wife a ring to let her know that he would be late. It was well past 6 pm now and whilst she wouldn't expect him on time, she would probably plan dinner around the usual 7.30. He picked up the phone and dialled. As the number rang, his mind turned towards Ingrid again. "Hello." "Hi Kim, just phoning to let you know I'll be late, won't be back until 10-ish I'd say. Got something on that can't wait."

"Oh Peter," she exclaimed. "Not again. I've done a casserole and it will be ready soon. I'm starving."

"You go ahead without me. Just save a bit. I'll heat it up in the microwave." He could sense the disappointment in her voice. He knew he should make the effort. He wasn't going to achieve much this evening but something made him reluctant to put himself out.

"It's not the same," he heard her say. "I don't want to be on my own all evening."

"I'll make it up to you, make sure I'm home early tomorrow."

"Oh forget it. Just make sure you're back by ten," Kim said and she put the phone down abruptly without waiting for a reply.

He could understand the way she felt. They had had many similar conversations before and he knew where it could be heading. In reality he knew that it wasn't wholly the work, that perhaps he used his work as an excuse, but he didn't want to explore these inner thoughts too closely. He wanted to put them aside for another day when he could think more clearly, or more probably to put them off all together.

It didn't require much effort on his part to put these thoughts aside and to concentrate on his next task. He was helped by an interruption. His DI, George Baker, put his head round the door.

"Can we have a word about this Philip Cassidy thing before you go Peter?"

He wasn't sure at first how the DI knew, but he didn't let that show in any way. "Yes Sir. I've just had another call from France, takes things forward a bit, they want us to be involved in the investigation this end. I was thinking of speaking to you first thing tomorrow – didn't know you were still here."

"I'm just finishing off a few things but I can spare you a few minutes now if you want, must be away by seven… I've got some charity 'do' this evening and I need to get home to change and pick up Lorna."

"I won't keep you too long I promise, I'll be up in a few minutes," Peter called out towards George's retiring figure but George was absorbed by his own thoughts and he made no reply.

Peter gathered a few papers together and wondered how George had heard about the Cassidy case, then he realised that all email communications into the office were monitored and Sarah would identify items which she knew should be flagged up. No doubt a communication from France was sufficiently noteworthy to bring to the boss's attention. George had worked in Broughton almost as long as he had and the Helen Grant case would be as much on his mind as it was on his own.

As he made his way up to the DI's office, Peter collected his thoughts. He had the sort of mind that could marshal information, put each piece in the right order in the right place, and then present it orally, ensuring that the conclusions drawn were fully supported by the facts. As such he was a difficult person to argue with. The problem he faced now was that he didn't have much to go on. What he wanted was an opportunity to get the Helen Grant case reopened and he knew that he didn't have enough evidence for that at present. He was prepared to take it one step at a time as long as it was in the right direction and he was convinced that he was about to take that first step. He breathed a sigh anticipating difficulties, knocked once on the door and entered without waiting for a call to do so.

George Baker was almost the exact opposite to many of his colleagues. He had a happy well organised personal life and an untidy desk. In fact, his whole office was an absolute mess. Peter moved some papers from the only chair that he could reasonably occupy. The others were piled high with files and boxes plus the odd loose set of forms and papers.

"Well, Peter what have we got then?"

Peter had set his chair slightly to one side and at an angle. The rather formal straight on position it had previously occupied seemed too much like an employment interview for his liking. He had many recollections of stressful experiences of that sort and the rejections that almost inevitably followed. He took a deep breath, looked across at the DI, and paused for just a moment or two. "You've seen the email from Ingrid Peterson and my reply, Sir."

The DI nodded. "I've spoken with her now. The name Philip Cassidy cropped up during an investigation about a missing English girl – Amanda Dawson aged 15. More details will be confirmed by a further email later tonight and we can expect to receive a formal request for information and assistance."

"We've got to play this by the book, you know that Peter don't you, no slip-ups."

"Yes, Sir. That's what I told them on the phone. Follow the regulations and we can't go wrong," and he breathed a sigh of relief that he had held back when he spoke with Ingrid Peterson on the phone and had not jumped in with both feet.

"You remember them?"

"What, the regulations. Some of it sunk in, Sir. I knew I needed to be cautious and speak with you first."

"It's the European Investigation Order. That controls everything now. All nice and neat as I explained on that training day last year."

"Bit complicated though."

George Baker knew that Peter was right. The Order was complicated, everything surrounding Europe was complicated these days but the arrangements were meant to help and make it clear that all member states were expected to cooperate with one another. And it worked for the most part. "So we can expect a formal request for assistance. Is that what you said we would need?"

"Yes, and served through the proper channels."

"Good, good. Leave it with me. We can chase it up tomorrow if we don't receive it first thing, ok?" George looked across at Peter and wondered how he was feeling. There were dark clouds hanging over both of them and they had become very good at hiding their feelings. "Did you say the Grant family live in Gravesend?" he said eventually.

"Yes, why?"

"Oh, no matter, just checking."

Peter sat for a while expecting George to ask something else but there was quiet between them for what seemed like ages. In fact George's mind had begun to sift through a sequence of events and decisions he had made that went back to the day Helen went missing and it was the mention of Gravesend that brought it to the forefront of his mind. "Why don't you go home now and get an early night. We can talk again tomorrow when we're both rested. It's been a long day already."

Peter didn't really need much convincing and he nodded his agreement. "Ok," he said as he got up from the chair and turned towards the door. "I'll be in at 9 am sharp. Thank you, Sir."

George was beginning to think that he would give the evening's engagement a miss. He wasn't quite sure what his wife would think and perhaps she wouldn't be too pleased but she would come round in the end. He heard Peter close the door behind him and he was left alone with his own thoughts.

George had had his own theories back in 2003 when he had been a fresh-faced PC but he didn't believe it was just a case of a missing person. He dialled his home number and listened to the ringing tone, counting up to seven when he knew the BT answer service would kick in. He didn't want to leave a message. He waited a few minutes and then dialled again. This time his wife answered on the fifth ring.

"Hello," she said somewhat out of breath.

"It's me," he said knowing that she would recognise his voice.

"Oh hello darling. Is everything all right?"

"Yes, but I've been tied up here. We've had a slight problem and I need to sort it out tonight."

"Does that mean we won't be going to the 'do' tonight? I've just showered and I'm almost ready. I was expecting you soon."

"Sorry love. It's going to be too much of a rush. Why don't we have a takeaway and open that bottle of sparkling wine. I can grab something on the way home. What would you like?"

"Chinese," she said in a somewhat impatient way, "but it will cost you more than just a bottle of wine and a Chinese meal. We can talk about that Mediterranean cruise you keep putting off. I've got the brochure here."

George smiled to himself. "Yes," he said almost enthusiastically, "that's a good idea." He forgot to ask what meal she wanted but decided to get a selection. He knew what she liked and disliked. Their tastes were very similar.

Having resolved the personal issue George took out a small black book from the bottom left hand drawer. Despite the apparent mess, he knew where most things were and was always lost when Sarah tidied up. He opened the book and leafed through a few pages stopping at a particular page and running his finger down the list of names. A noise from the outer office made him look up. It was Sarah and he could see her through the glass door that separated his room from the office next door. She walked from her own desk towards his room and knocked gently. "Ok," he called out and she pushed open the door and came in.

"I'll be off soon, do you want anything before I go?"

"No that's fine. Have a good evening Sarah."

"What about a coffee? I could get one from the machine downstairs."

"No, I'll be going soon, just got a few things to finish off."

Sarah had been his secretary for about six years. She enjoyed her work and she got on very well with him. He was a good boss she often thought to herself. They spent many hours together and she had admitted to herself long ago that she had fallen in love with him.

She never said anything but they both knew how she felt. It was an unspoken understanding. A love that would never be fulfilled or spoken about openly but George was not irritated by it and despite the fact that he knew he would never return the feelings, he was somewhat flattered.

When Sarah had left, George returned to the black book. It was his list of contact numbers he had kept over the years, adding to it from time to time and removing names reluctantly when he thought about it. So many of his colleagues had left the force or retired. Some had died. His finger reached the name Jim Packer, Kent CID, alongside two telephone numbers and an email address. He selected the mobile number, not the land line, and started to dial. Jim Packer had worked with him on two different cases over the years and they had grown close professionally. He felt comfortable calling him up and asking a favour.

"Jim Packer," came the reply in a confident cockney accent.

"Hello Jim, George Baker here, how's it going?"

"Yeh, fine thanks, how are you, long time no talky talky." Jim could quite easily switch on the professional face and style which he knew was necessary in his work at the level he had reached, but he wanted to promote a more a jovial, somewhat flippant side to his colleagues and the outside world and to avoid revealing too much about himself, about what really lay beneath the veneer of normality which he had built up, partly to hide the many scars inflicted as a result of the two undercover operations he had endured in Manchester and Birmingham, but also as a protection in other ways. George was one of the very few colleagues who had got anywhere near understanding the real Jim Packer but even he had only just scratched the surface. On the other hand, Jim knew almost everything there was to know about George Baker, and above all he knew he could trust him.

"Yes, we must think up excuses for meeting up more often, maybe a project of some sort. How about crowd control and anti-racism in the Premiership." George knew that Jim was an avid football supporter and could easily be tempted into a light-hearted banter about his beloved Tottenham, sometimes not so light-hearted.

"Sounds good to me. With expenses of course."

"Of course," replied George enthusiastically. George was conscious of a movement in the outer office and he looked up somewhat nervously. He looked at his watch. "Hang on a minute," he said to Jim. The time was almost 7.30 pm and he did not expect the cleaners to arrive until after nine. The security people rarely came round before the cleaners began, in fact he hadn't seen anyone from security on his floor level before except when they had been asked to attend meetings. He could now make out a shadowy figure making its way across the outer room in semidarkness. The only light came from his own office through the glass walls. It was Sarah and he breathed a sigh of relief. He hadn't realised how on edge he had been. He got up and walked to the door. "What's up Sarah? Is everything ok?"

"Yes, I didn't want to disturb you putting the lights on. I just remembered that I've left my library book here and I want to finish it tonight if I can. Is everything ok?" She had sensed his unease and was anxious about him.

"Yes, fine thanks, I'm just on the phone. See you tomorrow."

Sarah returned to her desk and took a book from one of her drawers. She was convinced now that something wasn't quite right. She was sure George would not interrupt a phone conversation unnecessarily but there was nothing she could do. She would probably worry all night.

George returned to his desk and picked up the phone. "Sorry about that," he said but did not enlarge or give any explanation. He watched as Sarah walked back across the outer office in the semidarkness and waved her hand in his direction. He waved back and waited briefly until she had gone. "Right, where was I?"

"A community liaison project, with expenses I believe."

"Yes, that's right, but what's really on your mind?" Jim could sense that George had something specific to talk about and he wanted to make it easier for him. Besides, there was a steak and kidney pie waiting for him at home and he could do with putting his feet up in front of the TV with a nice cold beer.

"Well two things really." George explained briefly about the communications from France. "This business of the Grant family, we may need help your end on that."

"Just let me know what you want and I will do what I can," Jim said "but what's the second thing?" Jim guessed correctly that it had something to do with the Helen Grant case and he could tell from the way the conversation had gone that George was leading up to it.

George wasn't quite sure why he had confided in Jim Packer all those years ago. It wasn't as though he had been a close colleague, but there was something about their relationship that made him feel confident, made him feel that he could trust him. The fact that he had had more than his usual two pints of bitter at the time made it easier to talk and he had needed to talk to someone. He had needed reassurance, someone to share in the dilemma. He hadn't wanted to let Helen Grant down in any way all those years ago, but he didn't want to do anything to make a fool of himself or be seen as someone who let colleagues down. George had chosen his confidant well. Jim could easily have blown the whole thing wide open. Instead he had implicated himself by his own actions and silence and they were now bound by knowledge that they alone were party to.

"We may need to meet up. I don't really want to go into any of this over the phone." George was torn between seeking the reassurance he needed at that moment and the importance of discretion. He felt nervous and uncomfortable despite the lack of secrets between them and he knew that he would need a good night's sleep and a clear head tomorrow. Part of him wanted the call from France to be apologetic. To say that the girl had been found alive and well and that they did not need help with the investigation. That at least would take the heat off. They could then go back the way they were, still waiting for the trigger to start a new investigation rolling. Nothing to change the status that had existed for the best part of 16 years. The other part of him wanted answers, wanted an end to the uncertainty. He knew he could never rest properly. Not the sort of rest that came with an easy conscience and with the knowledge that his instincts had been right. He had put all his other instincts aside with never a passing thought about them. He had absolutely no regrets about that. The two forces wrestled within him but he knew beyond any doubt that the desire for answers would win. His lifetime service with the police was probably part of the reason for that. The other part was about him as a person, not as a policeman and it was that part that took over and was the deciding factor. "I'll contact you tomorrow whatever the news. Is it ok to use this same mobile number?" Jim confirmed that it was.

"Have you spoken much with Andy Blackstone since his retirement?" Jim asked abruptly.

"No, why do you ask?" George said, wondering why Jim would change the subject like that. It seemed really odd and made him feel uncomfortable.

"It's just that I called in to see him just after his birthday in December. It's not easy now that I'm living in Gravesend. Andy had a brilliant mind and we all learned much from him but he's not been the same since his wife died. It's tragic really."

The uncertainty in George's mind intensified as he explored the reasons why the conversation had turned so abruptly to Andy Blackstone and, momentarily he was lost for words. It didn't take Jim long to pick up on this brief void in the conversation and he smiled to himself recognising his own perceptiveness.

"It's just that Andy said something that made me sit up and think. Something about the Helen Grant case. Probably wasn't anything. I'll explain when we meet."

George was shaken by this but he tried not to let it show in his voice. "Anything I need to know now?"

"I don't think so. "Look," he added "Andy rambles quite a bit and says odd things all the time. We can talk about it soon, when we meet."

George accepted this reluctantly as the uncertain feelings continued to build within him. "Ok," he said eventually, "I'll be in touch about the best time to meet."

George decided he couldn't do much more tonight, but he was reluctant to leave. He thought about the events in France, and like his colleague Peter Lord, was struck by the coincidence. Two girls missing. Philip Cassidy close by in both cases. He didn't believe in coincidence. There was usually a rational explanation for most things and his instinct told him that something wasn't quite right. He was sure that there would be some sort of connection when everything became much clearer. He sat for a few moments and let his thoughts wonder. Eventually he decided to make his way home but his mind was in a turmoil.

Chapter 5

The alarm rang promptly at 7.15 am. George Baker had slept badly and he felt irritable. The sheet beneath him was pulled across the bed exposing the mattress on his side. A sure sign that he had tossed and turned most of the night.

"Do you want a cup of tea?" his wife Lorna asked.

"That's all right. I'll get it. You go back to sleep." Lorna had lain awake most of the night worrying because she knew something was troubling him. She had sensed that he had something on his mind when he arrived with the Chinese meal the night before and he tried hard to cover it up but she knew him too well.

"Beef in black bean sauce, just what I fancied," she said "What else have you got?"

As usual, George had bought far too much for just the two of them and he listed the six or so dishes in a voice which faked joviality unconvincingly.

"Go and open the wine, I've put it in the fridge," Lorna said as she retrieved the heated plates from the oven and took them into the dining room with knives and forks. George took the wine from the fridge, peeled back the black film covering the cork and prised off the wire, then expertly pressed the cork loose with his thumbs and it came out with a loud pop.

Lorna propped herself up on one elbow. "Well, what was the emergency that kept you late at the office?" she asked.

"Oh nothing much, just something I had to finish. Sorry about the party." They had not spoken about the charity event the previous night, but in fact Lorna wasn't too upset about missing it. That sort of function could be enjoyable especially if some of her close friends were there, but generally she found the need to make polite conversation with people she didn't know very well somewhat taxing and she did not have the sort of outgoing personality that many of the other wives had. She much preferred a quiet night in with her husband, but she did not make a fuss about it. Socialising she thought was part of a senior police officer's lot, particularly where promotion opportunities were concerned. She understood that and was prepared to go along with it to the extent that she gave George the impression that she enjoyed the social side of his work.

"What are you daydreaming about?"

The words brought her back to reality and she eased her mind away from her thoughts. "Oh, just the holiday we spoke about last night," she said after a brief pause. "I was thinking of going to the travel agent and booking something soon," she lied convincingly.

George had brought a tray of tea upstairs and he was getting dressed looking at her in the mirror as he tied his tie. "Yes that's fine. Last two weeks in July, I've already put those weeks down on the holiday list."

"Ok I'll do it today. Did you find the clean shirts I put out for you? That one looks creased."

"It was in the top drawer, it will be fine when I tuck it in. Where's my trousers?" He was standing in his underpants and she thought he looked good. His legs were long and muscular and despite the time of year they still had a very healthy tan.

"In the cupboard on the right, where they always are, you just don't look properly." George walked across the room and found his trousers in the cupboard straight away. He muttered something under his breath which Lorna did not hear, but she chose not to say anything. "You've not drunk your tea, do you want me to get you a fresh cup?" George was ready now and he took the few steps across the room with the tea tray in his hand. "No, I'll just have a snooze for a bit. I'll get a cup later when you've gone."

As he reached the bottom of the stairs he turned towards the front door. He could see that the morning paper and the post had arrived. He picked up the few letters and quickly determined that it was all boring bills or junk mail. He left them on the side table for Lorna to open later and he took the paper through into the lounge and switched on the TV. He wanted to catch the early morning news before he left for work.

"Make sure you have something to eat for breakfast," Lorna called from upstairs.

"Ok," he called back but he did not intend to eat anything before he left and he sat reading the headlines and listening to the news, but nothing of interest emerged. After a short while he got up and put on his coat. He checked his pockets for wallet, loose change and car keys and when he was satisfied that he had everything he made his way to the bottom of the stairs. "I'm off now," he called up but there was no reply. Good, he thought, Lorna's fallen asleep and he closed the front door behind him quietly as he left.

George made good time on his way to work. He drove on autopilot and wasn't really conscious of the journey. He came the same way to work each day and he was often preoccupied, but today he was completely absorbed by his thoughts, especially his conversation with Jim Packer the night before. He arrived at the office just before Peter turned into the car park and they parked side by side.

Peter's evening had been more problematic. "Look Peter – we really need to talk about us, we're not the same together anymore. I sometimes think that you'd rather be with someone else, or on you own," his wife said as they sat on opposite ends of the settee.

"Don't be silly, it's just the job, everything's all right really."

"Well it's not all right with me. I've been thinking – I get a lot of time for that these days being on my own so much."

Peter was not in the mood for a discussion about their relationship and he didn't want to face a row. "Look can't we discuss this some other time."

"That's what you always say," Kim responded angrily, her voice taking on a sharper tone.

The conversation was heading towards the sort of row they had frequently over the past few months. Peter kept his cool but he knew the time was fast approaching when he would say more than he wanted to, when his temper would get the better of him, but for now he wanted a quiet life, wanted things to jog along without this sort of bitterness. However, he knew that these were his terms and that they could not go on forever. He took a deep breath and pushed out his hands in front of him in a defensive gesture. "We will talk about this, I know we need to, but now's not the time, not the time for me," Peter said in a clear and decisive tone as calmly as he could.

"Oh damn you," Kim shouted as she walked abruptly from the room. "I just can't take it anymore," she called back at him just before she slammed the door shut leaving Peter standing looking somewhat bewildered but genuinely relieved. Inside her head Kim was screaming out loud. Screams of anger, frustration and loneliness. She flung her hands up to cover her ears but that physical act did not muffle the sounds coming from within. If anything, it made it worse.

Peter and Kim often slept in separate bedrooms. The arrangement had gradually crept up on them and was another example of their festering and fragile relationship. They had ceased making love long ago but, when they had shared a bed there was a level of closeness which had disappeared from almost all other aspects of their lives together. That too was now virtually gone and they had developed a brother and sister type relationship which they tolerated for most of the time but which fundamentally was not what either of them wanted. They slept separately again that night, hardly speaking for the rest of the evening and in the morning they both seemed to take on the sort of act they played out most days. The events of last night were not mentioned by either of them. They prepared their own breakfast and coffee and ate separately, Peter in the conservatory and Kim in the lounge. Peter said goodbye when he left but that was the sum total of words spoken between them.

George and Peter greeted each other and, after locking their cars, made their way from the car park to the office building. Once inside they both headed in the directions of the staff canteen. George chose a toasted cheese and ham baguette, a large white coffee and a doughnut. Peter settled for a coffee and a sandwich which he would probably eat later. They both took their purchases with them to their office on the floor above. "Any news?" was a frequently asked question of Peter in particular as they made their way past colleagues who were already seated at their desks. He generally answered with a shrug of his shoulders and a gesture with his hands outstretched before him and a slow shake of his head from side to side. "Nothing yet I'm afraid," he said to the last of the questions.

"I've been thinking," George said as he paused outside his office door. "We do need to make sure we are ready in case this whole thing blows up again… sorry if I seemed a bit reluctant last night, get Lucy to give you a hand, but I want you to concentrate on the Helen Grant case, not the recent problems in France. We can do that separately when we know a bit more."

Peter was surprised "What do you want me to do exactly?"

"Get Lucy up to speed… go over the background with her… we need a new perspective. She's not been involved before so she will be able to look at everything with a fresh pair of eyes. Just an initial review you understand and keep me informed, ok?"

Peter didn't need any further prompting. "Thank you, Sir," he said over his shoulder as he walked away quickly before George could change his mind.

It wasn't long before Peter was sitting at his desk and deep in thought. The Helen Grant files had been retrieved from archives and were now stretched out in front of him and all of a sudden he felt overwhelmed by it all. He knew he needed a fresh pair of eyes, but he wanted to be alert, to be in control and in command of all of the facts. He had thought about everything too many times and, on occasions like these, the words on the hundreds of pages in front of him seemed almost meaningless.

Lucy Atkinson had joined the team recently as a detective constable and had quickly gained a reputation for spotting errors, inconsistencies or lines of enquiry which had not previously been considered productive. She had a first class degree in Psychology from Oxford University and it was obvious to everyone that she had a first class mind to go with it. Peter hadn't worked with her before but he realised from her reputation that she was exactly the right sort of person to support him in a review of all of the evidence. The problem he thought was that she could well uncover errors they might have made and if there had been mistakes he wanted to be the one to find them. Peter's thoughts were interrupted by the clicking of heels walking towards him and instinctively he knew that it was Lucy. He resisted the temptation to look up straight away but when he did, the first thing he noticed was her perfect smile and that eased his anxieties just a little.

"Understand you've got something for me," Lucy said as she moved closer towards him. "I need something to get my teeth into."

"I was going to give you a ring."

"No need, Sarah spoke to me just a short while ago. Apparently George wanted me to get cracking as soon as… is that ok with you?"

"Yes fine… Absolutely"

"Just tell me, what you want me to do."

"Erm… not sure yet… wanted to get organised… get my mind clear… but yes, I could really do with your help," Peter said and he gestured towards the papers laid out in front of him, as he took in one deep breath and pushed it out in one long sigh. It was a sigh of regret, but also an indication of the task ahead of them. A task made more difficult because he had done it over and over so many times both in his head and in reality.

"Sarah says we can use one of the interview rooms… is that ok with you?"

"That would be great… we could do with a bit of peace and quiet."

"Do you want me to help move some of these files, or would you prefer to do that? I could get a coffee for us if you want."

"No I can manage the files, but coffee would be nice."

"White no sugar?"

"Yes, how did you know?"

"Just intuition, but it probably ends there," Lucy said and she looked for the first time deep into Peter's eyes trying hard to decipher how he was really feeling. She held steady eye contact wondering how he would react almost willing him to open up to her because she felt that he was hiding something.

Peter was the first to look away and his mind went blank for a moment or two, but eventually he pulled himself together enough to respond almost casually "Not from what I've heard."

"Well I'll take that as a compliment and thank you. I've heard a lot about you too."

"All bad I expect."

"Not a bit of it, all good in fact," Lucy lied convincingly.

"Well that makes a change I must say, but hey let's get moving on this before George gets you working on something else."

It wasn't long before they were sitting side by side in Interview Room 2. The files were spaced out in front of them and Peter had one in particular open in front of him. "I know the background pretty well," Lucy said "George got me looking into all of the unsolved cases as soon as I sat behind a desk and Helen Grant was close to the top of his list.

"Didn't know that, but yes it does help… so what do you think?"

"Not sure I think anything at the moment, don't know the case backwards and sideways like you… so, how do you think I could help?"

Peter was beginning to warm to Lucy. He had felt challenged when she looked him in the eye but now he knew there was another side to her. She did not seem to be pushy or big-headed, just keen to get involved and that suited him just right because it enabled him to relax, to clear his mind and to focus on the key objective. "If it's ok with you I'd like to go over the case, bit-by-bit, see if there is anything missing, check that our conclusions were justified or…" and Peter hesitated momentarily "… did we make any mistakes?"

"That's fine by me, but you… are you ok with that?"

"Yes, definitely."

"Ok then, let's get on with it."

Peter paused and this time he was the one to look into Lucy's eyes. She held his gaze for a few seconds then looked away. She was aware that she was the one being scrutinised and she could understand that because she was about to scrutinise everything that Peter and his colleagues had done all that time ago and which they had agonised over, time and time again, during the intervening years. Then he turned away from her but not focussing on anything in particular. He took in a few deep breathes and then he began.

"I want to take each suspect one by one, examine their movements that night and anything else we know about them, anything that's relevant, but first I need to set the scene. So the Grant family. Ok. Right, Helen's mum and dad. Fairly straightforward. Mum and Dad, Rita and Ted, both working class, local, met at the local secondary school and took up residence at Lilac Cottage when they got married in 1984. Two daughters, twin girls born 1986 at the City Maternity Hospital. No police record. No social service involvement and no credit difficulties. Ted worked at the City Council Offices. He started there as an office boy and eventually became a senior manager in the highways department. Rita worked as a typist for a local estate agent before the girls were born and then got a job as secretary at the local primary school. The two girls Janet and Helen both home loving kids, no trouble with the police and no problems at school. Helen was the pretty one and apparently she blossomed in her early teenage years.

"And was Janet jealous?" Lucy asked.

"It's not clear. Mum and dad say not. Friends weren't so sure, but she wasn't all that much of a Plain Jane herself, it's just that apparently Helen was extra special."

"What did Janet have to say about it herself?"

Peter selected a page from the pile in front of him checking that it was in fact the statement he was looking for. "Janet's statement doesn't say much about her relationships with Helen in that sense," he answered when he had checked the relevant bit. "Doesn't get us very far and it's very much what she wanted us to know and doesn't necessarily reveal what she really thought, how she really felt. But as for Helen she wasn't a virgin by all accounts and if the rumours are to be believed she had at least two sexual partners. Her sister, Janet, on the other hand and by her own statement was a virgin at that time. They were meeting two boys, Tom Wilkins and Giles Silsby, that night. Both boys said in their statements that they had full sexual intercourse with Helen on a number of occasions. Philip Cassidy told us that it was common knowledge."

"Was there any animosity between Tom and Giles?" Lucy asked.

"Not that we could establish. They were close friends and if anything seemed pleased for each other. It was almost as if there was a pact between them. It didn't seem as though Helen had a preference for either of them," Peter explained feeling more confident in using Lucy as a sounding board and he anticipated her next question. "It's more difficult to establish Philip's attitude to all of this. He wasn't what you might call close friends with either of the other two boys. Philip was in the loop mainly because he was going out with Janet. It's not clear whether he was jealous of Tom and Giles or whether he felt disappointed that his own relationship with Helen's sister was less than fulfilled in that direction. Janet did seem somewhat protective of him and he did not give much away himself. There was something about Philip that I couldn't make out. He always seemed shifty to me – not giving much away, like he was keeping something back. He always seemed to be looking over his shoulder. It's just a feeling I had."

"And you know what, very often it's those feelings that turn out to be the key."

"Well, perhaps," Peter responded. "But I'm not sure I can trust my feelings when it comes to this case – it's just too important to be left to something so vague."

"Yeah, I know what you mean," Lucy responded.

"As we understand it Helen and Janet were due to meet the others in the summerhouse in the garden of the Parkside Pub. Tom walked from his home 17 Preston Road to Giles's house 23 Buxton Crescent, about 250 yards away. Tom said he left home at just after seven and that is confirmed by his mum. Also there were two witnesses who saw him leave his own house and one other who saw him just before he reached Buxton Crescent. Giles's parents were out when Tom arrived, but his younger sisters said that she was watching EastEnders when her brother left and that started at 7 pm. One other witness saw the two boys at the top of Paisley Road near the off licence which is only about five minutes' walk from the Parkside Pub."

"Were they all confirmed sightings?" asked Lucy. "Yes," said Peter "All the independent witnesses made positive identifications. Other witnesses came forward. In the main everyone else said they thought they saw the two boys at about the appropriate times but could not be absolutely sure. There was no evidence to suggest that the boys had been seen at other locations. Tom and Giles said that they arrived at the pub before 7.30 and went straight round the back to the summerhouse."

"How long would it take for them to walk from Buxton Crescent to the pub?"

"About ten minutes at the most. So it all fits. Both boys said that Janet arrived about ten minutes later."

"And when did Philip arrive?" Lucy asked as she looked up from the notes she was taking. "That's not quite so clear. Janet said that it was just a few minutes after she got there. The two boys thought it was more like 20 minutes or longer, but they all got chatting and no one was really conscious of the time. Philip himself said that he was sure he got there before 7.45."

"So, to recap we were able to place the boys Tom and Giles at the summerhouse just before 7.30 and have confirmation that they walked there together. Janet arrived within about ten minutes and Philip maybe 15 minutes or so after that."

"Ok then," Lucy said "Let's start there then if it's ok with you," and Peter nodded in response as Lucy looked down at the notes she had made. "Could be that it's a little too neat and tidy… just a bit too perfect. What about their families?" Peter thought for a while. He could recall making extensive enquiries about the two families and the first thing that had struck him was that they could not have been more different. Tom's mum was a single parent and had struggled financially since his father left just after he was born. He began to explain the background to Lucy, but he wasn't sure if she understood or could comprehend how difficult it had been for a single mother especially after the financial crash in 2007. But in fact he could not have been more wrong. Lucy had become very good at hiding her true emotions.

"But," Peter said almost abruptly, "but the Silsby family, different story. Not that they had a lot of money but they were comfortably off. And, both parents stayed together, so a more settled family atmosphere."

"Did they have jobs?" Lucy asked.

"Dad worked as a taxi driver and mum, Pauline, did a few shifts each week at the Harvester Pub – down by the cinema complex. They were both working that night, it all checks out."

Lucy looked down at her notes again and paused slightly. "Have you got the taxi drivers pick-up and drop-off schedules for that night?"

"Yes, it's in the file, everything is logged for his shift, we double checked everything, there is no doubt that he was where he said he was."

Lucy started flicking through the papers in the file Peter had pointed to until she found the page she was looking for. She took it out and studied it carefully. Peter watched apprehensively but he was certain that Stephen Silsby had been working all that evening and he remembered talking with the manager of the taxi company who had confirmed everything.

"All looks neat and tidy," Lucy said without looking up from the page she was reading. "And I see you've got a statement from the manager who was on duty that night."

"Yeh," Peter responded, "I spoke to him myself…. everything checked out ok."

Part of Lucy's strategy was nearly always simplistic. Whilst she knew that she needed to be thorough and not rule anything out without good reason, she would always seek to reduce the size of the problem and that is what she had done in her own mind in all of her previous reviews of the evidence before her now. She needed to put each suspect into a category, and she always found the traffic lights system suited her best, red, amber and green – and she was rapidly moving in the direction of placing both boys and their families in the green category. Having resolved that in her mind she moved onto her next question. "What about Helen's sister?" she said but Peter was already leafing through pages in front of him. He was looking for the aerial photograph of the parkland area. "Right! he said "You can see Lilac Cottage marked at the very top of the page. Just off the main road. That's where the Grant family lived. There's a circular path around the woods, open space on the extreme right – you can just make out some football pitches, marked out down that eastern side and there's another large open area with cricket and hockey pitches at the southern end. The whole area is surrounded by main roads. Tom and Giles walked up the road from the bottom right hand corner to the public house, there, just towards the bottom." Peter pointed to the position on the aerial photograph in front of him. "Janet said that she left her house at about 7.20 and walked around the circular path on the eastern edge of the wood. She said that Helen was still getting ready and told her that she would follow on shortly."

"No confirmed sighting of Janet I suppose?" Lucy chipped in.

"That's right. No sightings reported. There's no confirmation. We spoke to a number of people who were walking either up or down that side of the park. There's reasonable lighting there but it was a dark night."

"What was the weather like that night?" Lucy asked.

"It had been raining in the afternoon, until about 4 pm, so it would have been wet underfoot."

Lucy was already beginning to think about the category Janet Grant should be assigned to and she was verging on amber, but she thought that red was still a possibility. She was reluctant to make that decision at this early stage and in any case she did consider that Janet and Philip were more intertwined than they appeared to be on the surface. But before she made any rational judgement her thoughts were interrupted.

Peter was going through a similar thought process. He firmly believed that there was more of a connection between the two friends than they had ever admitted. "We can't just consider Janet in isolation," he said eventually. "I think Philip is the key but they are linked in some way I'm sure of it. I don't know why but I've always had this feeling and now I'm more sure of it."

"Where did Philip live?" Lucy said, thankful that she and Peter were thinking on similar lines.

"He lived at 14 Basford Way, there on the western side of the park." The position of that address was not shown on the aerial photograph and Peter was pointing off the map to give an indication of its location. "So his direct route would be down the path on that side. It's just a short distance to the Parkside Pub."

"And what did he say when he was interviewed?" Lucy enquired.

"That's exactly what he said, and he said he got there about 7.45. The group said that they waited about half an hour for Helen to arrive. When she didn't turn up Tom and Giles left. They went to the off-licence which is on their way home, bought a few cans of beer and then back to Giles's house to watch TV in his bedroom. Tom said that he went home at about 9.30."

"You say that Philip and Janet were going out together?"

"Yes."

"The thing I can't understand then, is why Philip didn't just go straight up to Lilac Cottage and meet Janet there. They could have walked down together."

"I think Janet and Helen were expecting to walk down together, but I get your point. Let's consider for a moment that either Janet or Philip is not telling the truth or at least have something to hide. My bet is that if one of them lied to us then both of them is involved in that lie."

Lucy got up and walked over to the window. The sun was shining and the light hit the ribbons of water droplets running down both sides of the glass. She was deep in thought. "Maybe we are looking at this from the wrong point of view," she said eventually.

"What do you mean?"

"One minute Helen was there, at Lilac Cottage and the next she has disappeared. Either she left in a vehicle or she walked."

Peter nodded.

"And, as she hasn't turned up after all these years, it has to be that she was taken and then driven away."

"Not sure that's the only option… but I agree it's the most likely," Peter responded.

"CCTV?"

"Nothing much in the area… We looked at some footage down by the cinema complex but that's about the extent of it, I'm afraid."

"Was she taken from the cottage or did she set out and was waylaid I wonder?" Lucy took a few deep breaths and her eyes darted from side to side "You know what I'm thinking… Was it premeditated or was it opportunistic?"

"Perhaps a bit of both," Peter replied. "But in the end we just put it down on the list as a missing person. Quite a few of us argued against that but we didn't have enough to go on."

"So if she was taken, a local or someone who knows the area reasonably well from previous visits." Peter nodded again. They had asked themselves those sorts of questions over and over but not coming up with anything concrete, anything that is that led them closer to the answer. "Who comes to this sort of park at night in the middle of March?" Lucy asked abruptly.

"Courting couples, dog walkers, youngsters up to no good, drug addicts, alcoholics… the list goes on and on."

"There has to be some element of planning in this… Someone came here maybe on the off-chance, but at least with the thought in mind that an opportunity might arise."

"And they would need a vehicle," Peter said almost to himself and his hidden demons began to rise to the surface again.

"When was Easter that year?" Lucy asked. She was thinking about possibilities and her mind was jumping all over the place.

"What... What do you mean?"

"They always have a funfair on the green and a circus... over Easter. I've been to it lots of times."

Peter was looking at his mobile "April 20," he said after a short pause. "What are you getting at?"

"I was thinking... maybe... but no, the date doesn't fit."

"Yeah, I see what you mean. Could be someone checking in advance about availability or just to discuss all the details with council officials beforehand... do you think they would need to do that?"

"If they did, I would have thought they would make contact by phone – can't see anyone making a special journey."

"No, you're right, but you brought it up," Peter said with a smile creeping across his face. He was pleased that Lucy was able to look at possibilities from a new perspective and was already accepting that she was beginning to make him think differently, not significantly, but with a slightly different slant.

Lucy moved back from the window and sat down, not realising the way in which Peter was beginning to view her contribution.

"You are a help, keep me on my toes," he said eventually, I was just searching about aimlessly before."

"Nice of you to say so, but what next, for me it's Lilac Cottage, did Helen take any of her belongings or just the clothes she was wearing?"

"We weren't exactly sure but it looked like she wore a black skirt, jacket and a blouse of some sort. Nothing much to go on except what mum and Janet thought were missing. Then there was the brown coat of course."

"Not sure I get the significance."

"We found her brown coat just by the path, it had Helen's DNA on it and mum identified it."

"Any other DNA?"

"Only family members, I'm afraid."

"So what did you think about that?"

"We weren't exactly sure, but the best guess was that she didn't really like wearing it and so she dumped it, before she got to where she was going."

"So in that case she was taken from the park and not Lilac Cottage."

"Yes," Philip said almost delivering the word in slow motion and a short silence developed between them.

"Could Philip Cassidy drive, do you know?" Lucy asked out of the blue.

"Don't think we ever found out, he was just short of his seventeenth birthday of course, so he could not have started driving lessons."

"Perhaps no real problem, what about access to a car?"

"No, don't think so."

"Where did you find the coat exactly?"

Peter moved the aerial photograph in front of him again and studied it carefully. Eventually his expression changed and he tapped on the page with his index finger "Here, about 100 yards past the car park, between the millpond and the next clearing."

"So that means if we are right, that Helen went in that direction and dumped her coat on the way. She must have gone round the top end of the park and down the other side, but that's… That's the long way round, isn't it?"

"Why would she do that?"

"Yes, it would have been much quicker for her to go the other way, down that side."

"Which way did Janet say she went, remind me."

"Yes, she said she went that way, the long way round."

"So," Lucy said, "what do you think… did they go together or did one of them follow the other, it only makes sense if they have got something to hide."

Peter sat back in his chair and closed his eyes trying to picture the scene. He had thought many times before about the relationship between Janet and Philip. He felt they had both been evasive about that in their statements, but there was nothing tangible the police could hang on to. They needed hard evidence.

"Mobile phones, what happened to them?"

Peter and Jim Packer had spent many hours going through phone records but the work go them nowhere. "Everyone gave permission for us to trawl through mobile phone records," Peter said eventually.

"But we couldn't find any trace of Helen's phone. We tried to get a fix on it but nothing. Janet said she would only switch it off if she had to. We got a dead end there I'm afraid."

"We haven't spoken about Helen's other friends. Friends from school, best mates. What have you got about that?" Lucy said realising that they needed to move on.

"She was very popular at school, with both boys and girls, but it didn't seem that she had any best friends. She was reasonably friendly with a couple of girls who were in care I seem to remember."

Lucy stood up again and went over to the window. The rain had eased slightly, but it was still grey and dismal outside. She looked out across the grey slate roofs, all wet and shiny but still looking dismal against the dark sky. She felt a cold sadness deep inside her and for a moment found it difficult to swallow. Her memory played tricks on her from time to time perhaps because she did not want to be reminded about that period in her own life, the time when she had been in care and when she had been at the lowest ebb of her life. It had been bad enough she thought, the sterile environment, the isolation and the lack of belonging. There had been love of sorts, but not the unconditional love that should be the backbone of growing up. She had not been abused but she had been vulnerable and she understood. Some girls were desperate to find love, affection and comfort wherever it might come from as long as it belonged to them and them alone. To be able to hear someone saying "I love you," and fooling themselves into believing it was true.

"You ok?" Peter said when he became aware that Lucy seemed to be distracted.

"Yes, suppose, gets you down though, when you want to be able to concentrate… personal stuff, gets in the way sometimes."

"Well it's got me, that's for sure," Peter replied not really understanding what Lucy meant.

"This guy Spencer Cassidy, the teacher, Philip's father… now he could be right in the middle of it," Lucy said after a brief pause.

"Everything points in that direction, except for his alibi."

"Ah yes," Lucy said, "and you're the one who provided it."

"He was there, right behind me at the boxing that night. He was there when I arrived and when I left. Jim Packer saw him there as well."

"How long were you there for?"

"Must have been the best part of three hours."

"And you are sure he was there all the time?"

"Yes, absolutely."

"But, if you were watching the boxing you wouldn't have been looking at him all the time would you?"

"This seems a bit like the Spanish Inquisition."

"Sorry, just try to think of it as though we are talking about someone else… that's what I try to do."

"But it's me."

"I know, but just try, trust me. What questions would you ask yourself... the witness I mean. Stand back from it a minute, ok?"

"Yes, you're right... I would ask those questions and I would also ask... could he have gone out and come back later without the witness being aware. And do you know, the answer is definitely not."

"Did you go get a drink perhaps, go to the loo?"

"Yes, but I wasn't gone for more than a few minutes... Spencer was definitely there all the time."

"Are you sure it was Spencer Cassidy? Did you know him very well?"

"Well enough... and Jim... he confirmed it, we didn't make a mistake I can assure you."

"Ok then, accepting that, the other possibility is that he wanted to establish a cast-iron alibi and what better way to do it?"

"He would have to know what our plans were for that night, we didn't exactly broadcast it."

Right from the very beginning Lucy had her reservations about Spencer Cassidy's alibi. Not that she didn't believe the circumstance, but because she preferred things to be neat and tidy. Peter Lord's involvement placed him on both sides of the fence and she was aware that should be avoided at all costs. She looked in Peter's direction now wondering if he felt the same way but she had no idea from his expression how he was feeling. "But in all other respects he would definitely be one of the prime suspects," she said eventually holding Peter's eye contact just a fraction longer than necessary.

"I know what I know," Peter said eventually, understanding that he was being scrutinised and realising the intensity of it. "He's got the motive, but not the opportunity. We need to stick to basics."

"Ah yes, means, motive, opportunity, we haven't spoken about that yet. It seems to me that there are a number of suspects who tick one or two of these boxes, but no one who ticks them all, but that's often the way isn't it?"

"I can see your point," Peter responded reluctantly.

"Everything else about him makes me suspicious and maybe, just maybe he is part of it."

Lucy could see that Peter was uncomfortable about this part of their conversation and she was right. Peter's heartrate was racing, he was flushed and feeling vulnerable. He had faced these demons before, but now he was being forced to look at them from a different direction. He could hear the words Lucy was saying and part of him had to acknowledge that they were backed by logic. There was just a flicker of acceptance within him but he kept coming back to the same stumbling block and that was based on his own knowledge, his own certainty, then Lucy said something which sent a shiver down his spine.

"He may of course have an accomplice."

Chapter 6

Ruby Delacourt was sitting at her desk. She worked as a journalist for the *Blatchington Post* and these days she spent more time working from home than she did in the office. Travelling from the little village in a remote country area where she lived to the office in town had become increasingly unpleasant and Ruby avoided such journeys whenever she could. She had stopped using her first name, Emma, when she had separated from her husband because she had wanted to start afresh, to consign to history those parts she could change. Her name was a significant part of her and she decided not only to revert to her maiden name, but more importantly to change her first name as well. Many acquaintances had difficulty getting used to it but her best friends, those she had confided in during the latter stages of her marriage, knew the significance of it and took to it readily. Her husband, Ben, had been everything she had wished for at the beginning, and it was some time before things began to change. At first there were just subtle issues, small things seemed to upset him more than most people would expect but before long the insensitivity gave way to callousness and their relationship deteriorated rapidly. She began to despise him. He began to seek new ways to punish and humiliate her, and he would invariably use sex as part of the dehumanising process. He had chosen the very thing that had brought them so close together to inflict pain both physically and mentally. The act of love between them deteriorated into an act of torture. Even now years later she could still hear the words, feel the humiliation. Ben had used her name in a sneering, malicious way. Spit jumping from his lips as he mouthed the word over and over and she had begun to associate it with malignancy and hatred. From the point she first became free of him she chose to be known as Ruby, partly because she didn't want to feel that Ben had won any sort of battle, but also because it was the name her dear father often called her by and she had loved her dad absolutely.

Ruby was working on a story about the health service. Originally she had interviewed six patients with similar conditions but living in different parts of the country. The story centred on the wide disparity of treatments provided across England and Wales, but other worrying factors emerged and she had agreed with her editor to broaden the scope of her investigation. She glanced up at the picture of her father on her desk. She found it gave her both inspiration and comfort. Her work brought home the memories of his death. His last days were painful and humiliating and she could never understand the attitude of those who were charged with his care, their lack of compassion and apparent disregard for his most basic needs and she had felt so helpless and alone in her struggle. Through her recent work she had discovered that her father's misery was not an isolated example of failure but was a familiar story. That knowledge gave her no satisfaction and certainly did not lift in any way the burden of guilt she felt and which she was sure she would take with her to the grave. The inspiration in looking at her dad's picture came from the knowledge that she expected to make things better for others and the comfort came from his caring eyes which looked softly back at her lovingly as they had when he was alive.

The phone rang and she brought her back to reality. "Hi, Ruby Delacourt here," she said into the mouthpiece in her usual cheery tone.

"Just ringing to let you know we've still not heard anything from Philip. Any news your end?"

Ruby had expected to receive some sort of communication from Philip by Friday morning at the latest. It was Saturday now and she had spoken with Ann, Philip's secretary, the previous evening just to check whether she had heard from him. Ann was a loyal and trusted friend as well as working for him and if anything she was more worried than Ruby was, especially at the outset.

"But he always keeps in touch. He never just goes off without letting someone know," Ann had said when she spoke with Ruby on the telephone the previous day. Ruby was not particularly worried when she had phoned Ann and, whilst the conversation had not made her feel unduly concerned, it had planted a seed of doubt in her mind which came to the surface now and the early stages of panic began to develop. Ann had probably reached that same stage hours before. "I've not heard anything at all," Ruby heard herself say as if the words came from someone else.

"We must do something soon," Ann responded. "I've tried his office mobile which he always carries with him but I keep getting diverted to the answer phone service."

"Ok Ann, I know someone who lives in Lyon, I'll give him a ring and see if he can help. I'm sure he will know what to do." As she said this Ruby was already moving the mouse to close down the computer screen she had been working on. Ruby had met Philip just four months before and had fallen in love with him completely. She didn't know much about him at first except that he ran some sort of import–export business and he was obviously secure financially. They had got talking after an exhibition, had a meal together that same evening and then continued their conversation well into the night. Ruby felt relaxed and confident in his company and it had progressed rapidly from there.

Ruby picked up the handset and dialled the numbers she had located for her colleague. "Hello Trevor, Ruby here. Ruby Delacourt. Sorry to trouble you but I need a bit of help." Trevor Bently did freelance work for the *Blatchington Post* plus one or two other dailies and she had worked with him closely on one or two assignments. They had got on well and it was in fact Trevor who had first introduced her to Philip.

"What's the trouble Ruby?"

"This may seem silly but Philip went skiing in Méribel last Tuesday. He was going to meet up with friends there I believe for a few days. He said he would phone me on Friday but I've not heard anything. I've spoken with his secretary and she has not been able to contact him. It just seems really odd."

"Where was he staying. Do you know?"

"That's the point. I've no idea. None of us have."

"Look, don't worry. There's probably some simple explanation. I've got a few contacts in Méribel. I'm sure they will be able to help. I'll give them a ring and get back to you. Did he have a car do you know?"

"I think he uses a small company based here in the UK, something like Car Hire Exclusive, does that ring a bell?"

"Don't think so, but leave it with me."

"Thanks Trevor. If I hear anything in the meantime, I'll let you know."

"You've got my number, haven't you?"

"Yes. I'll stay near this number. My home line. Hope to hear from you soon. Bye." Ruby felt guilty as she put the phone down. She hadn't asked Trevor about his wife who had been unwell the last time she heard. She made a mental note to ask him next time they spoke.

There were two desks in Ruby's office. Her office desk with the computer was in the corner away from most of the glare from the window. She hated working with the light shining across the screen but she didn't like shutting out the natural light. Her other desk contained her personal papers and she moved over to it when she finished her conversation with Trevor. She looked through a few papers in the top right-hand drawer but did not find what she was looking for. There were a few papers on the top of her desk, mainly household bills and financial documents which had arrived in the post that morning, which she now pushed to one side looking for the red file which Philip had given to her the night he had left for France. It wasn't long before she spotted it on the shelf at the back of her desk alongside a golf trophy Philip had won and which he had given to her. "Something to remember me by," he had said. "Two birdies and an eagle using the putter you gave me for my birthday." Ruby had bought the putter on Trevor's advice. She had no interest or knowledge about the game herself but Trevor had assured her that it was exactly what Philip wanted. Ruby's thoughts returned to the folder. Philip had stayed with her before he left for France and she remembered that he had taken his passport and other travel documents from the file before he left on Tuesday morning. The papers were loose and clearly not in any particular order. She leafed through details of a golfing holiday two years previously, some handicap certificates and printed copies of flight details with prices. There was written confirmation of a hire care agreement relating to a trip to France just before Christmas and a similar note relating to a car hire for the previous September. Both documents were in the name of Car Hire Exclusive. She was pleased that she had remembered the name correctly.

Ruby sat back in her chair and massaged the back of her neck with her left hand. She recognised the signs of tension creeping up on her. She got up and moved towards her other desk. She stood behind her office chair, put her hand across the lower part of her face and scratched her nose and chin. She was at a loss to decide what to do next as she gazed unseeingly towards the blank wall in front of her. She picked at a small piece of loose skin on the side of her thumbnail until it turned white and became a little sore. She wasn't usually this fidgety she thought as she set off towards the downstairs kitchen to make herself a cup of tea.

Ruby took a large mug of hot tea upstairs to her office and sat at her desk where the computer was located. She switched it on and waited for the Google search to appear. "Accommodation in Méribel," she typed in as soon as the screen allowed her to. Eventually she was presented with a list of bookable hotel accommodation, but it was a formidable list. Far too long for her to do anything with at present. Then the telephone rang. "Hello," she said.

"It's Trevor. I've got some news but it's a bit sketchy."

"What do you mean?"

"Well my contact with the local police in Méribel was very cautious and I've given an absolute assurance that we won't publish anything yet."

"What do you mean?" Ruby said again but this time with a nervous edge to her voice. "What has happened?" Ruby asked these questions hurriedly and with a sharp intake of breath which added a quiver to her words as she gripped the receiver tightly and held it firmly against her ear.

"They certainly know Philip's name and they are looking for him," Trevor said as he searched for the best way of explaining what he had been told. "It seems that he was staying at the Hotel Orion but he checked out on Thursday, the day before he was due to leave. They don't know where he is now but I gather that they are very keen to trace him."

"Why? What's the problem? Why are they looking for him?" The questions shot rapidly from her lips as her mind raced through the uncertainties that the conversation had raised.

"All I know is that a young girl has gone missing from the same hotel. There's a big search going on for her and for some reason the police want to talk with Philip about it. I don't know why yet but the fact that he's missing doesn't help. My contact wouldn't say much but it seems that it's more than just a question of him leaving the hotel early. Look, we seem to be getting more information. Can I ring you back? I won't be long I promise."

"Ok," Ruby said reluctantly, "but make sure you do," and her voice began to quiver again. Before Ruby could say anything else, Trevor had hung up and she was left sitting in her room being swallowed by the silence.

Ruby sat in her office with her head in her hands. She wanted to be distracted. To have something to do or at least to be able to talk with someone. She thought about phoning Ann just to be able to share her unease, but she knew it would be better to wait until she had more definite information. She also wanted to keep the line free so that Trevor could get through to her. All her instincts told her that Philip could not possibly be involved in the disappearance of a young girl. She had watched him playing with her own niece and was sure that he loved children. Nothing was too much trouble for him and he never seemed to lose patience even when Emily's demands were persistent and unreasonable, as they often were. Ruby prided herself on being a good judge of people and she was confident in her belief in Philip. Ruby looked at the picture of her father and could almost hear words of caution. "But you were wrong about Ben weren't you?" The very thought made her shiver, made her clench her fists and stare back at the photo defiantly. "But that was different dad," she said out loud. "I don't think I ever really trusted Ben. There was always the flicker of tension within him that frightened me. Something just below the surface. But with Philip it's different. I know I can trust him," and she took her father's picture in both hands and held it close to her face feeling the cold glass in the frame against her cheek. Ruby wanted to hear reassuring words, the sort her father had been able to deliver so expertly whenever she needed them. But she did not hear them now, even when she moved the picture away from her face and focussed unblinkingly into his eyes as if pleading for a response. Ruby put the photo back on her desk and looked at her watch. The second hand made such slow progress around the dial and two or three times she even thought that it had stopped. She liked being in control, being the one who made things happen and not the one waiting for others to get things done. Some people she knew were the opposite and she always wondered how they would react in a crisis. Would they continue to be calm and patient or would another side of their personality come to the surface. A side which she believed everyone possessed to some degree or other and which would take control when circumstances demanded. Then the phone rang. "Yes, hello," she said hurriedly.

It was Trevor phoning back as he had promised. "We've got a report through about Philip. It seems that his name is on record with the police your end. Something about his being involved in the disappearance of a girl in England about 16 years ago. Apparently it's one of those long-standing unsolved cases. No body. No nothing."

Luckily Ruby was sitting down as she received the news. Her head started spinning and she felt sick. She was sure she would have fallen to the ground if she had been standing up. She shook her head from side to side trying to clear her mind but it didn't seem to do any good. Eventually she drifted back to something close to normality. "Involved?" she said. "Involved in what way? How?"

"We haven't got all the details yet. The information comes from one of my colleagues. He has his own contact this end and he checked it out for me but I've only got half a story."

"So how do the French police have the information?" she asked almost pointlessly.

"They put a call through to the UK straight away apparently." Ruby was functioning on all cylinders now, her head was clear as the adrenaline streaked through her veins. As Trevor was about to expand on what he had already told her Ruby cut him short. "Ok. We need to get details and then go through the newspaper's coverage at the time. What was the missing girl's name? When exactly did she disappear? What were the circumstances?" Ruby fired off the questions without pausing for breath and for some reason she felt more in control again.

"We don't know her name, but I think it was March 2003. We haven't been given an exact location, but the feeling is that it was on the outskirts of Broughton."

"Look Trevor, could you keep digging your end. I'll get on to records. See if I can trace the press coverage at the time. See if I can identify the team that were working on it for the *Blatchington Post*. Some of them may still be around. Let me know if you uncover anything else. Use my mobile number. I'll keep that free for incoming calls. Thanks Trevor."

Ruby heard Trevor take in a short breath of air as if he wanted to say something else but the line went silent for a moment.

"Sorry about that," Trevor said eventually "but information keeps coming in we've heard about the car hire now."

"What's the news on that?" Ruby said rather hesitantly believing that the information might add an extra layer of uncertainty.

"Car Hire Exclusive, you were right about that. The news is that Philip did use them and…"

"And what?" Ruby said abruptly.

"Not good news I'm afraid. Seems Philip hired a car for four days, but it was returned out of hours at least 24 hours before it was due. That was on Thursday, I'm told."

Everything was tumbling around her and each piece of new information just seemed to add to the confusion. Ruby knew that she needed to concentrate, to focus on those things she had some control over and she knew that the events in France were completely out of her reach at least for the time being. She wanted answers to so many different questions and needed a period of calm reflection, to concentrate on one thing at a time, to get her mind working like a computer, taking small logical steps and not seeking to answer the final questions until the first pieces of the puzzle had been put in place. These thoughts had an immediate impact, she felt much better now, more like her old self and with a plan in her mind. She had not asked Trevor about his wife's health. The opportunity for that had not arisen and she had no regrets about that. There would be time for that later.

Ruby was fanatical about keeping diaries. Not the usual personal stuff, but records of business meetings, projects and key national news highlights whether or not she had been directly involved. Her recent diaries had noted for example the conviction of a teacher at Christ's Hospital School on charges of sexual misconduct down in Sussex somewhere, together with some of her own thoughts and ideas on the case. There were also entries about other prominent cases. It was a mismatch of information that had caught her eye for one reason or another. She never knew whether or not she would be asked to support the news teams in such cases and she always liked to keep in touch with background details just in case. Serial killings in particular were hot news and every reporter's dream. It was sad to think that the misery of some poor unfortunate families could be so eagerly picked over by the ambitious and glory seekers. But that was the way of the world, by the reporting world at least. Any titbit whether due for publication or not, that could be added to the story. In fact it was frequently the bits that were unlikely to be published that were the most interesting. Sometimes such information had a direct and close bearing on the case and would be shared with the police. Other times there could be spin-off details which emerged and which were not necessarily linked to the crime itself. For the keen reporter such titbits were often of more value to the story teller but they always had to be handled with great care. Not only was there a need to keep them out of the reach of rivals, but it was also necessary to avoid treading on the toes of the police, who always took a dim view of parallel but unconnected investigations. There was unfortunately a habit of the seemingly unconnected turning out to be an important aid in reaching the centre of a maze, or in escaping from it.

The diaries were kept in a bookcase in Ruby's spare bedroom. As she took the few steps across her office, she realised that the mug of tea she had made for herself some time ago lay untouched. She took it into the bathroom and tipped it quickly down the sink, spilling a few drops onto the floor. That could wait, she thought to herself and so could a fresh cup. "2003," she said out loud to herself as she stood in front of the bookcase and located the shelf. That was just two years after her short but intense affair with Graham. An affair which almost changed her life but which she had ended before it got out of hand. She still remembered it fondly and with a few regrets. The 2003 diary was easily located and she took the A4 volume off the shelf and returned to her office with it. "Right," she said again out loud to no one but herself "January, February, March," turning the pages a few at a time until she came to the month she was looking for. Then it hit her and rekindled memories.

She had made summaries at the end of each week and most of them had been about Helen Grant, a 15-year-old girl who had disappeared on 17 March. Ruby leafed through pages passing through April and May and it was some time before reference to Helen petered out and eventually disappeared. The amount of information in the early weeks had been extensive and she recalled that Graham Forbes had been a key figure in the news team following the case. It was Graham's name that had caught her attention when she was leafing through her address book earlier.

Ruby read through all the entries she had made all those years ago and then went back to the beginning to read more carefully those sections which appeared to be of most interest to her now. Philip Cassidy's name cropped up a few times and she wondered now why it hadn't rung any bells earlier. It seemed from the brief information she had that there wasn't any suspicion that he had been directly involved in Helen's disappearance. The focus about that fell on Helen's father. That angle was always newsworthy. Possible stories about the sexual behaviour of groups of teenagers was another lead for further exploration, but two other bits caught Ruby's eye. Apparently Helen had confided in her form teacher at school about difficulties in her private life but the details lacked any real substance. The interesting point was that the teacher concerned was Philip Cassidy's father. The second bit was less tangible, no more than a rumour really. There was a suspicion that there had been other potential witnesses present, but they had never come forward or been identified. The possibility of some high-profile public citizens being involved and having some influence on the investigation would have made one hell of a story. However, despite some careful probing nothing came of it, and like smoke in the wind there was very little to grasp and other passing stories quickly covered any tracks it might have left. Eventually she noted the case had been put down as a missing person, but a number of people directly involved had serious doubts about that.

Ruby was feeling hungry and thirsty by this stage. She didn't really want to be distracted by domestic chores but decided that it would be better in the long run for her to be refreshed. That would help recharge her batteries and mental powers. She moved quickly downstairs and felt almost light hearted as she bounced down each step one by one. Even though she feared the worst she felt she could tackle any obstacle in her way because she was convinced that her Philip would not be mixed up with the disappearance of teenage girls. She could not offer herself any tangible solutions to the web of uncertainty but she knew there would be one and she would find it. Her light heartedness continued whilst she prepared a sandwich and a fresh mug of tea.

Ruby returned to her office feeling better with a full stomach and she sat at her office desk. She would need to use the computer to download editions of the

Blatchington Post in the days following 17 March 2003. She was anxious about the next telephone call she planned to make. She had picked up the phone many times over the intervening years and dialled the initial digits of Graham's telephone number. So many times she had wanted to talk with him. To hear his strong voice and to feel comforted by it, but she knew he would take it the wrong way and she did not want to do anything to rekindle the pain she had caused him when she told him that their relationship was over. She knew how strong that pain was for him. He had shown it the last time they had met to say goodbye. Graham had done his best to hide his pain from her but his eyes and mouth had given him away. The eyes never lie she thought to herself as she avoided his gaze. She did not want him to know that she had felt the same way. Her decision had been made and she knew that he would be better off without her. It had taken Ruby many years before she had fallen in love again. Her first few meetings with Philip had been special. Now she was completely smitten but this time she promised herself it would last forever.

At last she began pushing Graham's telephone numbers into the keypad of her telephone and she felt anxious and uncertain. Their meetings in 2003 had been business-like and always with other colleagues present. They had not really spoken privately at all. Now she felt it would be different, at least the initial contact and the first few words. The number began to ring out and she almost put the handset down. Then he spoke in clear strong tones that she remembered so clearly.

"Graham Forbes here. Can I help?"

Ruby felt the mounting pounding in her chest and cleared her throat. "Hello Graham, It's Ruby. How are you?" she said and she was pleased to be able to keep a neutral, calm edge to her voice.

"Hello Ruby. How lovely to hear from you," he responded enthusiastically.

Ruby felt the beginnings of a flutter in her chest, but she pressed ahead. "You know that case you were involved in back in 2003? The missing girl Helen Grant? Something's come up and I need to go over a few details. Have you got time to help now or should I ring back?" Ruby thought she could sense disappointment in Graham's voice as he explained that he was tied up at the moment but that he would love to meet up later if that would help. "Yes, that's fine," Ruby responded thinking at the same time about the best location to suggest. They would need access to a computer and in the end she couldn't think of anything better than her home. "Is that ok for you Graham?" she said trying again to sound as neutral as possible and hoping he would see how logical it was. They agreed a time but she did not give any other details. If she had started it would have taken an age and she wasn't sure how helpful it would be for either of them.

Ruby's final call was to Ann and she explained in detail what she had done so far and what she had achieved by way of information. Ruby spent some time going over every conversation she had had so far and did not spare any detail. Despite some of the news being upsetting Ruby felt that at the very least she owed it to Ann to hold nothing back. Ann took the news better than Ruby had expected and they discussed some of the implications and arranged to speak again the next day.

After that final call Ruby felt exhausted and she decided to have an early night. She wasn't expecting to sleep well and anticipated a fitful night, but nonetheless she trudged off to make the attempt.

Chapter 7

The doorbell rang. It was exactly 9.30. Ruby had only just finished breakfast and put the few plates and the cup she had used into the dishwasher. She wasn't normally house-proud but for some reason she looked round the room to make sure it was reasonably tidy and satisfied that it was ok she moved from the lounge to the front door and opened it. Graham was standing there with a smile on his face and a big bundle of papers under his arm. It was a cold but dry day and he was wearing a dark blue zip-up coat and a white open-neck shirt. He was about six feet tall with dark hair swept back from his forehead, which he had gelled that morning, and it sat up on the top in a style which might have been fashionable a few years before but which suited his face perfectly. "Hello," they both said at once and then giggled somewhat nervously. "Thanks very much for coming over at such short notice," Ruby said as she opened the door wide as a gesture for him to come in.

"That's alright. Always pleased to help. You know that," he responded as he stepped into the entrance porch and wiped his feet carefully, gazing at the same time at her face and concentrating on her eyes. "You haven't changed a bit." Ruby began to protest about the effects of the passing of time before he added, "No it's true. You look absolutely wonderful," and he meant it.

Ruby showed Graham upstairs to her office. "Do you want a cup of tea or something?" she asked. "Not just for the moment, thanks," he replied as he looked around for the office door. "It's this way." Ruby led Graham past her own bedroom along the corridor to her office at the end of the landing. She had made sure she closed her bedroom door when she made the last few checks before she went downstairs for the last time that morning. She wasn't sure why, but it just felt better that way.

In her office Ruby had pulled up two chairs and positioned them side by side at her office desk which was bigger than the other one and the computer was located there. She had anticipated that they would call up the reported highlights of the disappearance of Helen via the internet, those that had appeared in the *Blatchington Post*, but Graham surprised her. He had brought some folders with him and he placed them on the desk in front of them.

"Well what do you want to know?" he said. "I've got my collection here, always thought it would come in handy."

Ruby had put on just a touch of her favourite perfume and the scent filled Graham's nostrils as it had all those years ago. The most primeval of the senses he thought to himself as he tried to avoid coming too close to her, in a self-conscious and somewhat awkward way. Ruby was aware of it immediately but she did not let it show. "What have you got there then? You look like you are protecting the crown jewels," she said light heartedly and with just the right emphasis to avoid any suggestion that she was teasing him.

"You know when you get a big case that just won't go away. The ones that are never resolved and stay just out of reach. Well for me this one comes top of the list. There's something about it that makes it stand out from the others. I don't know what it is but I've spent long enough going over the facts. Time and time again, and I bet I'm not the only one. It was never just a case of a missing person, I'd stake my life on it. Here in these two files is the result of my work. Months of it. And I'm nowhere near making a decent story out of any of it. Not now at any rate."

Ruby looked sideways at him feeling a slight crick in her neck. She adjusted her chair slightly so that she was able to look at him full on and it helped. She was about to explain herself, to tell him why she needed to know as much about this old case as possible but first she wanted to get something out of the way.

"It's lovely to see you Graham. I'll always have a soft spot for you. You know that don't you. I need your help now but we need to clear the air first."

Graham sat looking at her and nodding almost in time with her words. He felt uncomfortable and elated at the same time and he could feel his heartbeat quickening as her words penetrated the cocoon he had drawn around himself. The cocoon he had used as protection against his feelings, against the many dark days and against the truth. He had been able to exist and to flourish in the eyes of those round him, but it had been difficult especially in the early months. It was bearable now. "What do you mean?" he said as confidently as he could but lowering his gaze so that he wasn't looking directly into her eyes.

Ruby wanted to reach out her hand and to hold his arm but she felt instinctively that Graham would misunderstand the gesture. "We were very close all those years ago but it came to an end. We've both gone our separate ways since then but I'm sure we have never forgotten those very special months. They were very special Graham but they will never return. I loved you then, but now I love someone else with all my heart. I'm sorry to put it so bluntly but I need your help and I don't want you to help me believing that it could possibly lead to something. I don't want you to feel that I've used you in any way. Does that make sense?" Ruby placed her hand on top of his and squeezed gently believing that the gesture would be received as it was intended now that she had spoken the words she had prepared carefully in her mind.

"I can't pretend that part of me does not love you still, I can't pretend that I don't still think of you every day, or that I'm not jealous when you say you love someone else, but I want you to be happy and I'm really pleased that you are."

Ruby was a little taken aback by this. She had expected some sort of reaction but not perhaps in exactly that way. She struggled to find the right words to use in response and failed to find them when she said, "That's really sweet of you Graham."

"One thing would piss me off though. If I ever thought that I could help you in any way. Any little thing and you didn't ask me. Now that would be hard to bear. So let's get on with it. What exactly do you want?" Graham looked at Ruby as he spoke these words. He felt more confident now and far less uncomfortable. If he had been asked before he had arrived how he would react in these circumstances he would have said that it would tear him to bits, but in fact the opposite was true. Now he could behave normally, with his usual sense of humour and easy relaxed manner. That was the real Graham and there was no reason to hide it any more.

"I need to explain what's happened," Ruby said feeling relieved that they could move on to business matters. She sat with her legs slightly apart and she placed her left hand between her knees and pressed them together. She stared ahead but not at him, and looked as if she had drifted into a trance. She was in fact collecting her thoughts and considering where to start. As soon as she had decided her eyes took on a more purposeful expression, she turned towards Graham and began to outline the key facts that had emerged. As in her conversation with Ann the previous evening, she covered all the ground fully but this time she began to dwell on possibilities and theories that had developed in her mind overnight. She also told Graham a little bit about Philip and gave some information about their meeting and their friendship. Talking out loud and going over the details helped her. She was able to look at circumstances from different points of view, but always within the context that Philip was not involved in any way in the disappearance of Helen Grant or in the disappearance of the other girl in France.

"You are making a big assumption about my theories aren't you?" Graham said when he assumed Ruby had finished. He had allowed her to talk him through everything from the beginning without interruption. He hadn't taken any notes and he knew that he would have to go back over some of the details to make sure he had a clear and complete picture. That could wait for the moment. He preferred getting a good overview. Names, places, dates could be added later.

"What do you mean?" Ruby responded but knowing full well what Graham was getting at.

"Aren't you making the assumption that my pet theory in the Helen Grant case does not place Philip slap bang in the middle. My number one suspect!"

Ruby looked back at Graham with a cocky expression on her face. "You're forgetting," she said "You told me back in 2003 what most of your pet theories were and none of them featured Philip Cassidy. Unless you've changed your mind since then and, knowing you, I didn't think that was likely."

"Well given that you didn't have a personal interest in the case back then, I'm surprised you could remember all the detail about what I thought."

"You're forgetting my squirrel-like journalistic mind, and my diaries."

"Ah, ah, those bloody diaries. I remember now," Graham said with a teasing tone in his voice, "All right then I don't think Philip did it, but for my part I'm not going to rule him out completely."

"Thanks, that's what I thought," said Ruby. "But let's get down to business, as far as my notes go, there were a number of strands being looked at by the news team. The dad as suspect number one and, linked with that, the fact that Helen confided in a teacher at school and the three boys plus her sister of course. Then there was the potential newsworthy bit about teenage sex and finally the vague suggestion that someone was covering things up. What shall we start with?"

"Let's start with the teacher bit because that interests me most," Graham said as he opened one of the folders in front of him and started leafing through the papers.

"Ok then what have you got on this chap Spencer Cassidy?" she said when she was ready.

"The police didn't get any real dirt on the teacher and he a had a good alibi. When they had finished we did our usual bit and began pumping some of the other kids at school. We also put in a stooge. We got some very interesting anecdotes. The general feeling was that Cassidy senior was a bit of a perv. Bit touchy feely, but nothing too heavy. They all said that he was a bit odd. He had his own office because of his pastoral care work and some of the kids used to go round after school for tea and cakes. Apparently he was a very good listener, well you would expect that wouldn't you? He used to gravitate towards the kids with problems at home, the ones who were the most vulnerable, well you would expect that as well. But it did leave him in a very powerful position and some of the kids absolutely loved him. That's love otherwise than in the biblical sense. The interesting point is that he let the special kids, those he was helping most, call him by a nickname but only when they were meeting up on the special occasions – not generally in the school."

"What's so interesting about that?" Ruby interrupted.

"Yes, I can understand what you mean but I haven't explained yet. His first name was Spencer as you know and he was generally called that by colleagues and friends. For the special ones the secret was that he asked to be called Philip. That was his second name and presumably his son was named after him. We did a bit of snooping and found two thank-you cards from pupils – a boy and a girl and they were both addressed to Philip. They were at the very back of his desk drawer. Look I have photocopies here. It's not clear whether the cards were handed to him or whether they were left for him in the office. It was usually locked when he wasn't there but we found out that notes were pushed under the door sometimes and he picked them up later. As far as Helen is concerned, everyone in the inner circles thought that she was the number one special one."

"What did colleagues have to say?" Ruby asked.

"Oh, they all spoke very highly of him. Not one word against him. The bee's knees apparently."

"Did he keep confidential records of his conversations with any of the pupils?"

"No," replied Graham. "He told the police that he made it clear to each pupil that if any of them revealed any criminal act he would share that information with the Deputy Head and presumably ultimately the headteacher."

"And what did the Deputy Head have to say?" Ruby asked not expecting that this would lead anywhere.

"Yes, she confirmed that Cassidy senior was following school policy, but interestingly Cassidy did have a conversation with her about Helen just a week or so before she went missing. He told her that Helen had spoken to him about a lot of personal stuff and he got the feeling that she was about to make some sort of disclosure about her father perhaps, but that's only speculation. Apparently she hadn't said anything at that point but he told the Deputy that he thought she was leading up to it. He asked for advice and he was reassured that he should continue to support her in the same way as before."

"Where is this all leading us?" Ruby asked the question aloud, almost as if it was directed at Graham, but in fact it was aimed as much in her direction as it was in his. "Don't answer that just yet," she added, "we both need to think this through," and a look of steely determination began to form across her face. They were both quiet for a while, perhaps just half a minute or so, but it seemed to last forever and they were using the time in different ways. Ruby's first thought was about her own teenage years and the diaries she kept at that time recording her feelings, her hopes and her fears. She felt that if Helen had secrets that were too difficult to talk about it was just possible that she could have written about them. Words that were meant just for her and which could be less guarded because of that.

It was Graham who broke the silence. His own thoughts had been along completely different lines and he was in a little bubble of his own. "As I see it there are three people in this triangle, Helen, her dad and Spencer himself. So, what are the most likely issues for each of them, what's top of the list for you?" he asked.

"Go on, tell me," Ruby replied, not really concentrating on what Graham had asked, but still partly absorbed by her own speculation.

"She could be pregnant. That is the tops for me."

"Or," Ruby replied as she began to turn her mind to the point Graham was making, "the simple answer might be that she was sexually abused by her father."

"She would have said something. To her mother, her sister. She wouldn't have kept it to herself, I just don't believe it. But if she got pregnant by one of

She would go on of course, but he could ignore her without too many recriminations. Suddenly his daydreaming was interrupted.

Andy was getting impatient. His mind, which had begun to sift out some of the unimportant details and to bring more sharply into focus those parts of the puzzle which pointed towards a conclusion. "Have you finished your call?" Andy called over to him from the open patio door trying hard not to show in his voice how he was feeling.

"Yes, all done – just sitting here soaking up the sun."

"Bit chilly though isn't it?" Andy said as he walked across and sat next to him on the bench. "I come out here quite a lot nowadays," Andy said almost nonchalantly and nodding towards the hills in the distance. "I sit here and think about old times. Didn't really notice so much then, but since Jean died everything seems much clearer, especially the things we both saw together. It's a lovely spot here, but I haven't always appreciated it. Now sometimes I can't get enough of it, but it's not the same on your own." Andy let the words trail off gently and hung in the air for a brief second or two. "But we need to press on, we need to build this picture adding the bits we know about now and see where it leads us."

They took their places indoors once more. For a few moments neither of them spoke. Andy was the first to break the silence. "You didn't tell Sarah where you were, did you?"

"No, but she'll guess I'm sure. Don't forget she took your call and she must know that something's up."

"Yes, I suppose so," Andy said looking a little anxious. "Don't worry. Sarah won't let on. She won't tell anyone."

"Yes, George I know how lucky you were to get her. But she's in love with you, you know that don't you?"

"Don't be silly," George replied abruptly but without any anger in his voice. He knew that it was true of course, but he wasn't ready to admit it to anyone. Not just yet at least and probably never.

"Getting back to business," Andy said, "we need to take things on a stage further. Come on, you're the copper with the active brain, I'm just the retired one, what do you make of it all?"

George looked at the notes in front of him. He had already drawn three boxes and had started to fill them in. "Well, the first thing that comes to mind is that Peter is not the only one whose alibi has been blown away. There's Philip Cassidy's father, we can't rely on the siting of him at the boxing match now."

"That's exactly what I was thinking," Andy said.

"Two new suspects to add to the list," George said with some reluctance – "I don't like saying that about a colleague but we have no choice do we?" George noticed that Andy seemed to wince when he said that and he wasn't sure whether it was in response to a real pain or an expression of disgust at the prospect. He chose to ignore it as he replied, "But it does mean that if they were together that night, they can alibi each other or they might be in it together."

The pain which had started deep within him just a short while ago suddenly grew in intensity and this time it showed clearly on Andy's face.

"You're not ok, are you?" George said.

Andy took a few deep breathes seeking to regain some control. "Need to take something," he said at last and he reached for the packet of painkillers in his back trouser pocket. He had concealed his need for medication from everyone up to this point, but now he had no alternative. He took out two of the tablets and swallowed them one after the other with a little water. "I'll be alright in a minute," he said.

"What's up. What's the matter?"

Andy didn't reply immediately, partly because the pain continued to push aside all rational thought, but also because he just wanted to keep everything secret. It was so personal after all and he just wanted to face it alone. That was his way of coping. After a few minutes, with George fussing around him, he began pulling himself together and he knew that he would have to explain it all to George. It didn't take long and George just listened in stony silence. "Now you know, so you know why I've got to see this through. I don't like unfinished business."

"Neither do I, but why don't you rest a while."

"I'll get all the rest I need soon enough. Just trust me on this one." George wasn't entirely convinced and it clearly registered on his face. "No buts George.

I'm ok now and this is what I want." With that Andy started to discuss the case again but he had clearly lost momentum. He stumbled from one theory to another without reaching any firm conclusions.

In the end George interrupted. "Well Peter and Spencer have already lied once about what they were doing that night. And if that's the case they probably weren't up to much good. So, what are the possibilities? Come on Andy, think."

Andy tried to clear his head of the jumbled thoughts that had just gone through his mind seeking to push aside all of the minutiae and to concentrate on this one specific question. Slowly the fog lifted and he began to think more clearly. At last he responded. "One a teacher, the other a policeman. If they were working together on some fiddle, I'd say it's likely to have involved children. So drug dealing? Child abuse? Prostitution? Or they were just spending time together. That's what Jim Packer suggested."

When Andy had been working on a case he was often the one who would look for simple answers and his mind was searching for that now. All of the information available showed that Peter and Spencer had been together that night. That premise he thought was sound. He made a determined effort to visualise situations where any meeting between them might have taken place away from Pashley Park that night but he kept returning to Tim Sherwood's comment and the library card that George had found by the pond. He knew these facts put Peter Lord right in the middle of it and if he was there Spencer Cassidy had been at the park as well. It only took him a moment or two but he made his decision. He knew he needed to return to the basics, just to get a foothold and start the process of moving forward. His mind began to search for a simple answer, the sort he knew he needed to find. A reason for Peter and Spencer to be together, for a purpose far less dramatic than child abuse, and he started to nod to himself, slowly and almost imperceptibly at first, but then more pronounced as the answer came to him. He let out a small puff of air through his nose and the beginnings of a smile started to form at the corners of his mouth, adding just a hint of brightness to his otherwise dull eyes.

"We can't leave it like this," George said but he wasn't entirely convinced that there were any loose ends that they could clarify between just the two of them.

"Like what?"

"You said it yourself earlier, none of us had all the information, we each had just our own bit, but I get the feeling that you were not convinced about that. What are you thinking Andy? What is it that you haven't told me?"

"It's not clear enough, I can't say any more, not now at least, but just be careful, be very careful. I think one of us knows much more than they would want us to believe."

Chapter 11

Events unfolded rapidly whilst George Baker was away from the office. Detective Superintendent Mowbray Jackson had become directly involved and he was not one to allow grass to grow under his feet. Mowbray was another long serving officer who was coming close to retirement. He could remember the Helen Grant case and he still felt bruised by the recollection. Almost everyone who had been around at the time had their own memories and there was a common feeling of regret and sometimes of shame about the lack of success either in finding Helen or in tracking down her killer. Mowbray had supported the pragmatic decision at the time to close the case with a 'missing person' conclusion, but he had never truly believed that she had not been taken.

Mowbray was an ex-military man. He joined the army straight after university and graduated from Sandhurst achieving the Sword of Honour. His father and grandfather before him had distinguished army careers and it had always been expected that he would follow in their footsteps. "For goodness sake, don't tell your father, but I do wish you would go into banking or something safe like that," his mother had confided in him just as he began his final year at Oxford.

"Don't worry mum. You know dad wouldn't hear of it. But it's what I want to do. I'm not doing it just for him or granddad; I'm doing it for me, ok. I'll be safe don't worry," he had replied with a half-smile of encouragement and a small hug. He could feel the warm tears on her face, but neither of them spoke about it again. He had never seen his mother cry except on that one occasion and he wondered if her tears came at night when she was alone or whether she never cried at all. Mowbray's subsequent army career had gone as expected. He was ideally suited to army life and he never felt the need to settle down and marry any of the girlfriends his mother continued to push his way.

Some of these thoughts were going through Mowbray's mind as he sat contemplating the information he had been given in the past 24 hours. It was Tuesday now, almost a week since Amanda Dawson and Philip Cassidy disappeared and they were still missing. All the necessary procedures in accordance with the European Investigation Order had been completed by the French police and Mowbray had spoken directly with his opposite number in France about the support and information they needed. Everything was moving forward smoothly, everything was being done that could be done, the problem was that they needed a breakthrough. Mowbray knew that it was essential to collect hard evidence and he was convinced that they were most likely to find it if they could search Philip Cassidy's flat in Station Road. The difficulty was that they didn't have sufficient justification yet for seeking a search warrant. Then they had a breakthrough. Normally Mowbray was reluctant to act on information provided anonymously but this time he was prepared to make an exception. The telephone call had come through at 13.21 and Mowbray had listened to the recording three times.

"Could I have your name and address please caller?"

"I've got some information for you, that's all."

"But it would be helpful to know your name."

"Just listen."

"Ok then but perhaps you could let me know who you are."

"I can't be arsed with all that. It's about this Philip Cassidy bloke – just tell someone high up. That girl in Méribel – the one who's gone missing – you want to find out where she is before it's too late, just check Cassidy's flat ok."

Then the line went dead.

Mowbray thought it might just be enough and he wanted to be involved personally in drafting the submission to the local magistrate's court. But the more he thought about it, the more concerned he became. They needed more, he was certain about that and he would have welcomed the opportunity of talking it through with George Baker but his whereabouts remained a mystery, even it seemed to his PA, Sarah.

Then another unexpected piece of evidence arrived on their doorstep and Mowbray became even more convinced that someone out there was pulling all the strings, drip feeding them information and having one particular target in mind – Philip Cassidy. It was Peter Lord who brought it to him and he knew immediately that, although he was convinced that it was a set-up, it added just enough to what they already had, enough that is, to apply for a search warrant.

"I thought you should see this straight away, Sir."

Mowbray looked up expectantly "What's that then Peter, something helpful I hope?"

"Definitely looks like it, but I just have my suspicions."

Mowbray held out his hand expecting Peter to give him the paper he was holding, but he hesitated for a second or two wondering if he should say anything else. "It's just," he said again and then the words dried up in his throat.

Mowbray noticed Peter's reluctance but chose to ignore it as he took the paper out of Peter's hand before he could object in any way. Mowbray studied the page carefully and his eyebrows rose a fraction or two. "Where did this come from?"

"Arrived in the post this morning. Nothing with it to say who it's from."

Mowbray was looking at a photocopy of the picture pages from two passports, both with exactly the same photograph, but one in the name of Philip Cassidy and the other in Martin Denman's name.

"Well, well, well, would you believe it? Too much luck to be a coincidence."

"Exactly what I thought," Peter replied.

"Now I'm convinced, but I just can't make up my mind."

"In what way, Sir?"

"Either we are being led in a particular direction or…" and Mowbray paused slightly and looked Peter square in the eyes "… or we are being led away from something. Which is it?"

Peter was quiet for a while. He had similar thoughts the moment the envelope arrived. "But does it really matter?" he replied with a shake of his head.

"Got to keep the possibility in mind, but it's just enough with everything else. Enough that is to request a search warrant," Mowbray said triumphantly but his feelings of uncertainty were not far below the surface. "Thanks Peter," Mowbray said. "I need to get cracking on the submission to the local magistrates. Anything else before you go?"

"Not really, Sir, just let me know when we hear back, from the magistrates I mean."

"I'll let you and George know straight away, don't worry. Then we can discuss how we go about it."

"You know I want to be involved," Peter said emphatically and he nodded his head in time with his words."

"Yes, yes, we will see, ok," Mowbray replied.

It didn't take Mowbray long to complete the necessary forms. He had done it many times before and knew from experience how he needed to present the evidence they had in the best possible light. Mowbray arranged for the forms to be delivered by hand and he gave instructions that the PC should wait for the response and then report to him personally with the result.

Mowbray breathed a sigh of relief when he was told that the request had been granted. A team of police officers had been despatched with the clear message that they should tear Philip Cassidy's flat apart and not come back before they had some solid evidence. It wasn't clear exactly what they were looking for and whether there was an emphasis on the recent disappearance of the girl in Méribel, or Helen Grant's disappearance all those years ago. Peter Lord had pleaded to be involved and his request had been agreed. "I know you feel personally involved, we all do, but don't let that get in the way of your judgement. Get it right this time. Let's do it by the book but don't leave any stone unturned." Those had been Mowbray's words and they were left ringing in Peter's ears as he left Mowbray's office and headed in the direction of the police car park.

When Peter arrived at 15 Station Road, three of his colleagues were already there and had just gained entry. There was a brief discussion between them and an agreement was reached about the search process. The house was a very large mid-Victorian end of terrace now broken up into flats and in need of outside redecoration. The mood amongst the search team was jovial on the surface, but everyone knew the importance of the task and they all took their responsibilities very seriously indeed. And it certainly paid dividends. It wasn't long after the search had been completed before Peter was back at the station with a contented look on his face. Mowbray had asked to see him as soon as he arrived and it was a meeting he was looking forward to.

"Well, what have you got for me?" Mowbray said as soon as Peter stepped into the room.

The smile on Peter's face developed even more. "We found a dark red ski top down by the side of the bed and it had a key in the zip pocket… A key to one to the rooms in the Orion Hotel," he replied as he looked Mowbray square in the eyes. It was the sort of eye contact that he rarely, if ever made with Mowbray but he felt assured, relaxed even and more confident than he had ever been before in Mowbray's presence.

"And?" Mowbray responded.

"It wasn't hidden, just left on the floor for us to find easily, but that's not the only thing."

Mowbray sat in silence expecting Peter Lord to continue but he paused slightly partly because he wanted to enjoy the moment but also because he felt more in control of the situation than he had been in a long time. "We are being led in particular directions, we all know that, but…" and he paused again briefly, "… does it really matter? It's the results that count surely?"

"So, don't keep me in suspense. What else did you find?"

"Banik's got everything and he is doing the usual checks – he will get back to us as soon as. But, the items. A little box under the floorboards. Had a quick look, a 2003 diary with entries in up until 16 March and with Helen Grant's name inside the front cover, plus an envelope addressed to Philip Cassidy and a note from Helen inside. Plus," again Peter paused and took in a gulp of air and he remembered the feeling he had when he saw it for the first time, "Philip Cassidy's passport and his photograph just like the photocopy we got through the post."

"Well, well," Mowbray responded as his interest about the list of items increased. "Nothing in the name of Denman though I expect?"

"Not a passport, no, but there was a package next to the box and it was addressed to him – Mr Denman I mean," Peter said triumphantly "It contained a videotape – one of the old ones, Banik's going to check it through first and will let us know what it's about in his report.

"Well, well," Mowbray said again and he flicked the tip of his moustache with his bottom lip. "Sounds interesting."

Peter was thinking about the way in which the search team had found the items under the floorboards. One of the PCs, the youngest in the group, had called the rest of the team into the bedroom where the ski top had been found. He was standing with his back to the window and he pointed to the carpet at the foot of the bed. "Looks like the carpet's been moved when the bed was pulled out," he had said and he pointed to one of the exposed floorboards which was raised slightly. The team had made a thorough search of the area and the items were found in the section under the exposed floorboard. Peter began explaining all this to Mowbray.

"So," Mowbray responded, "the bed shifted out of position, the carpet moved back and one of the floorboards protruding. We didn't really need to engage in major detective work to sort that one out."

"That's about the size of it, Sir."

Peter, in particular, was pleased that the phone rang just at that moment. Mowbray listened for just a few seconds and then, turning to Peter he lifted his eyes and eyebrows skywards and shaking his head at the same time. Another second or two passed by and Mowbray's expression seemed to be frozen, but then, just as suddenly his eyes softened just a little. "I've been waiting to hear from you George, didn't know where you were, but something interesting has turned up. Could you come up to see me straight away please?"

Peter could not hear the words George spoke in reply but he watched as Mowbray listened in silence. "That was George," Mowbray said as he put the phone down "He's on his way up, best if you get off now. But I need to see you later ok, I'll be in touch."

"What's up?" George said as he approached Peter in the corridor outside. "Sarah told me that Mowbray's been looking for me."

Peter walked a few paces down the corridor in George's direction before he replied. "Yes, but I've given him some good news, I think he wants to talk to you about it."

They were standing toe to toe now and George leaned forward so that he could whisper in Peter's ear. He didn't want anyone to overhear but it seemed an exaggerated gesture in the circumstance. "I want to talk to you in private when you've got a spare moment. I'll give you a ring."

"What, about the Philip Cassidy case?" Peter asked with just a hint of anxiety catching in his larynx.

George waited a few seconds before he answered and watched Peter closely for any further signs of his being ill at ease. "Well to my mind it's the Helen Grant case and always will be," George said eventually.

"Yes, the same with me. It's just that Philip Cassidy's name is on everyone's mind at the moment. I've just come away from searching his pad."

"Yes, I know. You had better get off now and prepare your report. See you when I've finished with Mowbray." George had not planned how he would handle the situation when he encountered Peter Lord for the first time following his discussions with Andy Blackwell earlier that day. Perhaps it would have been better to say nothing at this stage, maybe wait until he had more information or at least a plan of action, but there again, he had to broach the question sometime. Now he made a small gesture, just a brief wave of his hand and moved off down the corridor towards Mowbray's office. He took two deep breaths to prepare himself for a potentially difficult meeting with Mowbray and reached out his right hand to grasp the door handle with almost as much care as he would if he suspected it might be electrocuted. "Come in, come in," Mowbray called out as George's figure came into view behind the opening door. The words were not spoken harshly as George had expected given his unexplained absence from the office, but he had already decided that he would not tell Mowbray about his meeting with Andy Blackstone, not just yet at least.

Mowbray wasn't sure why exactly, but he felt as though one of the many heavy burdens on his shoulders was beginning to lift. He knew that he expected too much of people working for him, but when it came to the Helen Grant case, he believed that they deserved a breakthrough and now at least there did seem the possibility that they were about to make progress. This latest enquiry was at least a new beginning and it was just possible that this time they would make a breakthrough, and it was this single strand of hope that enabled a glimpse of sunlight to enter the seemingly perpetual gloom in his mind. Whatever the reason he was grateful for it. "Come on in, here have a seat," he said as he gestured towards a chair beside his desk. "Sarah said she wasn't sure whether you had gone on to another meeting this afternoon, but no matter you're here now. Have you heard the news about the search of Philip Cassidy's house?"

"No, not really," George replied and Mowbray could not resist snapping back, "Well you either have or you haven't. Which is it?"

"No I haven't," George said unequivocally separating each word with a slight exaggerated pause.

Mowbray took great pleasure in explaining carefully everything he knew, not leaving anything out and then he sat back with his hands clasped behind his neck looking pleased with himself. "I've got this funny feeling that this time, at long last we're going to make a breakthrough and I want you to give it priority – drop everything else for now, ok?" Mowbray had kept his small military moustache and he had the habit of pushing his bottom lip forwards so that it just touched the end strands and then exhaling a few small short puffs. Most people found the habit annoying but George did not react to it as Mowbray went through the ritual a few times. "Peter has told forensics that they've got to give this priority. We might get something through in the next half hour or so."

George wanted to get away from Mowbray's office and he took the opportunity. "I'll go down and hurry them up. Anything else you want for now?"

Mowbray looked up "Good idea, yes do that George will you, got to keep those fellows on their toes."

"I'm in for the rest of the day now, I'll let you know what they say," George said as he got up and walked confidently towards the door expecting with each step he took that Mowbray would change his mind and ask him where he had been earlier but the only sound he heard was silence. As he closed the door behind him, he heaved a sigh of relief, turned and walked on down the corridor towards the stairs leading to his own office on the floor below. He knew that at some point very soon he would have to make his confession to the superintendent, but he wanted to delay that as long as possible. He was well aware that as soon as Mowbray knew what he had done he would be suspended from duty whilst the circumstances of his involvement were investigated and he knew that when that happened, he could have no more official involvement in the case. He wanted, at least, to be able to help bring all the loose ends together and to play his part in securing a solution. Yet his conscience was pulling at his resolve to remain silent about what he had done and what he knew now and he paused momentarily in his step, considering the possibility of returning to Mowbray's office but the other side of him took over again and he resisted that temptation.

"How was he?" Sarah asked as George walked towards her desk. "I tried my best to stall him, but I don't think he was happy. Sorry."

"Ok, he was fine. Sorry I left you in the lurch. Can you come in for a moment," George said gently. Sarah followed George into his office and sat down on the chair beside his desk. She watched as George first walked to the window with his back to her and then within just a few seconds he turned and without looking at Sarah directly he returned to his desk and sat down wearily. Sarah thought he looked tired and on edge and she was partly right. She sat forward doing her best to gauge his mood.

"Will you be able to stay late tonight. Mowbray wants me to clear the deck so that I can concentrate on the latest developments in the Helen Grant case. I'll need you to help with the paper work. Is that ok?" George asked.

"Yes, course it is."

"I'm just going down to forensics, see how they're getting on. See you in a bit. Could you make a start on the paperwork? You know the drill – the usual summary note for each case with a check list of all the completed work and the programme for the work in progress or needing to be started. It's a drag, I know, but I can't pass this lot on in its current state," he said looking around the room.

"Go on get off with you. I don't mind honestly. If I did I would have been gone long ago," Sarah replied and George looked back at her and blew a kiss.

George went along the corridor, down the steps and into the basement. It was darker than the rest of the building and had no natural light. His eyes took a few seconds to adjust and he made his way cautiously towards the large door at the far end of the first room. He knocked very deliberately and waited for the door to open. Banik Osama, the senior forensic expert, ushered him in without a word and George followed the overweight figure of a short bald man towards the examination area that was sealed from the rest of the room with plastic curtains.

"Sit over there," Banik said. "I've just finished and Tandi is finishing off," he said nodding in the direction of a blurred figure through the plastic screens. Banik went over to his desk and removed some of the protective clothes he was wearing, but for some reason he left the plastic shoes cover in place. "I'll give you and the Super a full report as soon as possible, but I can give you an outline now to keep you going." George listened to all that Banik had to say without interrupting once.

It was about 7.15 pm and George felt guilty about leaving Sarah alone with the paperwork on her own for so long. The office was deserted and in almost total darkness. George could just make out Sarah's profile as she sat at her own desk with her desk light switched on and angled down so that it cast it's light on the paper work in front of her. She looked up as George walked across the room. "You startled me."

"Sorry," he replied. "And thanks for all of this," he said waving his arm almost aimlessly towards the neat stacks of files which were now on her desk and obviously in much better order.

"I've said before, don't worry. I've left an Apple Danish on your desk. Go and have something to ear, you must be starving."

George walked towards his office but stopped before he reached the door. He turned and looked at

Sarah who was writing a note on one of the file covers. George looked down at the files on her desk. "Have you done it all, or do you want me to finish up here. I really do appreciate it. You know that don't you?"

"Yes, all done. Just go and eat your cake. I'll get you a cup of coffee from the machine," and before he could protest or say anything in response, she had turned and began to walk to the door at the far side of the room.

George walked to his office and was surprised how tidy it was. His desk was cleared almost completely. All that was left were his 'in' and 'out' trays and the files on the Helen Grant case were stacked neatly in the 'in' box. He sat, and saw the Apple Danish still in its paper bag. It made him remember how long it was since he had eaten. As Sarah returned with a plastic cup of hot coffee he was taking his first hungry bite. She put the coffee down in front of him and stood in silence looking at him. He didn't want her to say anything just at that moment so he said the first thing that came into his mind. "You know, I don't think Andy has got over it – losing his wife like that. Hope he'll be ok."

Chapter 12

DC Lucy Atkinson had spent a very unproductive morning sorting out paperwork and drafting reports. Sometimes she thought she should force herself into the spotlight, be more involved in hands-on police work at every opportunity but she knew the value of getting things done on time and of course presenting written information in the best possible light. These reasons alone were enough to persuade her to knuckle down. Lucy was fully aware that she needed to fit in, to be accepted as an equal and appreciated for the contribution she could make. Attitudes had changed significantly in recent years and the right words were often spoken, particularly by those in senior positions, but the prejudice had not disappeared completely. Lucy could understand that. There were some situations that required strength, speed and perhaps the ability to intimidate but they were in fact limited, and of course they were attributes that not all the men possessed. She needed to be successful in particular areas of work, to promote her special skills and abilities without making it too obvious or causing offence and, up to a point, she had been able to achieve that. When she first started with the police her academic skills were at their peak and, quite correctly, that is what she decided to concentrate on. Absorb information, analyse it, test it, refine it and reach credible conclusions. Those were the processes she took from university life into the world of crime and detection, and they stood her in good stead. Now she wanted to branch out, not in any substantial way as she knew that would be a mistake, but at least away from the quiet evaluation of the written word and into a more robust challenging environment. Sometimes she thought about it as if she had been playing chess but was now facing an opponent in the boxing ring, where reflexes and quick thinking became more important and she believed that the cut and thrust of the interview process would be an ideal step for her. Her first interview had been planned meticulously but, even then, there were times when she had to respond instantly to the unexpected and she began to love the rush of adrenalin through her bloodstream as various twists and turns developed instantly before her. She became very good, very quickly and it did not go unnoticed.

Detective Superintendent Mowbray Jackson was considering his options. The right choice could provide his third success of the day and his mood lifted even more when he thought about it. First the search warrant being secured and having proved so productive; that would have been enough on its own. Second, even in his wildest dreams Mowbray would not have expected such luck. He even had to pinch himself again now just to make sure he wasn't dreaming. The opportunity had been delivered to his front door, or to the police reception downstairs to be more precise. Everyone in the building down to the canteen staff, the cleaner and even the IT boffins knew the significance, knew how much they had all longed for this sort of moment. Janet Grant had come in off the street and quite simply had set a timebomb ticking.

The reception staff did not realise the significance at first, but it didn't take them long and, once the beginnings of a story emerged it spread around the building like an electric current.

"I need to speak to a senior officer."

"Could you tell me what about please?"

"I'm Janet Grant, Helen's twin sister, she's the one who disappeared 16 years ago. We didn't tell the truth then, none of us did, but I need to tell the truth now."

Mowbray Jackson wasn't the first to hear the news, but he wasn't the last and it didn't take him long to decide on a strategy. "Get me Peter Lord and Lucy Atkinson," he said abruptly to his PA, "and tell them it's urgent." He had made his choice and he had decided what his instructions would be. He sat for a while and his bottom lip flicked against his moustache a few times. His breathing was deep and rhythmical as he quietly contemplated what might unfold over the next few hours, believing correctly that this was a pivotal moment and needed to be handled with great care. There was one question in particular that kept jumping into his mind and he asked it of himself now, out loud without any restraint or embarrassment "Why now, why bloody now?"

After just a few courtesy questions, Janet Grant was escorted to one of the rooms which had been identified as suitable for difficult personal discussions. It was warm and pleasantly furnished, softly lit and the furniture was arranged in a non-threatening way. Lucy Atkinson sat opposite Janet Grant, just the two of them in easy chairs. Mowbray had stipulated that Lucy would take on this role and she only had the opportunity of the briefest discussion with Peter Lord beforehand. Peter had started to protest but he knew instinctively that Mowbray's decision was the correct one and the few words that he spoke were delivered without any real conviction.

"Just take your time, start wherever you want, I'll just make a few notes as we go along. Is that alright?" Lucy said when Janet Grant had settled into the seat opposite her.

"Yes, yes."

Janet shifted in her seat and took a deep breath. She wanted to be sure she got everything right. She didn't want to leave any loopholes, it had after all been 16 years ago but she had gone over all the details in her mind so many times and she was confident that she would be able to remember everything without prompting and without saying anything that would cast doubt on her belief. Then she started at the beginning.

"When I left home that night on 17 March 2003, I didn't go straight to the summerhouse behind the Parkside Pub. I lied about that."

"Why did you lie Janet?"

"It's all complicated and we were all so very young. Everything seemed so important then. I was madly in love with Philip and nothing else seemed to matter. Not my sister, not my family, nothing. That's the only reason I can think of."

Janet looked back at Lucy Atkinson meeting her eyes full on. She noticed Lucy's dark blue eyes in particular and was comforted by their warmth as they caught some of the soft light coming from one of the table lamps beside her. She nodded a few times, more a gesture to herself than a signal to Lucy and it seemed to act as a trigger for her to continue.

"I knew that Philip fancied Helen. Everyone did. She was so very pretty and an outrageous flirt. But I thought he loved me."

"What made you believe he fancied Helen?" Lucy asked as softly as she could.

Janet smiled again, more to herself than outwardly. She felt more comfortable thinking through her emotions at a distance of several years. At the time they had been a constant source of pain, gnawing away at her inside and forcing her to behave out of character. "Because he told me. Because he asked me to do the things that she would have done."

"I think I know what you mean," Lucy said and she reached out and touched Janet gently on the arm.

"We didn't all jump into bed with any bloke we fancied or even those we fell in love with. There were still some of us who wanted to be respected. But Helen wasn't one of them. Let's just say that she put it about a bit and she didn't seem to mind people knowing."

Lucy made a show of taking in what Janet had said. She looked thoughtful and nodded her head a few times. It was a ploy to give herself a few seconds to ensure that she had the right tone and emphasis to her voice when she asked her next question. Her main concern was to make Janet feel relaxed, more confident about getting to the point. She wanted the key elements of Janet's evidence set out clearly so that she could prompt her to go back over the details again, filling in the gaps, adding the small pieces of information so that they could be tested more robustly. It was almost always the small details that would trip people up.

"I can understand that, I know how you feel. I have often felt the same way, but you need to put that to one side for a moment and let me know what is truly worrying you."

Janet held eye contact with Lucy again for a second or two, blinking a few times, but not looking away. She could feel the tension rising within her, catching the back of her throat and leaving a taste of bile in her mouth. She had thought so many times about this moment, the very point where she could accelerate the process of securing the conviction of

Philip Cassidy for the terrible crimes she knew he had committed. But for some reason she was reluctant to come to the point.

"But I still loved him, I would forgive him almost anything, but it was always at the back of my mind that he would go after Helen if he thought he stood a change with her. But I knew her pretty well and I always thought she didn't really fancy him."

"Did you change your mind about that? I mean whether she fancied him or not?"

"She started acting suspiciously and I was convinced that she was keeping something from me. That wasn't like her. She was always boasting about what she had done and who with."

"And when did all this start?"

Janet considered this carefully before responding "I think it must have been about Christmas time or just after. Then I found her diary hidden in her bedroom."

"What did she write about?"

"Oh the usual stuff, but she added bits about her feelings. Mostly she wrote about meeting up with Tom or Giles but there was someone new on the scene. She referred to him as P. There was lots of stuff like 'Saw P briefly today. He needs to be careful, I must tell him.'"

"And did you read something in the diary that night in March 2003?"

Janet looked sad when she thought about this and Lucy noticed that she kept clenching and then relaxing her fingers in a rhythmical way, first the left hand and then the right. Then she tapped the desk lightly with her fingers in a drum like roll before she answered. "Yes, but I had become suspicious over the previous few days. I began to convince myself that the P stood for Philip after all she did not say a thing to me about any of it. I decided it had to be Philip. And then that night the entry said 'Left a note for P asking him to meet me in the Park. Fingers crossed.' So I followed her."

"And where did she go?"

"It was dark and she was wearing a brown coat so it was difficult. I didn't want to get too close. She went down past the car park and then made towards the millpond. I saw her stop and stand to one side of the path. I could hear voices and I assumed that she was waiting for people to pass by and didn't want to be recognised. I ducked back, near the car park and waited a few seconds. After a short while the voices disappeared and I crept down the path again, but Helen was nowhere to be seen. I followed the path for a few hundred yards and then I saw him."

"Who?"

"It was Philip and he got up from a bench in a clearing just off the path and walked over towards me. I could see straight away that he was surprised that it was me."

"Why was that? What did he say?"

"He sort of stumbled over his words. Mumbled a bit. 'You thought it was going to be Helen didn't you?'

I said to him and then he replied 'Did she tell you? Oh, I should have seen it coming.' Then he told me."

"Told you what?"

"That Helen had sent him a note asking him to meet her there. He still had the note. He told me that he often went to his dad's office at school for a lift home at the end of the day, we all knew that anyway, and that Helen had left a note for him there."

"You say he still had the note. Did you see it?"

"Yes, he showed it to me but I was pissed off with him and walked away. I started to walk through the woods, across to the summer house where we were due to meet the others."

"And when did you see Philip again?"

"He came after me straight away. He asked me not to say anything to the others. 'Look,' he said, 'here's the note, you take it.'"

"And did you?"

"What?"

"Take the note."

"Yes. I took it."

"And what did Philip do then?"

"He said he would catch me up later. I had calmed down a bit by then. He said he felt so silly and asked me again not to tell anyone. 'Promise me,' he said and I remember nodding. 'Thanks. I'll see you in a few minutes. It's best if we don't arrive together.' That's what he said. I took the narrow path through the woods. It was dark, but I had a torch and it was much quicker that way."

"And when did you see him next?"

"I arrived at the summerhouse and started chatting with Tom and Giles. They asked about Helen and I told them she would be coming later. Then Philip arrived. We all got chatting and when Helen didn't turn up Tom and Giles drifted off."

"What time was that?"

"I don't remember exactly. After about half an hour or so I believe."

"Why didn't you tell them about Helen going off to meet Philip?"

"I wanted to have a proper conversation with him first. Find out more if I could. I think I probably believed him about the note, or at least I wanted to believe him."

"Were you able to speak to him again that night"

"Yes, we had a brief conversation. Then we went back to my place. Mum and dad were out and we had the place to ourselves. In the end he convinced me that he hadn't been seeing Helen and the note from her came out of the blue as far as he was concerned. We had a good old cry together."

Lucy noticed a hardening of Janet's face, almost imperceptible at first but then more pronounced as if she had drifted off into her memories of that night and was reliving events which she regretted or found distasteful. Her top lip in particular rose and crumpled at the same time and a few short sniffs left her nostrils one after the other. "Bastard," she said simply, "bloody bastard," and she turned her head away as if recognising that she had given away too much of her true feelings.

Lucy thought at first that Janet's outburst must have been about the note Helen had sent to Philip and that did seem logical to her in many ways but she wasn't entirely convinced. "It's alright, it's ok, just take your time," she said eventually having decided to store the uncertainty at the back of her mind and, perhaps, to return to it later.

"Mum left a note saying she would be home about 9.30. Dad was working down the bypass. We didn't expect him until later."

"What time did your mum get back?"

"Philip and I came downstairs about 9-ish and we watched TV for a while then mum arrived. It was close to 9.30 I would say."

"What about your dad?"

"We were getting worried about Helen by then. Philip had gone home and me and mum were thinking of phoning the site office where dad worked. Then he arrived and we all went out to look for Helen."

"Did you tell your mum and dad about following Helen earlier that evening?"

"No. It all got a bit difficult. I'd promised Philip that I wouldn't say anything. We agreed that I would say that when I left to go to the summerhouse, Helen was still getting ready. So that's what I told mum. I didn't know that Helen had disappeared. I just thought she was out late seeing someone and I was pissed off with her anyway for sending that note to

Philip. And then it got later and later and Helen still didn't turn up. We were all getting really worried."

"When did your mum and dad call the police?"

"I know they spoke about it two or three times, but we kept thinking that she would turn up at any minute and we would just look silly. Mum phoned Tom and Giles first to make sure Helen hadn't met up with them later on. Then dad phoned the police. About 10-ish or just after I think."

"Did the police come straight away?"

"Yes, a police car arrived very soon. Mum and I spoke to a policewoman and the policeman had a look around outside with dad. We phoned two other schoolfriends but couldn't think of anything else to do. Then the policeman and dad came back. They asked if anyone had had a row with Helen whether she had ever stayed out late before, what she was wearing. That sort of thing. After a while they called someone else at the police station, someone in charge I believe, and it wasn't long before two other police cars arrived. They also sent cars to other parts of the park."

"Yes, ok, thanks for that. We've got it all logged. I know that a search started that night and continued throughout the next day. Can you tell me about you and Philip? When did you see him next?"

"I saw him again early next morning. Someone had phoned his home the night before to make sure Helen wasn't there. He came round to see if he could help and we went out together. There were lots of people looking by then. But we had a chance to talk.

Philip said we should stick to the same story. He said it could look very bad for him if they knew about the note. So I agreed. I didn't fancy the idea of changing my story anyway and as time went on and Helen still didn't turn up it got more and more difficult."

"When did the police ask you to make formal statements?"

"I can't remember exactly. It was probably the next day. The day after Philip and I spoke. I think Philip made a statement the same day but he was questioned again later in the week and the week after I believe."

"Did the police speak to you again?"

"Yes. I was asked again to tell them everything I could remember about that night. They also asked what I knew about Helen. Was she herself? Did she have any problems, that sort of thing? They also asked a lot about dad, which I didn't really understand."

"And you stuck to your story throughout?"

"Yes."

"What about the note? What did you do with it and what about the diary?"

"First of all I put the note inside the diary under the floorboards in Helen's bedroom. Then Philip asked me about it. He wanted to know if I had thrown it away. He came round again about a week later and I gave him the note and the diary. He said he was going to get rid of them. Burn them I think he said."

"Was there an envelope with the note?"

"I didn't see one but I think there must have been."

"Can you remember exactly what the note said?"

"I'm not sure I can remember exactly but I've a good recollection. It had his name at the top, and went on to say that she had wanted to talk to him for some time away from anyone else and could he meet her at the pond in Pashley Park. I remember the last bit clearly. It said please, please come."

"Well you have remembered quite a lot. It's been very helpful. But there is something I need to ask you. I'm sure everyone will want to know sooner rather than later and I want to make it as easy for you as possible. We all appreciate you coming to us now, telling the truth at last, but there must be a reason. Why are you telling us all this now?"

Janet didn't say anything in response straight away. ☒She sat open mouthed but with an otherwise blank face and not showing any real emotion. In many ways she believed her part had now been played out and nothing she could do or say would add anything or take anything away, but she was still cautious. "Start the ball rolling and then let them get on with it," that's what her daughter had told her, but she knew she had to answer this question.

Although Lucy had only limited time to prepare for the interview with Janet there were two clear messages still ringing in her ears. Mowbray had pushed aside Peter's words in his usual strong voice. "Don't let on that we've found items in Cassidy's flat, or where they were hidden", he added emphatically. "And get her to explain why it has taken her 16 years, ok – push her on that one." Lucy believed that she had now laid the groundwork for that and was ready to press ahead. She waited expectantly for Janet to answer.

Janet continued to look straight ahead hoping for inspiration. It had been her daughter's plan from the very beginning but Janet had been more than a willing participant and she had her own views about sharing their information with the police. Now Janet just wanted to blurt it all out, to unburden herself and then to step away, but Amanda had been adamant. Janet knew what her daughter wanted to do and, whilst she didn't approve, she understood. In that split second her resolve strengthened, her promise to her daughter would be respected, and she would do as she had been told. "Had to be some time," she replied simply.

"Yes, I understand, but there must have been some sort of trigger. What do you know about Philip Cassidy?"

"What do you mean?"

"Look, I don't want to pressure you, but it's about him isn't it? I'm not trying to trap you in any way."

"Course it's about him, I've already told you," Janet responded and a slight quiver became evidence in her voice.

Lucy decided not to say anything in response hoping that a period of silence would be uncomfortable for Janet and encourage her to add to the brief reply she had made. It worked.

"What do you want me to say?"

"It's a simple question, there must be something, something about Philip Cassidy, what do you know about him, something about him recently, that is?"

"I can't say anything more now. I don't want to be difficult, I just can't."

Lucy thought for a while, and another period of silence developed between them. It was unlikely Lucy thought that she could persuade Janet to say any more on the subject, at least at present so she decided to change direction. "You say Helen was wearing a brown coat, are you sure about that?"

"Yes, absolutely sure."

"You know they found it abandoned, why do you think she might have ditched it?"

"I don't know, I don't know, lots of reasons. It might have been pulled off in a struggle."

"Perhaps," Lucy said with no emphasis to her voice and then, in a more menacing tone, she added, "Do you think Philip had anything to do with her disappearance?"

"I don't see how he could have. I saw Helen walk down past the millpond, further down the path, then I saw Philip. It's just not possible, but everything about that night doesn't make sense. I just don't know."

"When you said earlier that you couldn't say anything more now, were you protecting someone? Has someone told you what to say?"

Lucy could see instantly that Janet felt uncomfortable facing this question. She had been fidgeting for some time, but she was more nervous now, her fingers were twitching almost uncontrollably but she did not seem to notice. She pursed her lips and the wrinkle by the sides of her eyes deepened as she sought to control the tremor in her head. "I don't know what you mean. We haven't, we haven't agreed anything."

Lucy knew immediately that she had made a breakthrough, but her instincts told her that she needed to tread carefully and she held back. "We do appreciate you coming in, we really do and you have been a great help, but you need to tell us everything. You don't need to tell us now if you don't want to. Go away and think about it. I'll get in touch with you tomorrow if it would help."

Janet breathed a sigh of relief, thankful that her ordeal was coming to an end, and satisfied that she had kept her promise to her daughter. "Yes," she said eventually, "yes please."

Lucy started to close the meeting and she moved away from asking questions about Helen's disappearance, but she was still hoping that Janet would add some seemingly innocent comments. She didn't want to prompt or to make her intentions too obvious and she noticed that Janet became increasingly more relaxed. "Is there anything else we can do for you now, or do you have any questions?" she asked.

"What will happen next, can you tell me that?"

"I will discuss with my Inspector but I don't think we have enough, enough that is to reopen the investigation into Helen's disappearance. Sorry."

"But you will talk with your Inspector?"

"Yes."

Janet watched Lucy closely trying to decide what to do. Her breathing was steady and rhythmical with no hint of anxiety or tension. She was falling into a trap of her own making. She couldn't resist asking one more question.

"I know you have searched Philip's house. Did you find anything?"

"Find anything? What did you have in mind?"

"I don't know. I'm not the policeman."

Lucy smiled, a warm gentle smile and she reached out to touch Janet on the arm. "I can't say. You know that don't you, but we are making progress and you coming in today, it does help, it does add to the picture, but we do need to talk again, perhaps not tomorrow, but soon, very soon."

Chapter 13

It didn't take Lucy Atkinson long to complete the formalities after Janet had left and she was now sitting in conference with Mowbray and Peter Lord. "I thought that went as well as could be expected, Sir," Peter said.

Mowbray pushed his bottom lip up until it reached his moustache and he flicked it a few times in well-practised movements. "Yes, not bad at all, but let's just be absolutely sure that we are all thinking the same way. You tell us Lucy, you were closest to it, we were just observing."

"Two things really. It's not just her, Janet I mean, there is someone else – she said 'we' when the going got tough, and that's not all."

"Ok," Mowbray said, nodding slightly, with an encouraging look on his face.

"Someone is in the background pulling the strings, but Janet didn't seem easy to control. I'm sure she wanted to say more."

"That's what I thought too," Peter interrupted "and she knew a lot more than she let on."

"So," Mowbray said, "what do we make of it all? What's the family background?" he asked looking directly at Peter as if he expected him to have all the information at his fingertips.

"We know they moved away, to Scotland I believe, the whole family that is, Rita and Ted Grant soon after Helen went missing, a few months after Janet's 16th birthday. We all thought they wanted to be far away from the memories."

"Anything else?" Mowbray said accusingly almost before Peter had stopped talking.

"We know Janet moved back down south, to Gravesend, not sure when, but that's about it, I believe."

Mowbray wasn't impressed and it showed on his face and in his voice when he spoke "Is that it? Didn't we keep tabs on the family?"

Peter wasn't to be intimidated about this part of the conversation. He had been the one who wanted to keep the investigation open when senior colleagues were calling for it to be scaled down and then dropped entirely a few weeks after the 'missing person' conclusion was reached. "Yes," he said emphatically, "that's all, we were told to drop it and officially that is what we did, Sir."

"Ok, ok, get the point," Mowbray replied in a clear calm voice. "But we need to find out more about the Grant family, I want you to do it now."

Peter looked across in Lucy's direction with a triumphant expression on his face. He knew a bit more about the Grant family than he had let on and he was more than a little keen to add officially to his pot of knowledge. "Yes sir," he replied simply and he breathed an exaggerated sigh of relief. "I'll get Lucy to give me a hand if that's ok?"

"No, I'll need her to help George this end. They need to review everything we have got so far and do an action plan to take it all forward. Why don't you get in touch with Jim Packer, he is working in the Gravesend area now. I'm sure he would be pleased to help."

Chapter 14

George arrived at the office the next day earlier than usual. He had slept badly partly because he felt guilty. Although George felt tired through lack of sleep, he also felt more alert than usual, his mind seemed to have opened up letting in the light and triggering the sort of mental clarity he hadn't felt in a long while. Now he could understand what he had to do and to plan the actions he needed to take. A smile began to form on his lips as he realised the significance. At long last he believed he would be able to put 16 years of torment behind him and to face the future, not exactly with a clear conscience, but at least without the dark cloud of silence that had sat just below the surface of his mind for so long.

There was a spring in his step and a clear purpose in his mind when he arrived in the office and he knew exactly what he was going to do.

He wasn't sure why exactly, but the first person he wanted to talk to was Sarah. "Thanks for all this," he said nodding towards his tidy desk as he stood in the doorway with his back towards her. Sarah realised he was talking to her and she got up from her own desk and walked over to him. "I need to talk to you," he said quietly over his shoulder as he sensed that she was close to him, and it wasn't long before they were sitting face to face and George was telling her everything.

"Does that mean…" Sarah started to say but the words dried up on her tongue before she finished the sentence.

"I know what you mean and yes. I'll be suspended, possibly dismissed, but I've got no control over that."

Sarah had a blank look on her face and she was shaking her head slowly from side to side, blinking a few tears from her eyes and clenching her hands tightly shut.

"But," George continued, "I have got control about when to tell Mowbray. I need to do that soon, but there are some things I need to do first and I'm more determined than ever now to push ahead with that and hope, really hope this time, that it will get us somewhere."

Sarah was still sitting quietly on the edge of her seat. "Do you really think it will come to that?" she said eventually.

"Not sure, but yes probably. They could sack me, I wouldn't blame them and then there's Peter. He will get mixed up in all of this in more ways than one."

"Will you tell him as well now?"

"Got to. I saw him briefly yesterday and he must know something's up."

Then the phone rang and it was Mowbray. George was uncertain at first how he was going to react when he heard Mowbray's voice, but he was able just to listen in silence with a calmness that surprised him.

"I want you to work with PC Atkinson, go through all the new evidence, you've seen Banik's report haven't you? I've spoken with her and she knows as much as you and Peter now so she is up to speed. Peter's off to Gravesend to check on the background to the Dawson family. I've told him to report to you when he gets back."

"Yes, thank you, Sir. I'm ready to go and really pleased to be able to work with Lucy on this one."

Chapter 15

Lucy Atkinson heaved a sigh of relief as she put the finishing touches to the note of her interview with Janet Grant and then finalised her report. She had been working at her desk long before George Baker had arrived at the police station that morning and she was now feeling hungry. Mowbray had asked to see everything she had recorded and she emailed the details to him straight away. She sat back in her chair with her hands behind her head focussing her thoughts on all that Janet Grant had said. She felt sure there were important details that Janet had not spoken about and she was keen to find out more. She knew that Peter Lord was on his way to Gravesend and she was looking forward to hearing what he had found out. She was convinced there was more to the family background and it intrigued her.

She started to daydream about the possibilities, but soon decided that was a waste of time. Mowbray had told her that he wanted her to work closely with DI George Baker that morning and she was expecting to hear from him soon. She did not have to wait long. She had worked with the DI on two previous projects, neither of which had been very interesting or challenging, but she had completed all that George had asked her to do with her usual efficiency. She recognised George immediately she saw him walking confidently towards her in the corner of the large office she shared with about ten of her colleagues. He looked fit for his age she thought and with attractive steel-blue eyes made more striking against his generously tanned and weather-beaten face. He looked like someone she thought she could trust.

"The Super says we will be working together on this one."

Lucy nodded in time with his words and she got up out of her chair as George drew nearer. "Yes Sir," she said as she stood almost self-consciously by the side of her chair. "I'm looking forward to it."

"Sarah's just getting me a coffee," he said as he looked down more at the top of her head than anything else. She was very small and vulnerable, he thought, but he knew that looks could be deceptive. "Do you want one?"

"No," she said, this time shaking her head from side to side and she smiled a warm smile in his direction. "Do you want to see my note of the interview with Janet Grant? I can print off a copy for you. I've already sent one to the Super."

"Yes please. Looking forward to seeing exactly what she said and then you can fill me in on what you and Peter think. What's behind her words I mean."

It was just a few minutes later and they were sitting side by side in George's office. It was quiet and they were both absorbed in the reports they were reading. "Well, well, well," George said as he came to the end of the note of Janet Grant's interview, "that didn't occur to me I must admit," and he looked across at Lucy to see if she had finished reading Banik's report.

In fact she had finished it a few minutes earlier but was now rechecking some of the important details. "I could say the same thing," she said almost to herself "There is much more to this than I ever imagined."

"Exactly," George replied "But tell me what do you make of it."

"So, the key they found in the pocket of the ski jacket, Banik certainly got a move on finding out about that"

George nodded a few times "Yes, there is a code on it and with the help of the hotel they have told him which room it's for."

"Room 214," Lucy responded. "That's Amanda Dawson's room, isn't it? Her room at the Orion Hotel?"

"Yes."

"And they are both still missing?"

"As far as we know, yes."

"And no report of him entering the country – ports, airports?"

"No, nothing."

Lucy lowered her gaze and pushed her short fringe to one side with her fingers as she took in a deep breath of air. "Doesn't add up," she said eventually. "He just wouldn't, would he?"

"What, come back to England somehow without being spotted and then leave incriminating evidence at his own flat. If he's got any sense he would know we were bound to search it."

"And so would Janet Grant," Lucy exclaimed. "I wondered why she should ask us about the search of Cassidy's address. She knew something obviously. But what's her game I wonder?"

George stood up and walked over to the window by the door overlooking the outer office. Sarah was working away at her desk, head down and obviously deep in thought. He was pleased he had told her the truth at last but he knew she would be worried about him.

"You ok, Sir?" Lucy asked when she noticed that he seemed distracted.

"Yes, don't mind me. This case has always unsettled me and I know I'm not the only one."

"But we may have a breakthrough now and maybe, just maybe, we can find out for sure what happened to her, to Helen I mean."

George smiled to himself. He understood exactly what Lucy meant and in many ways he knew that she was right. He also knew that the process of finding the solution would bring about his own downfall. He had no qualms about that. It was all that he deserved he thought. The clarity of his thought process which had been evident from the moment he got up that morning did not desert him now. "Everything Janet told us fits with Banik's conclusions, doesn't it?"

"I'd say so, yes but…"

"But what?"

"Banik's report is very clear. The box they found under the floorboards in Cassidy's flat contained three items, a note addressed to Philip, an envelope and a diary."

"Yes, the diary had entries for most days up until 16 March 2003 and it had Helen's name inside the front cover."

Lucy was looking at a particular section of Banik's report and she did not answer straight away. Then she found what she was looking for "It's the fingerprints Banik's found on the note and envelope that interest me the most."

"And I think I can see why that would be."

"But," Lucy said with a quizzical look on her face, "how was Banik able to make the comparisons?"

"Fingerprints were taken voluntarily from all family members in 2003 for elimination purposes and they were retained on the database. Cassidy's prints were taken at the same time."

Lucy listened to George's explanation and she was thinking through the implications. She wasn't sure whether or not the evidence was important, but it was definitely helpful, and she could see difficulties in using the information officially. That wasn't the important point for her at this stage. "We would all expect these prints to be on the note and envelope," she said eventually, "but it's the reference to Janet's prints on the envelope that interest me the most. Look, here," she said pointing to the section of

Banik's report that she had identified earlier. "He makes reference to Janet's prints in particular."

"Yes, I had noticed. He refers to them as being more defined and much clearer than all the others but he doesn't commit himself on the reason for that."

Lucy watched George closely expecting that he would explain what he meant but he just left his explanation hanging in the air knowing that Lucy would reach her own conclusion and she decided to follow her instincts. "Could be," she started to say tentatively. "Could be she touched it more recently. I'm no expert but I would definitely say that was a logical explanation."

This time it was George who was nodding as Lucy spoke indicating clearly that he agreed with her and she took comfort from his support.

"It all adds up," she said. "Could be it was Janet Grant who put the items in Cassidy's flat expecting that we would find them. She wants to incriminate him."

"And then she comes in off the street to stick the boot in. But what's it all for and why now?" George responded almost before Lucy had finished speaking.

"I don't think it's just her. There is someone else in the backgrounds I'm sure of it. We have the key, we have the note addressed to Philip and we have Helen's diary. But what's the connection?"

"The package addressed to Mr Denman. I think that's the connection. Banik has given us an outline of the contents but we are going to have to watch the video ourselves and you know what, I'm not looking forward to that one little bit."

Chapter 16

Andy Blackstone had thought about contacting Ruby a number of times since she and Graham had spoken with him, and each time he decided to put it off for one reason or another. Now he decided to make the call.

"Sorry I'm not available to take your call at the moment, but if you leave a message I'll get back to you as soon as possible." Ruby's voice was strong and clear on the answer phone with a gentle hint of sexuality.

"It's Andy Blackstone. Could you ring me on this number when you get a moment? Thanks." Andy's voice on the other hand was weak and with the hint of discomfort. He had been in pain on and off for about two hours. The painkillers he had taken were obviously not working as well as they had before. His doctor had warned him that he would need to change his medication in the next week or two, and now it seemed likely that he would have to make the change sooner than expected.

Andy looked at his watch and immediately thought about his wife Jean who had given it to him as an early birthday present the year before last. The both knew that it was only a matter of time for her and she wanted to make sure she celebrated his birthday with him before it was too late. Andy recalled the joy on her face when he opened it and Jean had taken it from him, placed it carefully on his wrist, securing the strap. It was a perfect fit. You can remember me whenever you check the time she had said and it had stuck in his mind. He had kissed her gently on the forehead and felt as close to her then as he had ever been. He was brought back to reality with a jolt as the pain in his stomach hit him suddenly with no warning and it was accompanied by a hot fizzy sensation rising up into his throat, burning each short breath he took making him cough and splutter against a fear of choking. He clasped his forehead with the open palms of his hands and pressed hard against his closed eyes with his index fingers. Why does death have to be so painful he thought with more self-pity than usual. The pressure on his eyes gave him temporary relief or at least something else to concentrate on. He opened his eyes and saw the time was close to 4.30 pm but it didn't matter much to him.

At exactly the same time Ruby was driving fast across town and heading in the direction of Marble Street. The telephone call she received from Philip a short while before had caught her by surprise and she staggered slightly as her legs began to shake when she heard his voice.

"Hi darling – it's me. I need to see you. Can you come over?"

Ruby stumbled over her own words as if she was speaking a foreign language. At last she blurted out "Oh Philip. I've been so worried, are you all right," and she sat clumsily in the chair next to the phone in the hallway.

"Well I've been better but I haven't got much time. I'm at my aunt's house – 17 Marble Street. She's away in New Zealand, so I've got the place to myself. How long will you be?"

"I can leave straight away. Is there anything you need? Oh, Philip I've been so worried."

"Get over here as quick as you can. We'll talk then, ok?" and he put the phone down before Ruby could reply.

Ruby's driving was erratic and she had at least two near misses soon after she left home. She knew she needed to take the second exit at the next roundabout which would take her down Carlisle Road and she positioned herself in the right-hand lane only barely aware of the car on her inside. As soon as the traffic from her right eased slightly, she pulled away quickly but she missed her gear change and had to fumble with the gear stick eventually forcing it into second. Usually she was a confident driver but her mind was in turmoil and it led to a lack of concentration. She was almost there, less than half a mile away and soon she found herself turning into the quiet cul de sac which bore the slightly faded sign – Marble Street. She could see the uneven house numbers on her side of the road and she counted down from 25 until she saw a parking space outside number 19. She stopped, turned off the ignition, pulled out her key hurriedly and pushed the driver's door open suddenly without checking if there was another vehicle going past. She was in luck and she stepped out of the car hurriedly and slammed the door shut. She ran as fast as she could to number 17 and was soon standing by the front door, panting slightly as she rang the bell. She saw a movement by the curtain in the side window and thought she made out a face but she could have been mistaken. Then the door opened suddenly just a few inches. "Come on in quick," she heard Philip whisper to her and he opened the door just a little more so that she could squeeze through.

Almost before the door was closed behind her, she flung her arms around him, turning and lifting her head so that she could kiss him, but he stepped back away from her.

"Did anyone see you?" he said looking out of the side window behind her.

"No I don't think so. It's all right Philip. I've been so worried," and she reached out for him again.

This time he did not seek to resist and they were stood wrapped in each other's arms as their open mouths met hungrily. After a short while Philip broke away from the kiss. "Come through into the lounge," he said turning away from her and leading her by the hand. The curtains in the lounge were closed and the room was in semi darkness. Philip sat on the settee under the window and Ruby released her grip on his hand and stepped back a pace or two. She reached up under her skirt with both hands and pulled down the white frilly panties she was wearing, held them in her outstretched hand and let them fall to the floor in front of him. Neither of them spoke as she knelt on the floor and put her head in his lap. Immediately she could feel the hardness rising up against her face and he thrust himself forwards adding to the pressure between them. Ruby reached for the buckle of his belt and fumbled with it for a second or two before Philip released the clasp himself, eased down the zip and pulled his trousers and pants down together. Immediately Ruby could feel the warmth of his arousal against her face and then the heady scent and taste which awoke a primeval part of her brain and she became almost frantic in her pursuit.

When their passion had been spent, they sat side by side on the settee. Ruby was the first to move as she picked up her panties from the floor attempting to step back into them as unselfconsciously as possible, but she lost her balance slightly and the manoeuvre was not accomplished as smoothly as she would have wished. Philip didn't notice, he was on edge and he could hear voices outside. Then the doorbell rang. "Did you tell anyone about this address?" he said with alarm in his voice and the veins in his neck began to puff up and take on a pinkness growing in intensity before her eyes. "No," she whispered back as the doorbell sounded again with growing persistence. "You get it," he said "Get rid of them as soon as you can. Don't say anything about me for Christ sake."

Ruby opened the door tentatively "Yes?" she said.

"That's your car over there isn't it?" the young man said. "Only I don't think you locked it when you parked, sorry to bother you but we've had lots of problems round here recently."

"Thank you" Ruby replied. She turned to pick up her car keys which she had left on the hall table, making sure that she kept the front door partly closed. "I'll come across and check." They walked together, side-by-side and when she was close enough Ruby pressed the key fob and they both heard the soft click as the lock engaged. "Thought so", the man said, "better safe than sorry."

The man was keen to engage in conversation about crime rates in the area and it took Ruby a minute or two to bring the conversation to an end. "Thank you again," she said as she walked away finally able to return to Philip without appearing to be too rude.

She rang the doorbell to number 17, still in somewhat a daze, but this time Philip pulled it open wide almost immediately. He glanced to the left and right behind her but didn't say a word.

"It's ok," Ruby said as she walked past him into the hall at the bottom of the stairs.

"Ok, ok – you stupid cow," he hissed at her through clenched teeth.

"It's sorted now – don't worry," Ruby replied calmly.

"I should have guessed you would alert the whole fucking neighbourhood," and he raised his arm as if he was going to strike her with his clenched fist.

His movement towards her was halted, but Ruby was aware that the anger within him was concealed only just below the surface ready to rise up again at the first provocation. She had never seen him like this before and she was afraid. "I heard what he said. How could you be so stupid… You, you…" Philip's words hung in the air between them and Ruby closed the gap, instinctively believing that Philip wouldn't harm her and wanting to calm his anger.

"I'm sorry," she whispered "but it's ok. There's no need to worry," and she gathered him into her encircling arms and felt his body begin to heave as his sobs echoed loudly in her ear. The warmth of his tears against her neck reminded her of her ex-husband's tears and she wondered if they were tears of shame or relief, as she fought hard to blot any comparison from her mind.

It was a minute or two before he was calm enough to speak "I'm sorry Ruby. It's just that everything's got too much for me. Please forgive me. I need you so much especially now, you know that don't you?"

"Yes, yes, I know and I understand – don't worry but I need to know what happened to you."

"One minute I was in Méribel and the next I found myself in this dirty bedsit in Calais with one stonker of a hangover."

"Just tell me what you can remember," Ruby said patiently and she watched his face closely.

Philip did not answer straight away. He sat next to Ruby on the settee in the lounge with his mouth open, eyes fixed on a spot on the floor in front of him, his breathing coming in short bursts interspersed with deep racking sighs. It was at least one full minute before he said anything and then he blurted out, "I've been set up, you've got to believe me."

"Just tell me Philip, tell me what happened and then I'll let you know if I believe you or not." This was the first time Ruby had admitted to herself that there was the slightest possibility that Philip might lie to her about something as important as this, but her trust in him had been weakened by all that she had learned over the past few days and tentacles of doubt had already begun to push against her blind faith in him.

"You're not going to like this," Philip said after a lengthy pause during which he had picked against a piece of loose skin by the nail on his thumb almost absentmindedly.

"Just try me," Ruby shot back.

"The girl in the hotel. I swear I never touched her but I did speak to her a few times. We both swam in the hotel pool and we got chatting because we were the only ones there most of the time. To be honest she came on to me in quite a big way."

"Came on to you – what do you mean?" Ruby said with a sarcastic edge to her voice. She watched him even more closely now, looking for signs that might show unease or dishonesty.

"Well she was always sort of waiting for me outside my room and we walked down to the pool together. She told me all sorts of stuff about her mum and dad and she kept making remarks."

Ruby was beginning to get edgy as she listened to Philip's explanation and he could tell by her face that he needed to explain what he meant.

"It was innuendo – you know the sort of thing. I was flattered I must admit."

"I bet you were," came Ruby's immediate response.

"She was young and attractive and very chatty, she came straight out with it. 'You like me don't you – I've seen you look' – that's what she said and then she went into the cubicle and started to change without shutting the door. She did it on purpose, knew that I was watching and when she came out, she came straight over to me. 'We can meet up later if you like and I'll show you the bits you didn't see.' Honestly that's exactly the way it was."

"And did you meet her?" Ruby said sharply.

Philip looked directly at Ruby, and she knew the answer before he spoke. Just as he started to protest Ruby interrupted. "She's only fifteen for god's sake. What were you thinking of?"

"I'm not sure what I was thinking but I couldn't let her down once we had arranged to meet."

"No, but you could have told her straight away that you weren't interested," Ruby shot back, her nostrils flared and her eyes caught him with a sharp glare of indignity.

"Anyway, she gave me the key to her room, said come round about 5-ish that afternoon. She said her mum and dad would be out."

"You stupid fool."

"I thought, just for a quick drink."

"Do you think I'm a complete idiot?" Ruby said and she got up from her seat and turned her back on him. She didn't want to look him in the eyes just at that moment and she didn't want him looking too closely into hers.

"I'm just telling you what happened. At least the bits I can remember. Nothing happened I tell you."

Ruby turned towards Philip now and she looked at him closely, at his mouth in particular, looking for any signs to help her make up her mind. She wanted to believe him but for the moment she wanted more answers. "What do you mean – as far as you can remember?"

"Well," Philip replied "I can remember arriving and letting myself in. She was next door and when she heard me, she called out – help yourself to a drink – I took a few sips and that was it. The next thing I remember is waking up in Calais – that can't be right can it? The thing is she must have planned the whole thing – but why for god's sake – it doesn't make any sense!"

"Let's get one thing straight first, you agreed to meet this girl and you expected more than a drink, so don't try to wriggle out of that." Philip began to protest but Ruby waved away his feeble excuses with the back of her hand as if she was discouraging an intrusive fly from settling on her nose. She was remarkably calm but continued to be uncertain about her feelings and her dark eyes held him steadily in her sight as she struggled to recall the parts of him which made her fall in love so completely just a few short months ago. As the seconds passed, her mood softened somewhat and she began to focus on the typical male frailty, their obsession with sexual conquest fostered somewhere in human evolution, but she couldn't forgive him completely, not by some distance.

It was Philip who broke the silence but his words came too soon. "The point is, nothing happened."

Ruby did not reply immediately. She had been relatively calm throughout and that calmness encouraged Philip to press ahead with his explanations but, inwardly Ruby was not ready to acknowledge any understanding or forgiveness and those emotions remained suppressed within her. Philip reached out to touch her on the knee which was another mistake and he noticed her recoil from his outstretched hand before it got anywhere near her, and she stood up abruptly taking a few steps towards the window standing with her back to him. Ruby couldn't see out the window because the curtain was drawn, but she flicked it open a few inches just to annoy him and a shard of light caught dust particles floating in front of her. At last Ruby broke the silence "I've already said, that's not the point, not for me anyway. You would have betrayed me, broken our trust, if you had the chance and there's no point in denying it, so let's just agree to disagree and maybe we can sort something out, but don't push me, not about that anyway."

Ruby was still calm and part of her was beginning to accept Philip's argument, but she wasn't about to give any indication that her steely resolve was weakening in any way, not for the moment at least. Philip, on the other hand, was a combustible mixture of emotions and unpredictability, built upon his determination that he had done nothing wrong and that Ruby's interpretation was no more than warped female logic twisted by an inability to see reason in such circumstances. For the moment he kept his thoughts to himself and his temper under control, but his cheeks were flushed with indignity and his breathing came in short angry bursts through his nostrils. He knew that he needed Ruby at the moment for all sorts of reasons and that now was probably the worst time for him to let his guard slip. He was convinced that the events in Méribel had been planned for a particular reason. He recalled waking up in Calais, but everything was a bit fuzzy and he willed himself to recall as many of the details as possible. His small case had been packed and was placed by the side of the bed, but his ski-top was missing. That didn't worry him too much but it did seem a bit odd. His main concern was that the parcel addressed to Mr Denman, which he thought he had hidden carefully, was definitely missing. Despite all the fuzziness he did remember that clearly and it worried him. He had thought fleetingly that there might be some connection with Helen Grant, but he had discounted that almost immediately. His main concern was that someone knew about the real secrets in his life and it was those activities which he didn't want Ruby to know about.

A further period of silence hung uneasily in the air as the dust particles continued to dance in front of Ruby who remained standing by the window. Again it was Ruby who spoke first. "That's agreed then."

"If you say so," Philip replied grudgingly but Ruby knew she was unlikely to elicit anything more genuine or sincere and decided to let it pass.

"Now we must decide what to do but first you must tell me everything."

"I've told you all there is to tell."

"That may be so, as far as Méribel is concerned, but the police have linked the girl's recent disappearance with the disappearance of Helen Grant way back in 03," Ruby said very slowly and deliberately and watching Philip closely as the colour left his face seemingly in stages until he looked ashen with dark shadows across and under his eyes.

"What do you know about Helen Grant's disappearance?" Philip said forcing himself to remain as calm as possible but the mention of her name had set his pulse racing and there was a tightness developing in his throat making it difficult for him to breathe or swallow normally.

"Quite a lot as it happens and I've been able to refresh my memory, but there are still a hell of a lot of gaps. I was hoping you could fill them in."

Philip was forced again to consider whether Helen Grant's disappearance had in fact been behind the problems he had experienced in Méribel. He still wasn't convinced, after all he thought to himself, there was only one other person who knew anything about that and, after all, she had kept quiet all these years.

"I've tried to forget all about Helen Grant. That's a part of my life that's buried and best left undisturbed," Philip eventually blurted out.

"But you will be asked about it again… by the police. You must realise they are longing to reopen the case, to put right past mistakes, to ease their consciences even after all these years?"

"I don't see why!" Philip said wanting to believe that everyone connected with the case felt the same way as he did, but fearing that Ruby might be right. But the uncertainty began to mount within him and his mind began playing tricks with his memory. He just stood there with a blank look on his face and nothing seemed to make sense any more.

"What is it Philip?" Ruby said sensing how uneasy Philip had become. "Please tell me, it can't be so bad that you must hide it even from me."

"What do you mean? Do you think I've got something to hide? I told the police everything 16 years ago."

"Then why do you look so worried now? I'm only trying to help, you know that don't you and I believe in you."

There was a delay in Philip's reply which Ruby noticed immediately and her father's words of caution came into her mind again. She knew that in many ways she was a strong and confident woman, able to tackle many difficult tasks but she knew that she did not always have the same confidence as far as her private life was concerned and she had made mistakes before.

It was the last few words that Ruby had spoken which eased Philip's anxiety. He smiled inwardly, not wanting to reveal any of his true feelings when Ruby had said she believed him. There were parts of his life that he had kept hidden from her and he intended to keep them secret for the foreseeable future, but the events in Méribel had, as far as he was concerned, been out of his control and he had been entirely innocent. But Ruby's belief in him was important now and he instinctively wanted to nurture her support. He turned towards her and looked deep into her dark eyes. "Yes I know," he said eventually and without any conscious effort on his part a lump came up in his throat adding to his false sincerity and it partly checked his next few words "I do love you so very much, but I always seem to destroy the things I love best." He put his hand up to cover his mouth and his last few words were almost lost amongst the tears that started to fall down his cheeks towards an involuntary quivering of his bottom lip. He was not acting, he was not seeking to put on a show. The whole effect came to him naturally and it was so much more convincing as a result.

Ruby reached out and cradled him in her arms. She could feel the warm tears on her own face and the rhythmical heaving of his chest as he fought unsuccessfully to suppress the sobbing rising up within him. Then there was silence and they clung to each other and gradually Philip became calmer. Ruby reached out and brushed the last of his tears away in a gentle affectionate gesture and she smiled at him spontaneously, receiving in return a nervous half formed chuckle as the tension holding him in its grasp began to let go.

"You've got nothing you need to hide from me," Ruby said eventually as she continued to caress his face with her fingertips, moving them higher up towards his forehead and then down across his temple, feeling his pulse so strongly that she thought she might be hurting him even with the lightest of touches. This time it was Philip who got up and walked towards the window with his back to her. Instinctively he felt it was easier to talk without looking into her eyes. I can't tell you just yet, not like this," and immediately he felt better as if some weight had been lifted from his shoulders.

"But you must tell someone... sometime," Ruby replied calmly. "It's obviously important to you... to everybody, but if you prefer to talk with someone you don't know... a professional perhaps, then I would understand."

Philip turned to face Ruby "You mean a psychiatrist?" he said in a voice just as calm as Ruby's had been.

"No, I was thinking about a solicitor, you'll need one anyway to support you when you give yourself up to the police and they will need to know everything if they are going to be able to help."

"Yes, it's that bad isn't it?" Philip said and he turned towards the window again but this time he drew back the curtains letting the daylight into the room. In some ways he felt relieved now that all the emphasis seemed to be centred on Helen Grant and he was happy to let in the light.

Ruby moved and stood beside him, looking out on a dry but cloudy sky as she linked her arm with his and held it tightly in an effort to demonstrate her support. "Ok," Philip said without looking away from the unspectacular view outside, "I'll talk with a solicitor, but I want you to be there too. Is that ok?"

Chapter 17

Commander Patrick Bouchard had most of the answers already. Bit by bit, layer by layer, a picture was emerging needing only one small extra detail to bring everything sharply into focus. Patrick was just waiting for Thierry Moureau to report back on his telephone conversation with the local police in Carcassonne and he didn't expect any surprises. The decision to upgrade the search for Amanda Dawson and to make it high priority had been correct at the time he firmly believed. It could have turned out so differently and it was always wise to err on the side of caution in cases like that.

He knew now that Amanda Dawson was in fact safe and well but he still had faith in Ingrid Peterson's judgement and her outspoken views at the time. Given the extra overtime involved he would now have to answer for that with his own superiors but he would not seek to push the blame elsewhere.

Patrick had arranged to meet with Ingrid so that he could inform her about all the latest developments. He half expected that she would know most of the detail already, as it seemed to be common knowledge throughout headquarters, but he was mistaken about that. For one reason or another Ingrid was often not included in the gossip among mostly male colleagues. That didn't bother her in the main because they mostly talked about trivial things – a bit like naughty schoolboys, but it did concern Patrick who often felt that it was indicative of an unpleasant attitude which belonged firmly in the past along with so many other prejudices.

Patrick looked out of the large window towards the south side of the valley and thought about the times he and Ingrid had met just above Méribel village. There were a few quiet parking places along the narrow road towards Courchevel and they often met there sharing a sandwich for lunch and having a quiet cuddle in the back seat of his car. Their relationship had started and ended there and he thought about these times fondly and with no regret.

Ingrid was also deep in thought as she drove down the hill towards police headquarters. She knew that Patrick wanted to see her to provide an update on the case and she had mixed feelings about it. Part of her wanted absolute clarity, an end to the process with all questions answered, but she feared that these answers would be embarrassing for her. She had been the one to tell all of her colleagues to drop everything, cancel social arrangements, and postpone family events so that they could take part in the search for the missing girl. To be fair they had all responded, with some grumblings of course, and the search had been extensive and thorough. Now Ingrid was tired and her mind began to wander. She had the beginnings of a headache and her eyes felt sore and gritty. She parked her car in one of the staff bays and sat for a while. She rubbed her eyes a little too vigorously and it felt like she was moving grains of sand back and forth irritating the skin around her eyes even more. It made her recall the one and only time she had sex on a sandy beach. She hadn't been very keen in the first place but her boyfriend made it sound quite romantic, a starlit night, the sound of the Mediterranean Sea breaking rhythmically nearby and the pleasant warmth from the remains of the day. The result however was far from romantic and she had told him to hurry up and get on with it. These distant thoughts were interrupted and she was brought back to reality by a colleague passing nearby and knocking on the passenger side window. It was Edith, one of the senior secretaries and she called out a cheery "Hello." Ingrid waved and smiled in Edith's direction but she didn't feel in the mood for small talk, so called out, "Won't be long – see you later," and waved again with a little more exaggeration. Ingrid sat for a minute or so pretending to be busy and then, when Edith was well out of view she got out, locked the door and headed in the direction of the main entrance, adjusting the lanyard around her neck which would give her access to all parts of the building. There were one or two "Hello"s, called in her direction as she made her way through the open plan office heading towards Patrick Bouchard's room and she returned them as cheerily as possible. "Going to get a good bollocking," one less than friendly colleague muttered under his breath, but clear enough for Ingrid to hear, but she didn't respond in any way.

Ingrid knocked confidently on Patrick's door and opened it immediately.

"Ah Ingrid, come in. Take a seat," Patrick said pointing to one of the three empty chairs in front of his desk. "You ok?" Patrick lifted his head slightly and looked directly into Ingrid's eyes. He could tell that she was in fact far from ok. Her eyes lacked their usual sparkle and the colour of her skin was ashen and tired looking. He paused slightly, not knowing whether or not to say anything, but chose not to and the silence between them became obvious to both of them.

It was Ingrid who broke it. "Are you going to update me or what?"

Patrick remained silent for another few seconds, still unsure what to say and he took a few deep breaths. "After this is all over, and it won't be long now, you have a good holiday – you deserve it."

"Is that an order?"

"No, just friendly advice, ok?" They still both had feelings for each other and at times like these it got in the way more than it should. Patrick in particular wanted to put his arms around her, to bury his face in her neck, to feel the warmth of her tears, but that was probably more about his needs and uncertainties. Ingrid just wanted him to be happy. Patrick took two more deep breaths seeking to push his thoughts to one side and to regain his composure.

"I probably will take that holiday soon, but we need to put this one to bed first."

"Yes, sure – you probably know that she's alive and well. I'll get Thierry in so that he can give you all the details."

"That would be nice."

Patrick took the few steps towards one of the windowed walls overlooking the main office. "That's Thierry with his back to you, the one with the dark hair." Patrick knocked on the glass seeking to attract Thierry's attention but all four faces nearby turned towards him. Patrick pointed directly at Thierry and beckoned him across to his office. Thierry was about six foot two inches, carried his impressive upper body in a relaxed but confident way and he made a physical impact when he walked into the room.

"Have you made the last call yet?"

"Yes, just finished a short while ago, I've got my notes here."

"What did they say?"

Thierry was just about to reply when Ingrid interrupted. "Could you take it from the top, don't assume I know anything at the moment."

Thierry looked directly at Ingrid and held her gaze for a second or two longer than necessary, but otherwise he did not show any particular emotion. "From the top it is. Mrs Dawson went home – back to England that is. On 19 March, just two days after

Amanda went missing. Mr Dawson left before that of course. We all thought it a bit odd that she didn't stay longer. I've been in regular telephone contact with them ever since."

"How did she travel?" Ingrid asked although she probably knew the answer but just wanted formal confirmation.

"Train back to Calais, then on the ferry to Dover."

"Was that the pre-booked return crossing?"

"Yes, all arranged in advance."

"So, what have they been saying then?"

"At first it was the usual. They sounded really worried, wanted to know what was happening. They chased me up a couple of times. Then yesterday it all changed. I had already spoken with them twice in the morning, then got a call just after lunch."

"And what did they say?"

"Full of apologies. Said they had heard from Amanda and that she was alive and well. Got in touch with them from Carcassonne it seems."

"Ok then, so what's the full story?"

"They say, and it's only what Amanda has told them, she met up with friends straight after skiing and did the usual round of bars – Barometer, Fifty Fifty, The Pub and then ended up at Ruby's Tea Bar. By the end of the evening they were all being picked up and were headed for the south coast. Amanda says she just got caught up with it all – she's had too much to drink. Apparently they got as far as Carcassonne and the partying went on.

"She would have phoned her mum and dad as soon as she sobered up. Do you really believe she left it – what – almost a week before making contact?"

"I'm just telling you what they said – I didn't say I believed it."

"And we did a thorough trawl that night and the next morning. All the usual drinking spots. You know what, Fifty Fifty is only a small place, someone would have remembered if she had been in there with a crowd. It just doesn't add up."

"I'm certainly with you there, but she definitely ended up in Carcassonne. Local police confirm it."

Patrick raised his hand. He hadn't spoken at all during the exchange between Thierry and Ingrid, but the mention of the Carcassonne police prompted him to interrupt. "I'll be interested in hearing what they had to say," he said.

"That's about it. They say everything checks out – it's definitely Amanda, they interviewed her before she left – got a statement and photos."

"Did they ask her about this guy Philip Cassidy?" Ingrid asked.

"No – all they wanted to do was to establish what happened and to know that she was safe."

"Do we know anything more about Cassidy? Has he turned up at all?" she asked with an accusing tone to her voice. She was beginning to think that the investigation had been slipshod but she knew that any protest on her part would be met with derision. She knew what many of her colleagues thought about her role in the earlier stages when Amanda Dawson went missing and some of them weren't afraid to say so.

This time it was Patrick who answered Ingrid's question. "All we know for sure is that he was booked on the return flight from Geneva to Gatwick on Friday but he didn't turn up."

"What about his passport details? Do we know if his passport has been used at all – another airport, channel crossing?" Ingrid asked with a flat tone to her voice. She was beginning to conclude that there wasn't much point in her pressing for explanations.

This time Thierry answered. "There's no record of his passport being used from any location in France."

"His bags were packed, his hotel bill was settled and his door key returned to reception," Ingrid said in a slow methodical tone seeking to emphasise each point.

"What are you suggesting?"

"He can't just disappear into thin air, perhaps we've been looking for the wrong person, what do you think Patrick?" This time she directed her question to Patrick in particular believing that he was more likely to take her enquiries more seriously.

"I think we could overanalyse this all day long. A girl was reported missing, we did all we could, the girl has been found safe. We had a suspect, but we don't need one now – so I think we should just step back, shut the case down and let the English get on with it. They were the ones interested in him."

Thierry was already beginning to switch off and to think about other things. He was convinced that

Patrick was correct and that they shouldn't waste any more time. "Do you want any more from me for now?"

"No, just get on with the other stuff. I'll see you later to catch up," he said and even before Patrick could answer he took a few steps towards the door.

The room seemed larger when Thierry had left and they both felt a little uncomfortable. "That holiday," Patrick said. "Just make sure you book it soon."

"Will do."

"And let me have your final report. I'll put all the finishing touches, make sure it's all complete and then we can put it to bed."

"What about the English. Do you want me to follow that up at all?"

"No Ingrid. I'll email their superintendent, let them know what we have established. They can take it from there. It all sounds a bit fishy."

"More than a bit, yes, but that's their problem."

"We've done all we can our end."

There was another silence and eventually Ingrid got up "I'll be off then," she said over her shoulder as she made her way towards the door.

"Yes, thanks Ingrid. Good work by the way and don't let anyone tell you otherwise."

Chapter 18

Jim Packer did not like surprises. He preferred to be in control and to be the one making all the decisions, dictating how events would begin and how they would unfold. In most aspects of his life he enjoyed being in that position. There was a murmur of voices in the far corner of the room which he ignored, preferring to concentrate on the witness statement he was reading. Then he looked up. At first he did not recognise the man standing there and uttering just three words.

"Hi. Long time."

But although the uncertainty lasted just a second or two, it unnerved him momentarily and it showed on his face. He took in a gasp of air and a smile began to crease his face when recognition finally arrived. "What on earth are you doing here?" he blurted out before he regained a semblance of control.

"That's a nice welcome I must say."

Peter Lord's face brought back the memories and Jim's mind filled with them now. They had all done their best, all strived to get a result, and Jim knew that Peter Lord in particular had thrown himself into the task of finding Helen Grant more than any of the others. Yet Jim wanted to protect him, wanted to spare him from the glare of publicity that would be inevitable if all the facts were ever out in the open, being scrutinised, being picked over and analysed. He knew it wouldn't look good. Not good for Peter that is and he wanted to shield him from that. "Just took me by surprise," is all he said in reply as his words failed to match any of his thoughts.

Peter could tell that Jim was on edge and he felt guilty about the possible reasons for that, especially now that the case was back in their faces again, but it was an opportunity and they needed to grab it. "You know," he said simply.

"Yes, George told me," Jim was beginning to relax and his pulse rate was returning to normal, or at least closer than it had been. He stood up and shook Peter warmly by the hand, cupping their interwoven hands with his free hand in a gesture emphasising warmth and friendship. And he meant it. "Gravesend, not the place I expected to see you. Is it the line of duty or a social call?"

"Bit of both I suppose."

Jim had regained his composure and he sat down indicating that Peter should do the same next to him. He had a corner of the office with a small desk, his office chair and a chair for visitors. He didn't get many visitors and that was the way he liked it. "Well what can I do for you? Let's get the business out of the way first so that we can concentrate on important issues over a beer or two later."

"Didn't George say?"

"Not really. Asked if I could help and of course I said yes. My DI is ok about that."

"We haven't kept tabs on the Grant family, don't know what happened to mum and dad. All we know is that the whole family went to Scotland and now Janet has moved. Down on the coast, here in Gravesend, we understand."

Jim nodded a few times as Peter was talking. He was in fact thinking about the information he had already obtained about Janet Grant and there was one important detail that intrigued him. He was sure that his very first thought had been correct but when he counted the months and years in his head and then rechecked them, he was certain. The marriage certificate and the birth certificate that he had obtained from the Registry Office confirmed everything. His thoughts now were directed towards using that information to get Peter off the hook. That, he thought, was the least he could do for him. "It's ok. I think I've found out all there is to know," he said in a clear comforting voice. "Everything adds up and I think I know what it's all about."

Peter sat open mouthed for a second or two expecting Jim to elaborate. Then, as Jim explained all he knew about the Grant family, his expression changed in stages from bafflement to clarity and his breathing became steadier as he absorbed the knowledge that Jim delivered. Everything did indeed fit neatly into place.

Just as they were finishing, there was a text alert on Jim's mobile phone and he looked down at it briefly.

Peter noticed a change in Jim's expression. "You seem on edge. Is there anything I can do for you?"

"Got a monkey on my back, not sure you could sort that out."

Peter was uncertain what Jim meant but he thought it must be important. He wanted to understand, he wanted to help, to begin to repay the debt of gratitude he felt, but he knew that any support he was able to give would be minute in comparison to what he owed.

"But if I could help, you would ask, wouldn't you?" he said eventually.

"Course, we've been mates long enough but there are some things," Jim hesitated and his mind shifted in a different direction. "We've all got problems and you know what, more often than not they are interconnected."

"Not sure I understand," Peter replied.

"No, nor do I. Let's just go and have that beer, shall we?"

Chapter 19

Ruby set off with plenty of time to spare. She drove carefully and she stayed in the inside lane at the roundabout leading to Marble Street. Her heart was pounding in her chest as she glanced left and right making doubly sure that there was no traffic even remotely close to her. At last the roundabout was clear and there was no other traffic entering from her direction, but another clumsy release of the clutch pedal resulted in her jerking forward leaving behind patches of car tyre engraved in the road surface and a knocking sound echoing around her.

Ruby had been busy since her meeting with Philip on Wednesday. There was still a part of her that was angry with him, but in the main her negative thoughts had been overtaken by her desire to protect him and to see only the parts of his personality that attracted her. As time passed these more positive feelings became stronger and it probably wouldn't be long before she would forget his anger and forgive his lack of self-control.

One of the first things Ruby had done was to make enquiries about the best solicitor to choose and the advice she received was unequivocal. Jason

Barnaby was a senior partner with Bell and Glover and he had a fantastic reputation. Despite his fees, which some might say were extortionate, she was not to be fobbed off with anyone else and she decided to move swiftly. She was in luck and was able to arrange a late afternoon meeting the same day for an initial consultation. But her first impressions were disappointing because it seemed to Ruby that she was doing all the talking and suggesting ideas. Jason just sat back and absorbed everything without comment and without making any notes but he took all of Ruby's papers placing them on one side of his somewhat small but uncluttered desk. "I'll see you both here tomorrow at 9.45 am and will advise the police that Philip Cassidy will make a voluntary statement at about 12 noon," Jason said as he offered his outstretched hand indicating that the meeting was concluded even before Ruby had the chance to protest. "It won't give us much time, but I don't want to run the risk of Philip being arrested in the meantime," Jason said putting on his best professional smile.

When Ruby arrived at Marble Street she was able to park right outside number 17. Almost immediately she had reversed into the space, Philip appeared at the side of her and she lifted the button to open the car door. Philip got in the passenger seat with just a nervous "Hello" offered in Ruby's direction. It was obvious from his body language that he was feeling very uncomfortable and vulnerable.

They arrived at the offices of Bell and Glover in Upper Preston Drive at about 9.30 and had been shown to Jason's office straight away. Coffee was offered by a young attractive PA but Ruby declined on behalf of both of them.

"Good morning. Please take a seat," Jason said as they arrived in his somewhat small and dingy office, with just enough space for two guests' chairs.

"Hello there," Philip said and Ruby nodded a greeting and smiled.

"I've told the police that you've agreed to make a voluntary statement and fixed an appointment for 12 noon, but I believe you know that already," Jason said in a business-like fashion and directing his remark towards Philip in particular. "We've got about one and a half hours to go over the important details and I'd like to start on that straight away. Is that ok?" Jason said, this time looking down at the file in front of him on an otherwise empty desk and flicking through the pages. Philip noticed that there were no personal bits and pieces on display, and no certificates concerning legal qualifications. This was the first time Philip had met Jason.

"Yes, that's fine," Philip replied and he looked across at Ruby partly for consent but also for reassurance. Ruby smiled at him in response and put her hand on his squeezing it gently.

"There are two separate areas we need to discuss. Firstly the disappearance of Helen Grant in 2003 and then the problems in Méribel recently. So, starting with the events that night in…" Jason looked down to check the date on a list at the front of his file. "Yes, on 17 March. Just talk me through the important details. Is that ok?" Ruby noticed that Jason had the habit of checking that each of his suggestions was agreeable before going ahead and she found it annoying. She tried her best to hide her irritation and she thought she had succeeded, but it had not escaped Jason's notice.

"I was going out with Janet and we were getting on fine. I must admit I did find Helen very attractive, all the blokes did, but I can honestly say I never did anything about it. I didn't chat her up or ask her out or do anything which would make her believe that I fancied her. She was an absolute cracking girl and Tom and Giles were always talking about her, but that's all there is to it. So when I got the note from her I was gobsmacked."

Ruby, in particular, was surprised by Philip's comment and she could feel her heart begin pumping more quickly, particularly when she glanced across at Jason's face and noticed his expression take on a more questioning look which was most noticeable around his eyes and mouth.

"I don't think I've heard about any note before," Jason said. "Please tell me more about it, is that ok?"

"Yes, out of the blue I got this note from Helen asking to meet me in Pashley Park at 7 pm that evening… on the 17th March that is."

"And did you decide to meet her," Jason said in a tone which did not suggest disapproval or disbelief.

"Yes. I thought about it a bit, but yes, I decided to meet her. I was only 17 for God's sake."

"Ok then, erm," Jason cleared his throat as he prepared to continue.

"Did you tell anyone?"

"No."

"Did you see anyone when you were there?"

"No, I don't think so."

"How did you get there? What route did you take?"

"I walked across the football pitches and took the short path leading directly to the clearing where Helen said to meet."

"So, presumably quite a few people must have seen you go that way."

"I expect so. I'm not sure."

"Did you arrive first?"

"Yes."

"How long were you waiting for Helen to arrive?"

"I'm not sure. About a quarter of an hour probably. I made sure I got there on time."

"And the note said to meet at seven."

"Yes."

"So, you got there at 6.45 or thereabouts?"

"What time did you leave home, do you remember?"

"Must have been about 6.30 or just before. I went straight there and it only takes about 15 minutes from where we were living."

"And when did Helen arrive?"

"She didn't. I thought I saw her walking towards me but it wasn't Helen, it was Janet."

"And what did you think when Janet turned up?"

"Crickey. I was shit scared. At first I thought they must have played a joke on me, but I soon realised it was something else."

"What did Janet say when she arrived?"

"Not much as far as I can remember, I told her about the note."

Jason put his arms on his desk and tapped the index finger of his left hand a few times. He was looking directly ahead but not focussing particularly on either of them. You could almost hear him thinking out loud. "Now I want you to consider this very carefully. When you told Janet about the note you got from Helen can you remember exactly what you said?"

"I shouldn't think I can remember the exact words, no."

"But tell me what you do remember. Ok?"

"Well," replied Philip looking towards Ruby for reassurance. "I told her about the note Helen sent me. I showed her the note, I remember that and then I told her I should have realised it was a joke. Janet walked off in a huff and I followed her. I gave her the note and said she could keep it. We had some sort of conversation and I told her I loved her. We agreed to meet up later to talk things through. Then she went off to meet the others as far as I can remember."

Jason tapped his index finger again. There were details in what Philip had said that didn't make sense and he wanted to get things clear in his mind. The sound of his tapping was particularly noticeable and persistent and he stopped abruptly when he realised they were both looking at his hand. "Right," Jason said. "What I don't understand is why you didn't sort it out there and then? Why let her go off to meet the others. You could have walked with her and talked on the way."

Philip looked back at Jason and gave the impression he was thinking it through. A slight movement of his left eye brow and the lifting of his hand were the only visible signals Jason could detect and he was watching him closely. "No," Philip said "I just can't remember."

"Ok then, but can you tell me what you did next. Janet had gone off with the note. You had agreed to talk with her again later. What did you do Philip?"

Philip was becoming agitated. Ruby was still holding his hand and she could feel the tension building up in him, just as it had when they met up before. "You don't believe me, do you? Crickey, if my own solicitor thinks I'm lying what chance do I have?"

Ruby was the first to respond. "It's all right, it's ok. We do believe you, but Jason needs to check these things. He needs to know where the problem areas are, and you need to be prepared to talk about them."

Jason nodded his head as Ruby sought to calm Philip. "She's right, you know that don't you. Be prepared, that's my motto, and don't be in any doubt, the police will want to question you closely about those same things. It's best if we go through them here first. Look, shall we take a break now? Would you like a cup of tea?"

"Yes, that would be nice," Ruby said looking at Philip and gently circling the back of his hand with her fingers. Philip remained sitting as Ruby and Jason got up. He looked a forlorn figure, head down and shoulders rounded. He knew they were right, but he did not know what to do. He had protected his secret for 16 years and he had never breathed a word about it to anyone. He looked up at Ruby as she waited for him a few paces away. "Let's go and have a short walk," she said, holding out her hand towards him.

"I'll keep your tea hot for you in the pot." Jason said but he wasn't convinced that a cup of tea would solve any of their problems. He had watched Philip closely and he was in fact well trained in spotting warning signs of unease, of tension and more particularly of evasiveness and he had detected all of those as Philip had answered his questions. The point he was uncertain about, however, was the likely reasons for those tell-tale signs to be displayed, and whether or not Philip was seeking to protect himself or someone else.

Philip was particularly quiet as he and Ruby walked round the block and back through the swing doors into the reception area of Bell and Glover, solicitors. This part of the offices was completely different. A warm carpet welcomed them back into the building and the receptionist's desk occupied only a small proportion of the imposing room. Freshly cut flowers were strategically placed around the room and discrete lighting added to some impressive paintings on the wall. Here too framed certificates of professional qualifications were proudly displayed, alongside notices about the range of services on offer. "You can go straight on up," the receptionist said sweetly with a well-rehearsed professional smile on her face.

Ruby led the way and she went straight towards Jason's office.

"I'll just pop into the loo," Philip said as he moved down the short corridor to the men's room which had been pointed out by the PA when they first arrived.

"I'll wait," Ruby said, and she leant against the wall next to Jason's office door wondering how the meeting would progress.

Philip went straight to the urinal, unzipped his fly and stood there waiting. He didn't urinate for quite a few seconds, partly because he didn't really want to go, and partly through anxiety. He had wanted to be alone for a few minutes to decide what to do and had used the toilet as an excuse. He was undecided, but he was closer to sharing his fears than he had ever been. His thoughts turned to Ruby, and the possibility that he could be separated from her for years, probably forever. After all, who could blame her for turning her back on him and making a life for herself with someone else if he went to prison? Although he had acted irrationally in March 2003 he had not committed any criminal act, apart from the inaccurate statement he had made to the police and there was nothing he could do about that now. It was the other part of his life that was the real problem he thought and there were a lot of loose ends he needed to tidy up, matters he should have resolved before, and he knew he would have to do that much sooner now.

"You ready to go in now?" Ruby said almost gently as Philip walked the few paces towards her.

"Yes, fine," Philip responded. In that moment he felt clear in his mind that he would explain everything about that night Helen went missing and then deal with the other issues later. Philip entered Jason's office first and went straight to the chair he had occupied earlier. Just for those few moments his thoughts were centred on himself, and he didn't really notice Ruby follow him into the room and take her own seat beside him.

"Tea?" Jason said looking first at Ruby and then at Philip. They both shook their heads and mumbled words of thanks. "Well Philip," Jason said, "we do need to move on, but it would help if we could get this bit out of the way first."

Philip looked across at Jason and made a small gesture with his right hand, as if to signify that he didn't need Jason to say anything else. Philip was ready now, and, whilst a small tear began forming in his eye, he knew what he had to do. "Ok," he said looking first at Jason and then towards Ruby sitting beside him. "I didn't say anything at the time, or ever since for that matter, but you're right, it wasn't just a question of letting Janet walk off on her own for no reason. I began wondering when I was waiting for Helen. You see, when I left home that evening my father was getting ready to go out. He said he was meeting some friends in the centre of town. When I left home that night and walked down towards the park my father's car went past me, but that was in the opposite direction from the town centre. I didn't think much of it at the time. Perhaps he was picking someone up."

"Did you see if it was your father driving?"

"I can't be sure, it looked like him, but it was definitely his car because I noticed the number plate." Jason nodded his head slightly in Philip's direction prompting him to continue. "Then I thought that perhaps he was following me. I was a bit edgy after all and all sorts of things were going through my mind. I decided to check the car park after Janet left. Sure enough, my father's car was parked there. It was very odd."

"Was there any other car in the car park?" Jason asked.

"Yes, I remember it clearly, a light blue Sierra, fairly new."

"And what did you do next Philip?"

"There was no one about, so I decided to have a quick look around. There are two ponds in the northern area of the park and I walked down the path towards the other pond, the millpond, that's what we called it, but I didn't see anything at first. Then I heard voices. There's a small clearing just off the path before the pond. There's a few benches and a picnic table there I believe. I got a little closer and kept well out of sight and saw my father talking with this other man. The light from the football pitches were just enough for me to see that it was him. I didn't stay for more than a few seconds and then moved back onto the path as quietly as I could."

"And what did you make of it?" Jason asked.

"Well, it did seem very odd, but I convinced myself that, at least he wasn't following me. I felt somewhat relieved I have to admit. When I got back to the main path I hurried back to the clearing where I had been waiting for Helen to meet me. I felt more relaxed when I got there but then I started thinking, and wondered what it was all about."

Jason looked expectantly at Philip. There was a silence for a few seconds before he replied.

"I had wondered all along about the note. It was so out of the blue I wondered if it was really for me. It was in a little white envelope with my name on it. 'Philip Cassidy – private' that's how it was addressed and the note inside had my name at the top. So for a while I was satisfied it was for me. But I couldn't understand why Helen had left it for me in my father's office."

"What do you mean, in your father's office?"

"I used to go to his office when I had arranged to get a lift home with him. When I got there I found the note on the floor, saw it was for me so I picked it up and opened it. Then, when I was waiting for Helen to arrive I had this awful thought. I remembered that sometimes my father allowed some of the pupils to call him by a nickname rather than stuffy old Mr Cassidy, but I believe that got out of hand. His second Christian name is Philip, I was named after him and I remembered another of the girls who spent a lot of time with him had called him Philip when she was talking to me and then had got red in the face and corrected herself."

"Was that Helen?" Jason asked.

"No, it was another girl. I never heard Helen call my father Philip, but it got me thinking and I wondered if Helen wanted to meet my father. So, that's what I did, that's why I didn't go off with Janet straight away." Ruby was looking intently at Philip. They were as close as any two people could be, she thought. They had shared secrets and fears, yet Philip had never breathed a word to her about any of this. She realised that it was something he wanted to forget, and that it must be very difficult for him to sit and talk about it in this way. "Oh Philip," she said lovingly, "if only I'd known before, we could have talked it through."

"I know," replied Philip. "But I buried it so deep and didn't even want to think about it."

Jason didn't think that Ruby's intervention had helped and he wondered how he could get the conversation back on track without appearing insensitive. "But you must think about it now," he said with as much warmth to his voice as he could muster. "However much it might hurt, or bring back memories you would rather forget, you need to tell us now. I'm sure you know that don't you?"

"Yes, I do," Philip responded "But there isn't much more to tell. I sat for a while just thinking things through and then I went down to the summerhouse as quickly as I could. You know the rest."

"Yes, ok, thanks," Jason thought for a while before moving on. "Did you ever say anything to your father?"

"No. The longer I left it, the more difficult it became. When we heard that Helen was missing all sorts of possibilities went through my mind. I became convinced then that Helen was meeting my father that night, but I couldn't understand about the other man."

"It could have been another teacher," Ruby said.

"Yes, I thought about that. I also thought about Social Services or the police even. I knew that Helen had confided in my father about some problem. I heard him talk with my mother about it late one evening when they thought I was upstairs asleep, but I didn't know any details."

"But they would have said something to the police if it was as straightforward as that," Jason said in an attempt to speed things up. He was worried that they didn't have much time and he wanted to cover as much ground as possible before they had to leave for the police station.

"Yes, that's what I kept coming back to. Nothing seemed to make sense I just couldn't understand why my father hadn't told the truth. He said that he went to a boxing match in the town centre that night. That's what he told the police. But I knew he was somewhere else."

"Did you think that he had something to do with Helen's disappearance?" Jason asked in a voice as calm as possible.

"I kept worrying about that. It kept going over and over in my mind, but I couldn't convince myself that he would do anything to harm Helen."

"Maybe he was covering for somebody else," Ruby said as she struggled to find a more palatable explanation. She could sense that Philip was becoming more anxious. His breathing was shallow, there was the occasional involuntary spasm on the right side of his top lip which he attempted to cover with the flat of his thumb and he had become noticeably more fidgety. She looked across the desk at Jason and he nodded his head in response with just the faintest of movements. He could tell that Ruby wanted him to introduce a new direction to the discussion, one that would enable Philip to concentrate on something more tangible and less painful. He had already decided that, although speculation about possible motive for events that night could be helpful, it was not productive use of the short time they had available.

"That's right," he said ""Your father sounds the sort of person who would do his best to protect others, particularly if he knew that they had nothing to do with Helen's disappearance." Philip looked relieved by Jason's comment, but he didn't say anything in response. Jason pressed on "At some point you must ask your father. What does he know about the recent problems in France?"

"Not a lot," Philip responded. "I don't keep in touch that often, but the police contacted him to find out if he knew where I was. He and mum were obviously worried but I was able to speak to them on the telephone just a couple of days ago. I said that, as far as I was concerned, I must have had some sort of blackout and that I couldn't remember much. They were relieved to hear from me but were very insistent that I should see a doctor for a check-up. I said that I would and would ring them again."

"And you didn't say anything about the missing girl?"

"No."

Jason looked at his watch. They had less than half an hour before they needed to leave. "Someone needs to speak to your father urgently," he said, "preferably you. But they will probably want to question you and it will take a few hours."

"Do you want me to go and see him?" Ruby asked.

"Yes, would you?"

"Course I would," Ruby said emphatically. Don't be silly." She was concerned that Jason had been unnecessarily blunt when he had referred to the prospect of a lengthy police interview, but Philip didn't seem to have taken it badly. Nonetheless she wanted to reassure Philip that she would be doing all she could to help him. "Should I phone him first do you think? and not just turn up on his doorstep?" she asked and her question hung in the air briefly.

Jason was first to reply "I don't think it would help to say anything in advance, but you need something in writing from Philip to give to him when you arrive."

As Jason spoke Philip was watching him intently as if seeking inspiration. There was something bothering him. "I don't want my mother to know about any of this. At least not until it's all cleared up."

"That's what I was thinking. You need to pick your moment carefully Ruby. It shouldn't be too difficult. Does your mother go to any regular meetings on her own, or anything like that?" Jason asked, looking directly at Philip who now seemed more relaxed.

"Yes, every Monday and Thursday afternoon, down at the bingo. I haven't known her miss for ages."

"Yes, that's fine with me, I can go this afternoon, I haven't got much on, but will your father be in during the week." Ruby said not knowing for sure whether Philip's father had retired yet from his job as headteacher.

"He will this week, it's the end of the Easter holidays and school doesn't start again until next Wednesday. He was telling me about his plans when we spoke on the phone. He wants to get the garage and garden into shape now that the decent weather has arrived. So he should be in."

"I'll just have to take the chance," Ruby said wondering whether she could remember the way. She had dropped Philip off at the house just after Christmas when she was on her way to cover a story. She hadn't time to call in then, and it seemed rude to just pop in to say hello. Philip had met up with her later and they had left the area straight away because they both had commitments back home. Yes, she thought, it won't take me long to find it.

"Come on then, you need to write a note to your father," Jason said offering Philip a pen and some writing paper.

"What do you want me to write?"

"You need to explain everything about the note and that you saw your father that night at the park. All the details. Don't leave everything out."

Philip winced slightly but he knew he had no alternative and soon he was immersed in his task. He was nearing the end when they were all distracted by a noise outside and Jason moved away from the desk and was looking out of the tiny window with his back to them. "What do you make of this?" Jason said, turning his head and motioning to the scene outside with his arm outstretched. Ruby was the first to respond and she took the few paces to the window followed by Philip. With their heads together all three of them peered down at the road below. Two police cars had pulled up and four uniformed police were getting out and making as much of a scene as they possibly could. "I don't like the look of that,"

Jason said. "Come on, let's go out the back way. You can finish writing the note to your father on the way."

"Where are we going?" Philip asked as Jason moved back to the desk. "We're going to make a voluntary statement. I don't want the police arresting you here. Come on. I'll get my PA to tidy up and put the papers away safely."

Chapter 20

It didn't take them long to go down the back stairs and out into the car park. Jason led the way with Philip and Ruby close behind.

"Best if we go on our own," Jason called back. "You can finish writing the note as we go and I will bring it back later."

Ruby wasn't expecting this arrangement and she started to protest.

"I think he's right," Philip said as soon as he realised that Ruby was about to insist on coming with them.

Ruby thought for a while. "I won't come in. I could bring the note back with me. Save you the double journey." They had reached Jason's car by now and Ruby got in quickly as soon as the door was unlocked, leaving Jason and Philip with little alternative but to accept her suggestion.

It was difficult for Philip to write the last few sentences of the note as the car was moving. "Can you read that ok," he said as he handed the completed note to Ruby sitting next to him in the back seat.

Ruby skimmed through it quickly nodding from time to time. Some of the words towards the end were a little unclear but she could decipher them ok. "Yes, that's fine," she said as she folded the note carefully and put it in the envelope Philip had already addressed to his father.

It wasn't long before they arrived at the police station. "I'll get a taxi back. Don't worry," Ruby said as she got out of the car. She put her arms around Philip's neck "Good luck," she whispered in his ear but he didn't say anything in response. Soon she was watching their retreating figures as they made their way to the main entrance. "I'll go and see your father straight away," she called out.

There were two administrative staff working in the reception area and they both looked up when Philip and Jason walked towards them and they both seemed to take on knowing expressions when Jason introduced himself. It was almost as if they were expected making Jason feel slightly uneasy and the atmosphere worried him. He looked over the taller one's shoulder, half expecting a senior police officer to be waiting for them, but all he saw were posters about road safety.

"Come through," the shorter one said as she ushered them towards an open door behind her on the right-hand side. George Baker and Lucy Atkinson were ready waiting for them. They had spent time preparing for the interview and the information Peter Lord gave them when he returned from Gravesend added helpfully to their pool of knowledge. They knew now that Amanda Dawson was safe and well and the report from Carcassonne police made it clear that her disappearance had nothing to do with Philip Cassidy. That line of enquiry was therefore closed, but they continued to believe that there were links between all the events and they decided to ask some questions about it and the reason for Philip's trip to France. They had everything ready – all the evidence Banik had provided and they had now viewed the video in the package addressed to Mr Denman. They were waiting patiently in Interview Room 2 with everything to hand.

Jason had dealt with George before and he knew immediately he entered the room that he would be dealing with an experienced officer but he had not come across Lucy Atkinson before. It was unlikely that they would be making silly mistakes he thought, and he continued to have a feeling that there was an air of confidence in the room.

It was George who spoke first and he dealt with all the legal requirements in connection with the arrest of a suspect and the necessary caution. Although Jason had expected that Philip would be questioned under caution he was surprised about some of the charges. Nonetheless he pressed ahead with his plan for Philip to make a statement and then give 'no comment' responses to all other questions, but George Baker quickly took control of the situation.

"We have a number of questions we wish to put to you, Mr Cassidy, and that may cover everything. If not, you can make your statement at the end," he said firmly looking directly at Philip and ignoring Jason completely.

Philip looked at Jason seeking advice and he nodded in response. "We have no problem with that at this stage, but I may need to confer with my client... depending on your line of questioning."

"We have some routine questions that's all. But yes, if you want a break at any time, just say."

George looked directly into Philip's eyes and held the gaze a little longer than necessary before he asked, "Can you tell me how you travelled back to the UK from France – did you fly or did you get the ferry?"

Philip didn't hesitate in his response. "It's a long story and I need to explain the details."

"We can explore that later. It's a simple matter. Was it by plane or boat?"

"I ended up in Calais, so yes, I took the ferry."

"And what passport did you use?" George said as he picked up his pen indicating that he was about to take notes.

The question took Philip by surprise. This was an area he would prefer to avoid. He had not said anything to Jason or Ruby about the precise circumstances of his homeward journey and now he winced momentarily not quite knowing how to respond. This momentary lapse did not go unnoticed by either George or Lucy. They had discussed beforehand the point at which this potentially difficult question should be asked and their decision to do so early in the interview now seemed to be paying off.

"My own of course," Philip eventually replied but he sensed that he was being led into a trap.

"There is no record of any passport in the name of Philip Cassidy being used for a journey from Calais to Dover on any day between Wednesday 16th March and yesterday 23rd March," George said in a quiet calm voice.

"Then there must be some mistake," Philip responded but his voice had a hesitant edge to it and the palms of his hands were becoming cold and clammy.

"Unlikely to be a mistake, not much chance of that I'd say," George responded and then he hesitated for a while, took on a more serious expression and lifted his face so that he was making direct eye contact with Philip. "Who is Mr Denman?" he said suddenly and the whole room seemed engulfed in silence for a while.

The very mention of Denman's name drew the moisture from the back of Philip's throat leaving his mouth parched and momentarily he was unable to form words of reply. The effect was immediate and was accompanied by a spasm of shivers down his spine and he hunched his shoulders in an attempt to halt their effect, but he was unable to hide his discomfort completely. He took in a few deep breathes and regained sufficient control to reply, "Not sure I know a Mr Denman, why?"

"Then tell me, where have you been living since you returned from France?"

"I've been staying at my aunt's house, 17 Mabel Street."

"And when did you last visit your own flat – in Station Road?"

Jason Barnaby had been sitting beside Philip whilst these questions were being asked and he had thought about intervening before. He could now sense that Philip was becoming more agitated and nervous. "I'm not sure I can see any relevance to these questions," he said eventually.

"They are straightforward and routine that's all," George said.

"But what have they got to do with the charges? Has Amanda Dawson turned up yet?"

"I don't think she ever went missing," Philip interrupted emphatically and with a hint of anger. "I've been set up. That's what all this is about. I've not been to my flat yet if that's what you want to know. I'm housesitting for my aunt…. I've told you already."

"It's just that we've found some items at your flat which we believe you had with you in France."

Philip was silent for quite some time as he wondered what items they might have found. The thumping in his chest abated slightly and he was able to think more clearly. He reminded himself that he had not been to his flat since he got back from France and he began to think that this must be some sort of trick question.

"Well?" George prompted.

"I've told you already. I've not been in the flat or anywhere near it… So… You've got it wrong. It's as simple as that."

George had a small pile of papers on the desk in front of him and other items on the floor next to his chair. He reached down and selected a large evidence bag containing a red ski top and passed it over to Lucy.

"Recognise this?" Lucy said.

Her introduction into the conversation made Philip feel even more unsettled and it showed on his face. "Well, it looks like my ski top but there must be hundreds like that."

"This was found in your flat."

"Well I didn't put it there, so I can't help."

Philip had told Jason about the ski top when he had been explaining the circumstances of his waking up in Calais. Jason wasn't entirely convinced that Philip had told him everything however and he thought now that there were enough loose ends to prompt Philip into revealing all the details. He knew that he needed to be able to see the whole picture, warts and all, and he felt that this was the moment when he could persuade Philip to confide in him.

"I need to talk with my client in private now – so could we have a break please?"

"Yes, that's fine," George replied.

"But before we do, are there any other items, down there, that we need to know about?" Jason said as he pointed to the pile by the side of George's chair.

"There are other items – items found at Flat 2, 15 Station Road, that we would wish to put to Mr Cassidy and to seek his explanations. We can do that now, or, we can do it later, after a break. Which would you prefer?" George said in a clear calm voice.

"Well take a break now please if that's ok."

"Ok, that's fine. You can have the room next door," George replied. "I'll show you."

When they were alone together Jason was the first to speak. "You need to tell me everything – don't keep anything back, ok."

Philip thought for a moment. He wanted all the help he could get, but he was reluctant to put himself in a position where he would be vulnerable. "Can I trust you completely?" he said eventually "Would it be something like a confessional?"

"I've never heard it put quite like that before, but yes I suppose it is. Whatever you tell me is in complete confidence. I won't reveal it to anyone else unless you want me to."

"I don't feel comfortable talking to you here. Can we go somewhere else?"

"They won't allow that… at least not just yet. I'm pretty sure about that."

"Perhaps we could buy some time. Could you tell them that you've been called away to an urgent meeting of some sort? Come back in a couple of hours perhaps?"

"I don't think that world help."

"Give me time to think and you could see Ruby and reassure her. I'd like that."

Jason sat back, lifted his chin slightly and thought through the options. He wasn't convinced that

Philip's suggestion would achieve much, but he could see that it might help Ruby if he could let her know how things were going.

"Is that what you really want?"

"Yes – definitely."

Philip had his own private thoughts about the line of questioning the police had adopted. His initial thought was that they had found something incriminating and were building up to it. He convinced himself that there could be nothing to find about the missing girl in Méribel, but he could remember that George Baker had been involved in the investigation into Helen's disappearance. That connection made him wonder if this was all really about Helen – they would, he was sure, still be obsessed about that and desperate to see someone brought to justice. He needed to think, to plan and if necessary to cover his tracks. There might still be a chance for him to do that, and he now wished he had done so before. Philip sat and thought for a while longer. The mention of Mr Denman's name had unsettled him. It had come so unexpectedly and he knew it was the area where he was most vulnerable. He felt relatively confident that, on its own, the contents of the package would not be sufficient to incriminate him but he knew that there was always the chance that it could be linked with other items hidden in his flat and he just hoped that they had not been found yet. As these thoughts were going through his mind he knew what he had to do. The trouble was, he couldn't see how he could put his plan into effect while he was being held in custody in the police station. There was no one on the outside he could trust sufficiently, not even Ruby, because that would reveal a part of himself that he wanted to keep secret at all costs. Then slowly, bit by bit, a plan began to emerge in his mind and it was accompanied by a half-smile on the side of his mouth.

Jason sat quietly watching Philip closely. He had a feeling that Philip was planning something, but he knew he could only be of limited help if he didn't know exactly what the problems were.

"I don't feel at all well," Philip said suddenly. "Could you get me a glass of water please?"

"What's the problem?"

"I feel… I feel really dizzy. Please hurry."

Jason got up and moved towards the door but almost immediately he turned, took a few paces back towards Philip and whispered in his ear "Don't go doing anything stupid." Then without waiting for a reply he turned sharply, walked away and called out over his shoulder "I'll get you a glass of water, alright."

When he was alone Philip began to develop the plan that had begun to form in his mind. It was a long shot he knew, but it was all he could come up with. He knew that he was unlikely to fool Jason but he didn't think he needed to. He just needed to do enough to convince Inspector Baker or at least to play him along a bit. He waited until he heard Jason's footsteps returning just outside and he was in luck because the sound was accompanied by voices.

He paused, waiting for the precise moment when the door handle moved just a fraction, and then he let out an almighty scream and threw himself forward into a chair and grabbing hold of anything around him which would come crashing down on top of him. It worked much better than he could have wished. As he fell he caught the side of his face just above his right eye, on the back of the chair and a generous amount of blood soon began weeping down his cheek and into his open mouth. Jason was the first to witness the scene closely followed by George and Lucy.

"Oh my God," Jason exclaimed in an almost theatrical tone as he rushed forward seeking to help Philip to get up off the floor. A small part of him had doubts about the seriousness of the situation and whether or not Philip had actually fallen over on purpose, but he brushed these doubts to one side as his instincts to offer immediate help took over. George and Lucy on the other hand were caught up straight away in thoughts about Health and Safety and their desire to be seen to do the right thing.

"Get him to the medical room," George called out "We can get the first-aider to have a look at him, and I'll contact the duty doctor, get her to come straight away."

Philip was aware of the commotion around him, but he was shaken up and a little disorientated. He got to his feet with Jason's help. "What happened, where am I?" he mumbled as he took in gulps of air and released them in short panting breaths.

"It's ok, I've got you."

Blood was spurting generously from the cut above Philip's right eye leaving vivid red splashes on Jason's white shirt as he held him firmly and helping him towards the door which was being held open by George. They staggered together the short distance down the corridor towards the medical room with Peter leading the way.

"I'll call the first-aider," George called out to them as he turned and made his way back towards his own office.

Just a few minutes later Philip was lying on the small bed in the corner of the room. A young PC had visited and had applied a dressing to Philip's forehead, applying a little pressure, in a successful attempt to stop the bleeding.

Philip continued to complain that he felt dizzy and nauseous. "He needs to go to the hospital," the PC said "Might be concussed. I can't do any more."

George was hovering outside and he knew immediately that the PC was correct. He whispered his agreement into his ear and the officer went off to call an ambulance.

Jason waited patiently in one of the spare interview rooms. He made a number of telephone calls but was unable to contact Ruby as her mobile was switched off, but he decided not to leave a message. Some time later George and Lucy came into the room. It was George who spoke first. "We have taken the precaution of calling for an ambulance," George said "and we will contact the hospital so that they can make all the necessary arrangements. Philip Cassidy continues to be under arrest of course, but he will receive all the necessary medical attention he needs."

"Can I see him?"

"Yes of course but he's resting now."

"But he is ok?" Jason said.

"As I said, we have taken the precaution of sending him to hospital. I'm sure they will do more tests there."

Jason thought for a while, he wasn't sure what to do. There were a number of things he needed to attend to back at his office and he would have to deal with them tonight. He was reluctant to leave, however, without seeing Philip, but he couldn't see a way round it.

"I need to go soon," he said eventually, "but I want to be able to keep in touch. It's important that he has his mobile fully charged up and with him at all times when his is in hospital." George was surprised by the request but he did not let it show as he replied. "As I'm sure you understand, Philip Cassidy will remain under arrest and all of the rights and conditions will continue to apply. His personal possessions will be retained by the police, but he will be given the opportunity to make any necessary phone calls."

Jason nodded his head a few times as George was talking acknowledging that he did understand the conditions that would apply. "But I will have access to him in hospital?" he said eventually.

"Yes, you can attend and advise him, unless of course that would be contrary to any medical advice."

Jason wanted time on his own to think through all the possibilities. He was reluctant to leave before he was satisfied that he had done all he could and he went through everything in his mind just to be sure. Most of the time he could analyse situations in a flash, identifying key issues and their solutions and he wasn't fazed by the spotlight. In fact he performed better when the pressure was on. That was probably the key to his success, but he still recognised the importance of detailed preparations and that part of him was making sure that there were no loose ends for him to tie up before he left. He still had a nagging doubt that he had missed something crucial but he just couldn't put his finger on it.

Chapter 21

Ruby sat in her car across the road from Spencer Cassidy's house. She had been there for about 15 minutes and was reasonably sure the house was empty. She could see Spencer mowing the front lawn and she had watched the stripes appear behind the mower as it buzzed loudly up and down. Just to make sure she dialled the telephone number she had carefully noted on her pad, taking the risk that Spencer would not hear it ringing over the clatter he was making. Sure enough, he was not distracted from his task as she counted the ringing tone through to seven and then promptly ended the call. She felt confident now that Spencer was alone and by the look of things it wouldn't be long before he finished his work.

Ruby waited a few minutes and then saw Spencer begin emptying the grass cuttings onto the border in front of the house. She watched as he put the mower away in the garage and closed the up-and-over door behind him. Ruby assumed that there would be a side door leading from the garage to the passage way between it and the house, but the view was obscured by a large wooden gate. She decided to wait a few minutes longer.

Ruby hadn't seen Spencer Cassidy before. She had wondered whether he would look like an older version of Philip but there wasn't any similarity, which surprised her. Spencer was overweight, not very tall and his hair which was thinning slightly was a shade somewhere between blond and ginger. She had noticed, when the mower was temporarily silent, that he had an irritating nervous cough and had the habit of blowing his nose loudly on a large white handkerchief every now and again. Her impression was that the kids at the school where he was headteacher would take the mickey out of him something wicked.

She decided to watch the second hand of her wristwatch until it had turned full circle. That would be her cue to make a move and she counted to herself as each second passed. She was feeling uncertain about how she should handle the meeting with Spencer and her heart began to pound within her chest, prompting a tightening of the muscles at the back of her throat. She took a few deep breaths seeking to ease the tension as she got out of her car and slammed the door shut. The noise seemed to echo up and down the road and she was sure that everyone in earshot would be looking at her as she crossed the road, but in fact none of the residents noticed.

She held her head high and did her utmost to walk confidently up to the front door. The doorbell sounded to her touch and she didn't have long to wait before Spencer answered the door. He was still wearing the same shirt and tie he had on when he was mowing the lawn, but now they were joined by a surprised look on his face. "Hello," Ruby said willing her voice to sound as casual as possible and seeking to remove from it all traces of nervousness. "I need to talk with you urgently about your son Philip. He asked me to come. I'm his girlfriend Ruby."

Spencer's initial look of surprise was replaced with one of suspicion and he glanced over her shoulder as if to make sure that there wasn't a gang hidden waiting to push past him into the house. When he was satisfied that she was alone he turned his attention back and focussed on her face. "That sounds very odd to me."

"Look, I've got this note for you from Philip. It explains everything," Ruby said as she handed over the envelope which Philip had addressed to his father. Spencer held out his hand, somewhat suspiciously, but he accepted the envelope and looked closely at his name handwritten on the front. He seemed to be satisfied that it was in Philip's handwriting and he began to open it. "Is it ok if we go inside?" Ruby asked feeling that it would be much better for Spencer to read through the contents indoors. Spencer looked up at Ruby again scrutinising her face closely. She could tell by the concentration in his eyes that he was deciding what to do. After just a few seconds he made up his mind. "Yes, ok," he said, making room for Ruby to pass by him in the doorway and then closing the door carefully behind her.

There were three settees in the middle of the room. Two were facing each other and the third was positioned so that the attractive open fireplace made up a cosy square, with a low wooden coffee table in the middle. Spencer sat down without speaking and motioned for Ruby to take a seat opposite him. When he was settled he opened the envelope, took out the A4 sheets inside and read through the contents carefully nodding occasionally when he apparently recollected the events described but otherwise with no visible sign of emotion on his face. At long last Spencer looked up at Ruby and took a deep sigh. Ruby could see the colour draining from his previously pinkish face as the burden he had kept hidden for all these years came like a wave upon him.

Momentarily Ruby felt sorry for him, but she knew she needed to put such feelings to one side. "Philip told me all about it," she said looking across the space between them. "Now he needs your help." Ruby could see Spencer taking everything in as if weighing up his options and she didn't want to hurry him unduly.

"I'd rather speak with Philip face to face," he said after a few seconds. "It just doesn't seem right talking to a complete stranger. You must understand that."

"I don't think you've got much choice, I'm really sorry. Philip sent me, you can see that from the note and now he's in custody. I can understand it's difficult for you but please, we need to know what went on back then when Helen disappeared. For Philip's sake."

Spencer leaned back in his seat, closed his eyes and took two deep breaths before he focussed on Ruby again with a look of defeat beginning to appear on his face. He wasn't ready to explain all the intimate details to her but he was getting close to it.

They sat in silence for some considerable time. Ruby knew that she needed to guide the conversation in such a way that they could begin to talk about Philip's note. She felt that she needed to break the silence but also to give Spencer a chance to think things through on his own.

"How about I make us a cup of tea?" she said.

"No, it's ok. I'll do it, then I can explain what I was doing that night and why I was reluctant to say anything before."

Ruby was relieved. She got up and took a few paces around the room when Spencer went into the kitchen, hoping that the tension had been lifted slightly. It wasn't long before Spencer returned with the tea and he put it down on the coffee table with an exaggerated flourish. Whilst Ruby was beginning to warm to him but there was still something about him that made her feel uncomfortable. His looks, his mannerisms and sometimes the way he spoke were so unlike Philip's that she found it difficult to believe that they were father and son. She tried to put those thoughts to one side but she felt herself looking at him somewhat obviously.

"What's the matter?" Spencer said feeling one penetrating glance in particular.

"Oh nothing. I was just wondering when you were going to offer me a biscuit," Ruby said deflectively. He offered her the plate of biscuits he had brought in with the tea and a weak smile of acceptance began to appear on his face.

Spencer sat down and coughed slightly. The sort of cough that Ruby had noticed earlier. "Probably a nervous reaction," she thought to herself. Then he blew his nose once more and he put the handkerchief away in his trouser pocket. He was sitting with his hands in his lap as he began to explain what happened that night all those years ago. Ruby had not anticipated the explanation he began to outline but it did not come as a complete surprise to her.

"It was 2003 and there was still a stigma whatever people might say. I had known for some time that I was different and it wasn't long into puberty that I realised I was gay – homosexual we called it then. I didn't do anything about it. In fact I started dating Mary. She was my one and only girlfriend."

"And she's Philip's mother I take it!"

"Yes, we married in 1987 and Philip was conceived straight away. Then I met Peter. He spoke at a training day I attended, about child protection of all things. Ironic isn't it?" Spencer seemed perfectly at ease talking to Ruby, and in some ways it seemed easier to explain things to her than to someone he knew. "And it wasn't long before we began our secret relationship.

Everything seemed right about it at the time, but looking back it now seems rather grubby and sordid. We'd meet up in secret, always fearful that someone would see us, so the sex became hurried, and the chance just to sit and talk was limited – we'd go the pub sometimes but that was about it. I think we were reaching the point anyway where both of us wanted to put an end to our double lives."

Ruby was watching Spencer closely and she noticed a change in his expression. "And then came the night Helen went missing," she said.

"Yes. That brought it to an end. We never met up again after that. Well not as a couple if you know what I mean. I was a little relieved in a way,"

"Tell me about that night Spencer," Ruby said in a clear calm voice.

"We had arranged to meet at about 7-ish I believe. We arrived at the car park separately. It was quiet and there were no other cars about. We went to our usual spot and everything was fine as far as we were concerned. We didn't hear anything or see anyone else. We weren't there very long, less than an hour I would say. We went back to our cars and drove in convoy to one of our favourite pubs. We just had a couple of beers."

"What happened after that?"

"Peter's colleague – a chap called Jim, I remember – was covering for Peter that night. There was a big boxing match and Peter and I agreed that we would go there from the pub separately."

"And did you?"

"Yes. Peter's colleague Jim was on surveillance work. He was the only one who knew about us and sometimes he covered for Peter when we met up. When we got there things were beginning to break up, the big fight had ended and people were starting to leave. I stayed with Peter a short while and then decided to go home. I think I saw Jim coming out, but there were lots of people about and I'm not absolutely sure."

"How did you feel about someone else knowing about you?"

"I was never completely at ease about it, but Peter seemed to trust Jim completely."

"Was he gay?" Ruby asked wondering whether that might be the link which gave unity to this unusual triangle.

"No. Not a bit," Spencer said emphatically.

"And you went home you say?"

"Yes – my car was close by. It only took me a few minutes."

"When was it that you knew about Helen?"

"Well I knew that night but Peter phoned me on my mobile the next day. Said we needed to talk urgently. So we met at lunchtime. He told me everything the police knew."

"How did you feel about lying to the police?"

Spencer got up from the settee and walked towards the window and stood with his back to Ruby. She sensed that she had hit a nerve and she was reluctant to say anything more just for the moment. He turned to face her but she could not see the detail of his face against the light behind him. Maybe he wanted it that way she thought to herself.

"We both had our doubts," Spencer said moving back towards his seat, "but in the end, we didn't seem to have any alternative. After all we had no information which would help the police. We didn't see anyone and we both arrived together and left together.

"What about the note from Helen. Now you know about that, do you think it was meant for you?" Ruby asked.

"I don't know what to think. She certainly hadn't sent me anything like that before and had never spoken about meeting up out of school. She did have problems. At home I believe, but she did not say anything specific. Our relationship was friendly but I always kept it on a professional level," Spencer was beginning to look anxious. "It's just that Mary will be coming home soon, in about 40 minutes and I don't want you here when she arrives. I need to tell her about this but I want to do it in my own way and my own time. You understand that don't you?"

Chapter 22

"Come and sit down. I've got something important to tell you," Spencer said as his wife came into the lounge.

"That sounds ominous," she replied.

"Over here, next to me," he said patting the seat beside him and looking up at her with uncertainty. He had decided to tell her straight away and he wasn't looking forward to it. They had met as teenagers and had been married now for more than 30 years. Time and time again they had each vowed that they had no secrets from each other, yet here he was about to reveal the biggest secret of his life.

"What is it Spencer. What's the matter?"

"I had a visitor today. Someone I had not been expecting. It's about Philip and that missing girl all those years ago."

Mary sat in silence as Spencer told her the whole story. He didn't leave out any detail. When he had finished he handed her the note that Philip had written, but she didn't read it. She sat with her hands clasped tightly together in her lap. So tight that they had been drained of colour and were hurting. The pain was at least a distraction for her but it did not register in her mind. After a lengthy silence during which Spencer looked directly at her face Mary said "I've always wondered"

"Wondered what?" he replied.

"That perhaps you didn't love me, not deep down, not as much as you said you did."

"But that's silly. Of course I've always loved you. Don't do this Mary." As he spoke, he moved closer to her and knelt on the floor in front of her as if he was proposing marriage all over again. He wanted to take her hands in his but she recoiled slightly and he chose not to touch her. Instead he placed his left hand on the seat beside her, partly to steady himself.

"Get up from there, I don't want you pleading, I can't help the way I feel and nothing will change that, not just now at least." Spencer was slightly heartened by her final words. He would give anything to get back into her heart even if it took forever. For the first time she looked directly into his eyes. "Get up," she said firmly "and let's talk about this. Why would Helen send you a note – what was going on between you?"

"Don't be silly, nothing was going on," he said almost before the words had formed on her lips.

"Yes, you've told me that and I believe you. In some ways I'd rather that was true than the other." Spencer started his explanation again but Mary brushed him aside abruptly. She had always been stronger than he was and now it showed even more. "You need to get someone to represent you and we must make an urgent appointment for first thing tomorrow morning." She looked at her watch. "Let's phone now, if there is no one about we can leave a message." Spencer looked bewildered. "It's no use being like that," she said.

"Like what?" he replied.

Mary folded her arms across her chest and exhaled deeply. Spencer knew what she had meant and he started to apologise. "That firm of solicitors who drew up our wills recently, you know. Their office is just behind the bus station. They must have people who specialise in criminal work." As she spoke, she got up and went over to the wall unit beside the fire place. She took out a file from the top drawer and returned to her seat with it. "Yes, here it is," she said taking out a page. "I'll give them a ring now." Spencer was more than happy for his wife to take the lead and he watched her pick up the phone and dial the number. He started to speak but she gestured him to be quiet with a dismissive wave of her free hand.

Spencer did not react in any way and he sat meekly watching his wife as she waited for her call to be answered. It was soon obvious that an answer machine had been switched on and he heard his wife leave a detailed message, without any nervousness or uncertainty in her voice. Finally, after emphasising for the second time the urgency of her call, she hung up and looked back at Spencer as he sat with his head bowed and his shoulders sagging.

"Now then," she said more loudly than was necessary. "I want to talk to Philip. We need to let him know what we're doing."

"He's going to phone me tomorrow morning if he can," Spencer replied almost apologetically.

"Don't be ridiculous," snapped Mary as she turned away from him and picked up the note Philip had written which she had put down on the side table.

Mary read through the note carefully and then reread parts of it again. "What a horrible secret my little boy kept all these years," she said quietly to herself. She could feel tears welling up in her eyes as she imagined the anguish Philip must have suffered that night when he was little more than a boy, but she blinked them away and willed her steely determination to return again. She put the note back on the side table and looked into blank space, not really focussing on anything. Then it came to her. She remembered Philip's 17th birthday and his reluctance to do anything special to mark it. They had always done something before, bowling or dry slope skiing she recalled in particular. Early April was unpredictable and indoor activities always were the best bet. She recalled Philip being unusually difficult and argumentative in the week or so before his birthday. But it was the day itself that she recalled now so vividly. She had gone to Philip's bedroom with a cup of tea first thing and she thought he had been crying. When she asked him if everything was ok, he had turned away and when she spoke to him again he swore at her aggressively for the first time and had knocked the tea out of her hand. She had forgiven him of course and they never spoke about it again. The incident had been pushed below the surface of her memory, but as she thought about it now she nodded her head slightly to and fro in a gesture signalling to no one but herself that she now understood.

"Are you ok?" Spencer said as he noticed the vacant look on her face.

"Course I'm not," came her swift reply. "Why should I be ok? Don't you realise what this must have done to our son? Having to grow up knowing that his father lied to the police and having to protect you with his silence all those years."

"But I didn't know, did I? Don't you think…?"

Mary didn't let him finish protesting. "I don't want to hear your excuses, you miserable object," she shouted. He sat in his seat open mouthed and with an expression on his face which told of his inner turmoil. "Look," she said eventually. "This won't get us anywhere. I'm sorry but you must understand how I feel." Spencer nodded in response not wanting to inflame the situation further. "Your visitor, this woman Ruby Delacourt, I'll ring her now. She may have a contact number for Philip. I need to talk with him."

"Yes, she gave me her mobile number. I've got it written down here," he said as she passed her a notepad. "I'll phone her from the line in the office upstairs. I'd prefer to be on my own."

Spencer waited patiently and was tempted more than once to go upstairs to be with his wife as she spoke on the phone with Ruby. He decided against it and the time passed slowly. He felt more alone than ever knowing that Mary was in the house but wanting not to be physically close to him. At last his wife came into the lounge and sat in the chair opposite him. "She says she doesn't think the police will allow any more calls today, but she's given me the number for the police station so that we can check with them."

Mary picked up the house phone and punched in the number. She waited a few seconds and then Spencer heard her say, "Hello, is that Woodbridge Street Police Station?" and then after a short pause, "My son Philip Cassidy is being held in custody and I would like to speak with him on the telephone. Could you get him to the phone please?" Spencer sat watching his wife as she cradled the phone between her chin and her shoulder. She seemed remarkably calm and in control. He knew that, below the surface, her emotions must be boiling over, and he marvelled at her ability to present an exterior calmness which was almost unreal. With her hands free she was reaching out for Philip's note on the side table. Spencer felt so helpless watching her and he could feel his heart beating so loudly that he almost expected his wife to hear it from just a few feet away and complain about the noise. He tried to relax as he listened to the one-sided conversation with short gaps between her questions.

"Why can't I speak to him now?

"But I'm his mother. Could I speak with your superior officer please?

"When will he be available?

"Isn't there a senior duty officer you could call in an emergency?

"It might not seem like an emergency to you, but can't you understand my concern?

"And is there really nothing you can do to help me now?

"Well thank you anyway. I wasn't trying to get at you personally.

"Goodbye and thank you for your patience."

Mary put the phone down, got up from her seat and walked across the room to return the file she had previously taken from the drawer in the wall unit. She obviously did not intend to explain what the police officer had said, but Spencer had a good enough understanding from the questions she had asked. "Can I get you something to eat?" was all he could think to ask and he was surprised when she said "Yes."

She watched as Spencer left the room. She did not want anything to eat but she wanted to be alone with her thoughts. She heard a few cupboard drawers being opened and the chink of saucepans being lifted out, but she was soon miles away. Her first thoughts were of Philip sitting in a cold prison cell. She imagined him with his head in his hands and despair in his heart. She wondered if he was thinking about her or about his girlfriend Ruby. He had been a mummy's boy right from the start, not wanting to leave her side even when Spencer offered to take him fishing or for a walk along the river bank. But he had never

been frightened of adventure or taking risks as long
as she was close by. She remembered the first tree
he had climbed, much against her wishes. "I'll wave
to you mummy from the top," he had shouted out
to her as he ran towards the tallest tree in the park.
Some of the other boys about his age had tried but
had turned back when they got about half way up,
but Philip had overcome any fear he might have felt
and had reached the top at his very first attempt. He
had waved to her with no self-consciousness and she
had been happy to wave back enthusiastically. These
thoughts were going through her mind as Spencer
returned to the lounge "Won't be long," he said, "just
beans on toast I'm afraid, but you need to get some
food inside you. So do I for that matter."

"I'll have mine upstairs," Mary said as she got up
and left the room as soon as Spencer sat down. "On
my own," she added emphatically. She started to
make a list of the things they needed to do the next
day. It wasn't a long list but she needed to keep busy.
She knew that as soon as there was nothing else she
could do to keep her mind occupied, she would start
brooding again and she wanted, for some reason, to
delay it as long as possible. Spencer left a plate of
food on the desk she was working on. He didn't say
anything and Mary didn't even look up. Soon she
started daydreaming again and she was surprised
that when she next made a conscious effort to look
down at her plate it was empty. She must have eaten
the snack without being aware of it. Her inner

thoughts were all that she wanted to concentrate on, and she had recalled a mixture of happy memories about Philip's childhood. Every now and again she let her memories dwell upon her early relationship with Spencer and it made her feel physically sick. She had only had two serious boyfriends before she met Spencer. At first, she recalled, she hadn't been attracted to him at all, but he had been particularly attentive and persistent. She had grown to like him and felt she could trust him. She had never been in love with him she thought and had, in the end, settled for a future based upon security and friendship. After a while everyone expected them to get engaged and although she had some doubts, when he proposed she had accepted straight away. An unhappy marriage had been made bearable when Philip arrived, but she decided not to have any more children and their sex lives came to an end soon after Philip was born. Neither of them seemed to want to make the effort.

It was his ginger hair that put her off originally. It was that bright conspicuous shade gaining in colour down towards his sideburns. But, of course, it wasn't only his hair, but that seemed to be the catalyst for all the other things that she disliked about him. And now she had no reason to stay with him. At least the events she had stumbled upon on her return from bingo that afternoon, had forced her to face up to an assessment of their relationship. For that alone she was grateful. She would leave as soon as this mess about Philip had been resolved she thought to herself. Part of her wanted to leave straight away but she didn't want Philip to worry about anything else at the moment. But her mind had been made up and she was grateful for that.

She re-read the list she had written and picked up the pen once more. At the very end she wrote 'start new life' as she smiled to herself with the sort of inward satisfaction that she had not felt in a long time.

"What are you doing?" Spencer said as he walked into their bedroom. Mary had taken the two pillows from her side of the bed and put them together with her pyjamas and dressing gown on the chair next to the door.

"I'm moving into the spare room," she replied.

"But there's no need for that."

"There's every need. If you think I'm sleeping with you tonight you've got another thing coming," she said tilting her head back slightly and flaring at the nostrils. She wasn't prepared to discuss the matter and when Spencer started to protest she put her hand out in front of her with the open palm towards him. She shook her hand from side to side to add emphasis to the gesture. "I've made up my mind," she said as she turned to pick up the items from the chair. Clutching pillows and bedclothes under her arm she left the room and made her way along the landing. "You can use the en suite, I'll be using the bathroom," she called back to him over her shoulder.

Spencer stood in the doorway motionless. He hadn't really been in control of his emotions since he made his confession to his wife, but at least they hadn't got out of hand. Now he could feel them rising up within him but the shame and regret that had once dominated were being pushed aside and in their place he felt nothing but anger. "It's that precious bloody Philip," he shouted down the landing "Not about you and me at all. It never has been, has it?" He followed his words the few paces between himself and his wife. As he got closer to her the years of mounting resentment drew heavy lines across his face and his eyes were thrust forward menacingly. His colouring had turned almost crimson from the pressure of the blood vessels opening wide across his whole face.

"You look pathetic," Mary responded as Spencer moved closer to her. "Short, fat and ginger. Don't think I can be frightened by a jerk like you. Pathetic, that's what you are and that's what you've always been."

She turned away from him and he grabbed her by the shoulder, pulling her round to face him. "I've always known," he shouted at her and she began to laugh at his anger.

"Known what?" she scoffed sneeringly.

"That Philip was your darling and he couldn't do any wrong in your eyes."

"Well, what of it and now I really know what made the two of us cling to each other. We may not have known about your perverted filthy preferences, but there was always something about you." Mary did not raise her voice and in a way that made her words penetrate even more. Years of bottling up his feelings and suppressing his emotions were being released and there was nothing he could do to stop it.

"I think Philip killed that girl, just like he killed so many other lovely things, just because he couldn't get his own way," he shouted at the top of his voice.

Now it was out in the open at last and the effect on Mary was immediate. In a split second she lunged at his face, clawing it with her nails and ripping two jagged lines across his forehead and down his cheek. "You stupid bitch," he yelled at her but his words were swallowed by her own screams of anger. He pushed her away violently and she fell back onto the bed behind her. He put his hands up to his face instinctively and looked at the blood on his open palms before him.

As he started moving away down the landing to the bathroom, Mary got up and followed him. This time she did not make any attempt to scratch, bite or punch him but she wanted to. Instead she shouted at him with such anger that he could not make out what she was saying.

Now it was Spencer who was more in control and without raising his voice he said "That's what I've believed all these years," he repeated his words until he was convinced that she had heard him. He knew it would be difficult enough at the best of times to make her listen to his concerns, let alone to consider them, but he had no choice now. He had to press ahead. "You must listen." Her screams of anger began to die away, and he placed his hands on her shoulders, his arms outstretched so that there was at least some distance between them. He feared that she was going to kick him, as she pressed forwards against the weight of his grip, but it was more a reaction to her being unbalanced and unprepared for his actions. "Please, please listen," he said again in a more urgent tone, but this time she spat towards his face and pulled away from his grasp. His grip on her shoulder was more effective in keeping her away but she had little difficulty in knocking his arms from her shoulders and moving away from him.

"Don't you touch me. Don't you ever touch me again," she shouted with temper rising again within her. Then she fell to the floor in a crying heap, sobbing uncontrollably and covering herself with her arms crossed tightly above her head. Her face was held closely down towards her chest and her whole body seemed to be curled into a defensive ball.

Spencer thought about putting his hand on her shoulder but immediately realised that would only make matters worse, but she looked so pathetic that he wanted to comfort her in some way. "Come on," he said holding out his hand. "Come and sit down. We must talk about this." At first she didn't move, but her sobbing had stopped and there was silence. After a while she began to uncurl herself and, lifted her eyes towards him. As her face rose up from her chest be could see the tears still falling down her face, but they were unaccompanied by the sobbing that had been there before. "Come on," he said again, but still she made no movement.

Spencer felt a chill in his back and he shivered. He wasn't sure whether the temperature in the house had fallen or that the shock of seeing his wife on the floor had affected him more than he realised. "I'll get you something to put around your shoulders," he said as she turned and walked back to their bedroom. He quickly found a cardigan and returned with it under his arm. Mary didn't protest as he put it around her as she sat on the floor unmoving "Come on, let's go downstairs, it will be warmer there." This time she seemed to accept his suggestion and she got up. She put her hand out between them making it clear that she did not want him coming near her. She felt a little weak in the legs and she stumbled slightly as she took the first step down the stairs, but she quickly steadied herself by holding the banister with her right hand. Spencer followed her downstairs.

"Go and sit down in the lounge," he suggested and she did so without protest. "I'll just put the heating on for a while. Do you want a cup of tea?"

She didn't answer him. She was in a zombie-like state and nothing around her seemed to make any sense. As she sat listening to the noise he was making in the kitchen the feelings of anger began to return, but this time she was able to switch them off. "What did he mean," she thought to herself, "that Philip had killed Helen and so many lovely things?" but in her heart of hearts she knew.

"We've not talked about this before," Spencer said as he came back into the room and stood a few feet away from Mary's chair. She looked up at him and he thought he could see anger building up in her eyes again. But he was mistaken. She turned her face away and looked out of the window taking in the view of the trees in the garden outside.

"No, and I don't want to now," she replied.

"But we can't let it go unspoken again. We both know how things have been ever since he was very little. We're not doing Philip any good by pretending to ourselves that everything's ok. It's not ok and you and I both know that don't we?"

"Just because he had problems, doesn't mean he's ever killed anyone."

"Please Mary I don't mind too much what you think of me. I'll probably never be able to change that now. But we need to talk this through. Decide what we're going to do." Mary was much calmer now and Spencer felt it was safe to press ahead. He sat down and looked across at his wife by turning his head towards her. He didn't want the openness of talking to her face to face. That would probably be too much for both of them. "Who was it who said that the eyes were the windows into our souls, he thought to himself," and he looked down at his slippered feet in an exaggerated effort to hide his own soul and to avoid opening a passageway into hers. Talking things through was one thing, baring their souls to each other would be a leap too far. After a minute or two of eerie silence he asked "How many other families make three fresh starts but always end up with the same problems they started with?"

"But each time we moved it was because of your career," she responded quickly.

"Didn't we just use that as an excuse? I know you remember really, and we're going to talk about it now. We can decide what to do afterwards and I promise I won't say anything to anyone unless you agree."

"But it's true. Every time we moved, you secured a promotion. We had to move around for that didn't we. You told me that yourself."

"Yes I know, that's true, but I wasn't the real reason for moving. It was just a helpful byproduct and we were able to hide behind it because we didn't want to confront the real problem. But we need to face up to it now." He could see signs of acceptance in her, but he wasn't quite sure what to do next. He sat silently for a brief moment trying his best to keep his breathing as even as possible. He thought Mary seemed calm enough. She remained quiet, head bowed and with her eyes apparently concentrating lazily on an unspecific spot just a few inches from her face. He took a deep breath. "When we lived at Finches Avenue. You remember, our first house and Philip had those pet mice. He didn't want to go to school, but I made him. You do remember I know you do, but we've both buried the memory because we didn't want to face up to it. Eeny, meany, miney mo – that's what he called them – and he was laughing as he watched them,"

"No. No," Mary cried out.

"Yes. You must listen. You saw them first. They were running round in circles. Philip had cut off one leg from each of them with your pinking scissors. You remember him laughing at first and then he just got up and walked out as though nothing had happened. But that wasn't the only time was it. In the end we were never sure. He always denied it, and you wanted to believe him so I just went along with it. I'm just as much to blame as you are." He could hear Mary crying softly. This time it wasn't prompted by anger but that made it even more distressing. Spencer got up and sat next to his wife. She didn't protest but he accepted that it would be too much to expect that they would ever be the same again with each other. He just sat by her side for a short while.

"I want to tell someone about my fears. I want to tell his girlfriend. She seemed a nice sort of girl. She will be on his side but she seemed sensible enough to know what to do for the best. What do you think?" Mary looked defeated. She didn't say anything at first, just sat back taking in his words. "Or are they going unheard?" he thought to himself.

When she replied Spencer was surprised. "If you feel you must but don't expect me to agree. As far as I am concerned, family matters should be kept in the family. I don't want to talk about it anymore. Just do what you feel you must, but don't keep going on about it to me."

Mary got up slowly and turned towards him as if she was going to say something else. Spencer looked up at her, catching a very brief eye contact. He could sense that she was reflecting on all that had been said in the last hour or so and he was right. They would never look at each other again in the same way. Mary left the room and at the same time left behind the life they had shared for 30 years. She didn't feel any regret, but Spencer knew that there would be no new beginning for him.

Chapter 23

Ruby Delacourt was growing impatient. She had expected to hear from Jason Barnaby when she returned home after her meeting with Spencer, but almost a full hour passed without any news and he did not answer his mobile phone when she tried to contact him. Then the phone rang and it took her by surprise. It was Jason and she listened carefully as he explained what had happened. She didn't interrupt at all, allowing Jason to provide a full account of the interview and Philip's subsequent accident, but her heart was pumping fast and she had an empty feeling in the pit of her stomach. Jason kept his account factual and he made no reference to his suspicions, but he did emphasise that he did not believe that Philip was badly hurt and that the decision to send him to hospital had been precautionary.

"The police can keep Philip in custody for 24 hours, but can of course apply for an extension," Jason said abruptly but Ruby was thinking about something else and his words did not really register with her. There was a short eerie period of silence. "Did you hear me?" Jason said.

"Yes, yes," Ruby responded "I was just wondering when I could see him."

"Best wait until tomorrow. We could make a request first thing. I don't see a problem in the circumstances."

"Ok then, I'll call into your offices first thing. Could you make arrangements please."

"Make it about 9.30. I should be free by then and will do my best to make the necessary arrangements. If there is any news before then I'll let you know."

Ruby knew one of the front office admin staff working at Woodbridge Police Station and she decided to contact her. As soon as she finished her conversation with Jason she began to look for her telephone number, but before she could find it her phone rang in her hand. It was Philip's mother and she sounded off-hand and impatient. Ruby hadn't spoken with Mary before and she was surprised, given the circumstances, how curt she seemed to be. All she wanted was the telephone number for Woodbridge Police Station and she did not enquire at all about Philip. Ruby provided the number as requested but otherwise she did not say anything else.

Ruby stood in stony silence for a moment or two after the conversation ended, not quite believing how indifferent Mary had seemed to be during their short telephone conversation. Then a thought came into her mind from long ago which provided part of the explanation. Ruby had never experienced the special love a mother has for her child, but she believed she could understand it. The sort of love that was unconditional, never ending, and despite the severing of the umbilical cord there remained a bond that would never be broken. Now Ruby began to wonder if it was this bond that was driving Philip's mother, a bond that didn't need approval or support, and which enabled Mary to focus wholly on a process towards keeping Philip safe.

Chapter 24

Ruby arrived at Jason Barnaby's office at 9.30 precisely. She felt terrible and wasn't looking forward to her meeting with Philip one little bit. Her conversation with Spencer Cassidy the previous afternoon had unsettled her more than she realised at the time and she had spent a restless night thinking through all the possibilities. Nothing seemed straightforward and she had a recurring feeling that more bad news might be just around the corner. Ruby was pleased to have the opportunity to hear all of Jason's news first hand and to update him on her meeting with Spencer. They each spoke relatively briefly, but made sure they covered all the essential points. Jason in particular wanted to know and understand as much of the background detail as possible and he made a number of notes as Ruby was speaking. Then he began summarising everything and from time to time he referred to the notes he had made. At various points he paused and asked questions almost of himself. On the face of it, Jason Barnaby was talking to Ruby, but in reality he was thinking out loud, trying to recall the details Ruby had outlined and to analyse the relevant bits. He did not wait for an answer. He knew that he would have the opportunity of talking with Philip privately before the formal police interview was reconvened, but none of the new information Ruby had provided would be relevant for that purpose. It did however add considerably to the overall picture and made him even more convinced that Philip was hiding something. "We'll need to get going soon," Jason said eventually. "I'll call a taxi. We can talk on the way there."

They were soon sitting side by side in the back of the taxi taking them to Woodbridge Street Police Station. Almost immediately Jason's mobile rang and he answered it straight away.

"Well," Ruby said looking across at Jason, "what was all that about?" Ruby had the feeling that the call had been about Philip although she had not heard anything which made that connection obvious. "Can you stop the car?" Jason called out to the driver "Over there somewhere. Just for a second or two."

"You want a bit of time on your own?" he called out over his shoulder as he parked the car and before waiting for a reply he took his keys out of the ignition and opened the door "I'll be having a smoke over there," he said pointing to a bench seat overlooking a nearby park.

"That was the police. They say that Philip is not fit to be interviewed again just yet. The medics say best wait until tomorrow morning, but they have asked to see me now."

"But is he ok?" Ruby said simply.

"They say he has concussion and a constant headache, that's all. It's still just a precaution I'm sure of it."

Ruby thought for a while. She felt reasonably calm, the tension she experienced earlier had subsided and her mind was clear. She felt confident that Philip was not seriously hurt and she began to consider what she could do to help him now. That was her priority. Her thoughts turned towards Philip's mother and father and she began to wonder if they had got any more news. She doubted it somehow. "We need to let Philip's father know. I'll ring him now," she said. "Is there anything else I need to tell him?"

"Not really, no, that's all we know at the moment. "Do you want me to contact him?"

Ruby thought again for a moment or two. She didn't really want to get into another conversation with Spencer. "Yes, would you?" she replied simply.

Within just a few seconds Ruby was calling out the numbers and Jason was keying them in on his phone simultaneously. Jason put the phone to his ear and waited the short time before the ringing call at the other end brought a reply. Ruby could only hear one side of the conversation and Jason was doing most of the talking. From time to time Jason looked directly at Ruby sometimes with what looked like a questioning expression on his face as if he was expecting her to provide information for him. "Yes," she heard him say and this time he was definitely nodding in her direction. "Yes, she's ok, but I'm sure she will be pleased to see you at the hospital. How long do you think you'll be?" Again Jason was nodding towards her but this time it seemed to be a more distant look in his eyes as if he was trying to focus on some object but not really succeeding. "About half an hour, ok, I'll tell her."

Almost immediately Jason was signalling to the taxi driver, who had just finished his cigarette. He dropped the butt on the ground and twisted his right instep in a quarter circle grinding it into the pavement and then kicking the remains away with the side of his foot in a casual well practised movement.

"You going to be ok?" Jason asked nodding in Ruby's direction.

"Yes fine," Ruby replied but in fact all of a sudden she felt apprehensive and on edge. It was the thought of witnessing a meeting between Philip and his father that worried her. She knew there would be tensions and she expected that more secrets would begin to emerge, the sort of family secrets that could fester the longer they remained unspoken. She did not want to be there when they were brought out in the open.

Jason thankfully broke the silence. "Could you drop me at the police station and then take the lady on to Broughton District Hospital? I'll settle the bill in full when you drop me," he said to the driver. Soon they were pulling away from the kerb and joining the flow of traffic going in their direction. "Philip's mother was out," Jason said almost apologetically, "but Spencer said it's probably best if he breaks the news to her later. When he knows a bit more." Ruby could hear Jason's voice but to her it sounded unreal and distant. She remembered coming round from a fainting fit some years earlier when the sounds around her seemed disjointed and strangely unconnected with reality. She had a similar feeling now and she wondered if she might be losing consciousness. She took a tissue from her handbag and blew her nose vigorously. That helped to clear her head a little and she opened the taxi window to allow the cold wind to sweep across her face. Soon she felt a lot better.

They arrived at the police station and the taxi drew up abruptly. The journey had been delayed because of traffic and the driver seemed to be taking it personally. "I'll ring you at the hospital when I've finished here," Jason said. Ruby's whole attention was focussed on getting to the hospital as soon as she could and her brief acknowledgement was lost in the wind. It was raining slightly but she was almost oblivious to it as the taxi driver slammed the door shut.

Jason's meeting with George Baker did not last long. George's main concern, Jason believed, was to make sure that all the Health and Safety issues had been dealt with and he had asked Jason to add a section to the accident report that had been prepared. Jason had some reservations about that, but they had nothing to do with the witness evidence he was able to provide and he wrote a brief summary about what he had seen without any hesitation.

It wasn't very long before they had dealt with everything and Jason returned to the reception area. He arrived there just as Spencer Cassidy came in through the front door. Jason had never met him before but, instinctively he knew who he was. The age, the agitated state and the constant movement of his head from side to side as if seeking out a familiar face were exactly what Jason expected. "Hello. I'm Jason Barnaby I believe we spoke on the telephone."

"Yes, good afternoon... I'm sorry I don't know what to say." Spencer's voice was shaky and his hands trembled as he clasped them in front of him.

"It's ok, I know how you must feel. It's obviously such a shock," Jason said in his most polished professional tone. He hated the idea that he would be thought of as condescending but in these circumstances he always felt he must come across as shallow and insincere. In fact the opposite was true and Spencer warmed to him immediately.

"Yes, the news of Philip's arrest and subsequent accident really knocked me sideways and it couldn't have come at a worse time. You see I've been saying all sorts of things about Philip, especially to Ruby and I really feel terrible about that. Oh dear you must think I only care about myself – I didn't mean it to sound like that. I'm so dreadfully sorry." Jason could see the tears welling up in Spencer's eyes and the first stifled sounds of sobbing coming from deep within his chest. All of a sudden Spencer could no longer control his emotions and he clutched his face in his hands, bowed his head and sobbed uncontrollably. The sounds coming from the deep recesses within him were primeval in their intensity. Spencer hadn't cried for a very long time and now he just let go. Jason put an arm around his shoulders. "I thought you were going to meet Ruby at the hospital," Jason said after a few minutes silence between them. "I wanted to come here first… to get some answers and I couldn't face Ruby straight away. My outburst just then, I knew it was coming and I didn't want to upset Ruby any more, didn't want her to witness it. Do you understand?"

"Yes," Jason said knowing that he didn't need to elaborate.

Chapter 25

Ruby was a mixture of emotions as she drove home from the hospital. She had spent almost an hour with Philip and was relieved that his condition was described as comfortable. She had been told that he was concussed but he seemed reasonably relaxed and chatty although he did not seem interested in talking about the incident at the police station. In any case the nurses had suggested that it would be better if she did not raise the subject and as a result their conversation seemed strangely unreal. All that was missing was a bunch of grapes and a get well card!

Ruby had decided to take the circular route home via Broughton bypass but she soon regretted her decision. She had returned to Jason's office by taxi and collected her car which she had left in one of the visitors' parking spaces and the bypass seemed the obvious choice avoiding the town centre area during the rush hour. Now Ruby could see the red glow of hundreds of rear lights ahead of her flickering through exhaust fumes which hung in the stillness of the damp air. 'Damn and blast' she whispered under her breath as she pulled up behind the car in front. Immediately she switched on the local radio station hoping for a travel report, but all she got was a tiresome phone-in programme about abortion. She listened to that for a few minutes before the voice of the reporter got on her nerves to such an extent that she couldn't bear it any longer and she switched it off. She noticed that there was no traffic coming in the opposite direction and her mood deteriorated as she concluded that there was probably a serious accident ahead.

After about ten minutes someone knocked on the car window beside her and she wound it down revealing the face of a middle-aged man who seemed delighted to tell her that there had been a landslide ahead causing half the carriageway to be swept away and as a result the road was closed in both directions. "But we haven't had any heavy rain for ages," Ruby said in reply.

"These things happen," the man responded as he made his merry way to the car behind preparing to deliver the same depressing message.

It was 6.30 when Ruby eventually reached home and she felt exhausted. As she closed the front door she noticed a small envelope and she bent down to pick it up, assuming it was some sort of charity appeal which had been hand delivered. She put it on the hall table and went through to the lounge. There were three messages on her answer phone plus the message she had saved from Andy Blackstone two days previously. She felt guilty that she hadn't returned his call yet, but she had been busy and she just hadn't got round to it. The new messages were from Jason Barnaby, Spencer Cassidy and Graham and she decided to answer them in that order. But first she needed a drink. She resisted the temptation of a glass of white wine, seeking to keep a clear head, but she promised herself a whole bottle before bed to help her sleep. Instead she made a pot of tea and it wasn't long before she sat at her desk, steaming mug in front of her and reached for the phone.

Jason had left his mobile number and she punched the eleven digits carefully into her own house phone. As she waited she took a sip of tea and it almost burnt her lip. Jason answered on the fourth ring and he sounded breathless and impatient. "Hello, it's Ruby returning your call, I've been held up in the traffic... sorry."

"I'm just in the middle of something now, can I phone you back in half an hour or so?"

Ruby was disappointed by Jason's request as she had hoped to get an update from him about his discussion at the police station especially as she had so little to go on given her inability to talk things through with Philip at the hospital. Jason sensed this from the tone of her voice. "It's just that I'm in the middle of something and I might have more news for you in a short while," Jason said and he added "I won't be longer than absolutely necessary... promise."

Ruby replaced the receiver reluctantly and took a longer drink from her mug of tea. She wondered what Jason could possibly be doing that was more important than helping with her problems, but then she thought he probably had other cases to deal with and every client would believe that they should be given priority. She reached out once more for the phone intending to respond to Spencer's message but at the last moment she held back trying hard to recall Jason's precise words which hadn't registered properly with her when she first heard them. "More news for you soon," she said to herself adding, "I'm sure that's what he said so he wasn't working on another case after all." Her spirits rose immediately and the feeling of being overwhelmed and unsupported was lifted in the split second of her realisation. Ruby considered returning the calls from Spencer Cassidy and Graham but she decided that she would do that later. She wanted to sit for a while and reflect on all that had happened and she needed to do that on her own. Her thoughts raced through all of the details that had been thrown at her over the past few days and she tried, but failed to make any sense of everything. It was as if pieces of a jigsaw had been dropped on the floor in front of her and she was struggling to arrange them in any helpful order or decide what pieces were missing.

Then, when the phone rang again it made her jump and her voice probably sounded startled or anxious. Jason Barnaby didn't seem to notice. "Sorry I've taken so long to get back to you, but something interesting has come up."

"What's that?" Ruby said as the alarm in her voice became more pronounced and her pulse quickening markedly.

"It's alright… it's not about Philip," Jason responded sensing Ruby's anxiety. "I've got a contact… a private investigator… He keeps his ear to the ground and he feeds me information when he thinks I might be interested. I've already started to use him to do some background work for us. Anyway I've been down to the bypass with him. You've heard it's been closed I expect,"

"Yes… but," Ruby began but Jason cut her short wanting to get to the point.

"Part of the road has collapsed. A whole section has fallen away and they have been investigating the cause since late afternoon. It seems that some of the drainage ducts weren't filled in properly when the road was constructed."

"I don't see…"

"You will in a minute. The word is that a decomposed body of a young woman has been revealed and the whole area has been sealed off by the police."

"You mean it's Helen Grant?"

"Not certain yet of course, but everyone is jumping to that conclusion.

Chapter 26

Jim Packer had been as careful as possible about his personal contact details, but he always knew that he was vulnerable. He had received a text message from an unknown caller when he had been speaking with Peter Lord which worried him and the similar message he was reading now confirmed his suspicions. He was close to his final resettlement and he would make sure then that he could never be traced, but the text messages convinced him that there were some tasks he needed to complete as soon as possible. He had shared some of his concerns with the police resettlement team and they had offered him the opportunity of another move and they suggested either Hull or Southampton. Now he needed to make up his mind.

Both locations had their advantages, large urban sprawls, people coming and going all the time, and, he thought, far enough away from Gravesend. But he wasn't convinced. To be honest he had probably made up his mind when he had spoken with Peter Lord just a short while ago. He decided to return to Broughton but he didn't expect to stay for very long this time. As he sat thinking through his plans for the future two things caught his eye. The first was a fly buzzing about his feet and he went to kick it away. The second was the immaculate shoes he wore every day and he watched the shiny toecap as it swung lazily away from him.

Jim Packer had made enemies, he knew that, and some of the people involved were vindictive and persistent. He had been offered counselling by the police and they had supported him in many ways but there were some things he needed to do for himself, and the planning for his final move was the most important part of that. There would be no record, no paper trail and no loose talk to give him away. That was the way he wanted it.

He also wanted to narrow down the list of people who were most likely to be the ones who wanted to track him down. He had started to do that some months before and now he was faced with just two names. Making the final selection was difficult, they were both inventive, both influential with many willing contacts and they both had good reasons for seeking revenge. However, Jim Packer was beginning to convince himself that one of the names was more likely to see the logic of discretion, and had the ability to act more rationally, with more purpose and to put aside pointless vindictive pursuits and was therefore unlikely to be the one. That analysis enabled him to make his decision and now he believed he knew, not only where he was going, but also who he was running away from.

As soon as his decision was made he set about putting it into effect. He knew that time was of the essence and without any delay or regret he picked up the phone and contacted the emergency number he had committed to memory. Then everything took off and gathered pace rapidly. Mowbray Jackson was contacted at the highest level and that very same morning, Jim Packer was on his way returning to Broughton with a clear purpose in his mind.

Chapter 27

Peter Lord was sitting at his desk thinking about going home. It was about 6.30 pm but he wasn't looking forward to the end of his shift at seven because it would mean facing his wife again and he knew that sooner or later they would have an almighty row and he would probably say things that afterwards he would regret. If only they could just survive as they had for the last few years, with neither making any demands on the other. That life suited him quite well and he didn't have to face up to his feelings, either about himself or their relationship. When his telephone rang it was a welcome distraction and he answered it enthusiastically making Lucy wonder if Peter had been expecting a call from a long-lost friend.

"Lucy here... you ok to talk?"

"Yes, course I am... always pleased to help, you know that."

Lucy took a deep breath, she knew that there had been many false hopes raised over the years about finding Helen Grant or her body, but this time she was almost certain that the breakthrough she knew her colleagues craved had arrived and she was pleased to be the one to break the news. "I'm down at the bypass, expect you've heard that there's been a landslide and it's closed?"

"Yes, but what's that got to do with us, shouldn't traffic be dealing with it?"

"Traffic are already here in force. I'm here because of the body that's been found. Looks like she's been dead for quite a few years but we'll know more when Banik and his team are through."

"You said 'she'. Has the sex been determined?"

"Banik's not confirmed that, you know what he's like but the remains of the clothing suggest a female."

"I'm on my way," Peter said and he almost threw the receiver back into its cradle in his haste to rush to the scene. The possibility that it could be Helen's body had entered his head immediately Lucy had referred to a body being found and his heart was beating fast.

The first face Peter saw at the scene was Jim Packer and it took him by surprise. "Long way from your patch, but it's nice to see you again though," Peter said with genuine feelings.

"I've been transferred up to Broughton Central. Anyway, it will be nice to see out my time on my old patch.

"And it could be that you've arrived just in time."

"Yes, I couldn't believe my luck, almost my very first call and it turns out to be…"

"No, don't say it yet… we've had too many false hopes over the years. Come on, let's go and find Banik."

There was a large area screened off with stakes and the usual blue and white plastic ribbon running between them. A large canopy had been erected and the light-coloured canvas sheets were billowing in the wind. Peter could see a familiar female figure dressed from head to foot in protective clothing. "Lucy," he called across to her, "what's the news?"

"You'll need to talk with Banik, you know that, but if you want to have a look now there's some spare protective clothing in the side tent over there."

It wasn't long before they were both dressed in the white zip-up plastic smocks, wellington boots and the sort of head cover that Peter normally associated with a bakery. They looked at each other and grinned.

As they were approaching the main tented area, Banik emerged, looked up towards the sky and took a deep breath seeking relatively clean air. For some reason the protective clothing did not make him look as stupid as everyone else and even the large white mask which covered his nose and mouth did not look drastically out of place. Now the mask was pushed aside. "I've known much worse," he said as Peter and Jim got closer to him.

"Worse what?" Jim asked.

"Decomposed bodies have a habit of stinking especially in a confined space. Not seen you before."

"Oh sorry Banik, this is an old colleague of mine, Jim Packer," Peter said as they reached Banik's side and attempted to look around him into the area behind. "What have we got then?"

Banik looked directly at Pater but his face gave nothing away. "I'll be able to tell you a bit more when I've got the remains back to the lab and had the chance to study them properly."

Peter sniffed and started to jab his index finger in Banik's direction "Don't give me all that wait and see claptrap, what's your best guess at present?"

"I don't go in for guesses, but I can say that the decomposed body has probably been lying here for quite a few years – at least ten I would say and possibly as many as 20. Female clothing and shoes... size four I'd say. I'm pretty sure the body has been in the same position... not been moved at all, and it's in a sort of sitting position. Her hands – I say 'her' but only because of the clothing, that's not confirmed yet you understand – her hands are secured behind her back."

"I need to see," Peter said bluntly.

"Ok then, but wait just a minute... I'll call you in, ok?"

Banik put his mask back over his nose and mouth, turned and held the heavier plastic sheeting to one side and disappeared into the tent. "It's got to be her," Jim said almost to himself and Peter nodded agreement cautiously. "The bypass was due for completion about the time Helen went missing, I remember it well."

"Yes," Peter replied simply, and his thoughts were hurtling back to the period 16 years ago trying hard to focus on his recollections of the searches that they must have made at the time. "We will need to check with the Council, find out all we can about the way the road was constructed, precise dates when each section was completed and which firms were involved, that sort of thing. I will get cracking on that as soon as we are all finished here."

"Anything I can do to help?" Jim said.

"We were in at the beginning – together – don't see any reason why we can't see it through together."

"We'll see," Jim shot back as Banik appeared from the tented area and called over to them.

"All right, come across now, but be careful and don't touch anything."

Jim followed Peter cautiously. It seemed eerie in the half light and the hairs on the back of his neck bristled against the cold sweat that crept up on him clouding his mind for a moment or two and forcing him to remember. He had visited sites like this a few times over the years but this was very different. The area inside the tent was lit by arc lights and they could both see large concrete slabs about six feet apart with drainage pipes running between them. The pipes were at an angle of about 30 degrees falling towards the area where they had entered the tent and then disappearing into the ground in front of them. The area to the right was darker but they could just about make out a pile of rubble.

"Over there," Banik said pointing to the rubble – "that's where the landslide occurred and over here is where the body was found," Banik took a few steps towards the first two concrete slabs and gestured to Peter and Jim to follow.

In the confined space under the drainage pipe the air was putrid and the lighting wasn't so good, but there was no mistake. The body was propped up against the wall, head slightly to one side, and what looked like a full set of teeth smiling in their direction. They both stood looking, not saying a word, each with their own hidden thoughts.

Peter was the first to break the silence. "You said her hands were tied... I can't see anything." Banik adjusted the nearest arc light so that it was directed towards the left-hand side of the body. "There," he said, "just there," and he pointed into the shadow. "Yes, you're right," Peter said as his eyes caught the area where Banik had indicated. "I can see it now."

"Anything else?" Banik said. "Only I'd like to get the body back to the lab so that I can do a proper analysis."

"No, I don't think so, that ok with you Jim?"

"I've seen enough," Jim replied with a weary look on his face. He stood back and focussed on the head of the corpse sitting in front of him noticing in particular the deepset eye sockets, the scraps of hair and the teeth almost grinning back at him, not quite believing they could have belonged to a young pretty girl, but he knew beyond any doubt that it was Helen Grant.

The area outside the tent was very dark by comparison and they both needed a short time for their eyes to adjust to the light, making it difficult for them to see Lucy who was right in front of them. "Well, what do you think?" Lucy said.

"Well if it's not her I'd be bloody surprised," Peter responded. "You go back to the station Lucy. Let George Baker know, tell him I'll be back soon."

"I'm staying here. I'll go back with Banik, I want to be by his side on this one from start to finish."

"Are you sure that's wise?" Jim said.

"What do you mean?"

Jim looked down at his feet and he kicked a loose pebble with the toe of his shoe absentmindedly moving it just a few inches and a vision from long ago flashed across his mind. He lifted his eyes towards Peter but his head remained almost motionless. He was thinking hard trying to decide the best way of handling the situation and wanting to avoid Lucy overhearing what he had to say.

"Let's get this stuff off first," he said at last.

"No, I need to avoid contamination if I'm staying with Banik."

"I think it's best if Lucy stays with Banik," Jim said with a firm edge to his voice.

Peter began to protest "Not here," Jim said emphatically and he took Peter's arm in his hand seeking to guide him gently towards the area where they had changed. Lucy could sense Jim's reluctance to talk in front of her. "I'll see you back here in about five minutes, I just need to check with traffic down the road," she said as she began to walk away.

When they were alone Peter said "What's all this about… what's the problem?"

"We're all too closely involved… all of us who were on the case at the time. We need to keep our distance now that's all."

"Keep our distance… what the bloody hell do you mean?"

"I mean we don't want anyone pointing the finger, saying that we're prejudiced or worse even."

"And you think I am… prejudiced, and even if I am what difference does that make?"

Jim was more confident now, and the uncertainty he had felt a few moments before was evaporating fast. "We made mistakes back then, we all did one way or another, and I for one don't intend…" Peter turned suddenly and he pushed his right arm out towards Jim's shoulder with the open palm of his hand coming to rest just inches short. It was a gesture of denial more than aggression and Jim eased his body to meet it, cupping Peter's hand in his own, feeling that the physical contact would help defer Peter's rising anger.

"I'm not suggesting that we should not be in there on the case… as you said, we are the ones who need to see this through, not just for our own sakes, but because we care passionately about it, and none of us will leave a stone unturned, but when it comes to the forensics we all need to be very careful… keep our distance. It's not just you Peter, it's everyone, me included."

Peter moved his hand away from Jim's shoulder. He was beginning to see the logic in what Jim was saying, but there was something still worrying him. "I can understand the prejudice bit and the way in which some smart-alec lawyer might seek to twist things around, but you said… what was it, that there might be something else."

"I'm probably wrong, but I've always felt that someone close to us might be implicated in some way." Jim moved close to Peter, close enough to whisper in his ear "I don't mean us," he added in hushed tones. "That's different, but something has always – I don't know – has always been there at the back of my mind."

Peter moved away slightly but they were still close together, but now looking directly in each other's eyes. "I wasn't where I said I was that night and that's constantly at the back of my mind so your little something must be about me."

"I'm not saying that."

"No… you didn't have to. I could read it in your eyes – you have got doubts haven't you?"

"All I'm saying is, it's better for you and everyone else but especially you, not to put yourself in a position where your motives are questioned. If I thought you had anything to do with Helen's disappearance either directly or indirectly, I'd shop you straight away. Don't be in any doubt about that. Just be extra careful, that's all I'm saying."

Peter nodded vaguely. He felt dejected. He had always believed that if he ever had the chance to find out exactly what happened that night his own behaviour could finally be put behind him and that nobody would be any the wiser. Now he felt he had the chance to be part of finding the answers but it seemed that this part was getting in the way. "But I need to be involved, you know that. You must understand more than anyone else."

"I know and I do understand. Get involved as much as you like, work 24 hours a day if it helps but just keep away from the forensics, that's all I'm saying."

"Or what?" Peter said sarcastically.

"Or nothing, but I know you and I believe you can see it makes sense."

"But I don't like the implication."

Jim looked at Peter with an exasperated expression on his face, taking short regular breaths through his nose and with the palms of his hands partly open as if he expected to catch a beachball. There was silence between them as if they both realised that it was pointless saying anything else. To an outsider the sight would have been reminiscent of a pantomime or a circus act featuring two warring clowns. They were still wearing the protective clothes and hats and if only they could have seen themselves, they might have been able to see the funny side. But they were each concentrating on the words that had been spoken and for the moment it was those words, and not how they looked, that shaped the way they felt. "We're not going to fall out over this, are we?" Jim said at last. "I've told you what I believe and it's meant as friendly advice, but if you want to ignore it, well it's up to you. I won't make a fuss."

Peter was calmer now, but he was not ready to acknowledge his acceptance of what Jim had suggested, not verbally at least. He hated being in a position where someone else had power over him, but he had admitted to himself over the years that Jim had never done or said anything that made him feel vulnerable or indebted. He had felt that his secret was safer with Jim than it could have been with anyone else he knew but now that fragile feeling had been weakened and he knew it made him react irrationally. He had had moments of uncertainty like this over the years but usually they came to him during periods of restless sleeping in the early hours of the morning and they had been less frequent recently. Now he faced a more conscious turmoil of emotions and he couldn't hold on to his feelings any longer. "I've got to tell them, haven't I? It's the only way to get this demon off my back."

"Tell them if you must, but not because of me. Just stop and think for a day or two we can discuss it again properly if it helps."

"Thanks Jim… I'm sorry… You're right. Whether I say anything or not I need to be careful about this now. I'll get Lucy. She can stay with Banik."

"I'll tell her if you like."

"Yes, thanks Jim, I'd appreciate that. Come on we need to get this clobber off."

Chapter 28

Jim Packer sat outside the tent where he and Peter had changed back into their civilian clothes watching Peter's retiring figure and immediately noticed that he wasn't walking with his usual confidence. He looked drained of life and with no real purpose in his stride. Jim wished he could help, wished that there could have been another way, but now it was out of his hands, he had no control even if he wanted it. The timebomb was ticking and very soon the hour for detonation would arrive. It was a matter of survival and if he had to see it through to a conclusion, then that is what he would do. Then his thoughts were interrupted.

"Anything else I can do here now, Sir?" Lucy said as she approached.

"Peter's gone back to the station. He'll have a word with George Baker and the Super if they are about. He's asked me to stay on here a bit and to have a word with you. Peter says I can trust you, is that right?"

"What do you mean… trust… course you can."

"Only this may sound a bit unusual."

"Unusual I can handle… anything else… well I'm not so sure."

"I'm not talking about anything dodgy if that's what you mean. I don't know you well enough for that. In any case all my dodgy dealings, if there were any that is, are well in the past."

"Well, what have you got in mind?"

"I want you to stick to Banik like glue, make sure that nobody can say that there are any weaknesses in his security arrangements. We don't want any difficulties with the forensics later you understand."

"That seems fairly straightforward!," Lucy responded and she did understand. She had overheard part of Jim's conversation with Peter and she knew that there had been tension between them Now she assumed that must have been about the security of forensics and if Jim Packer had been the one to take a firm stance on that, then she supported him wholeheartedly. Jim was watching her closely and she was aware that she was being scrutinised. "You can trust me, Sir," she said wanting to break the brief period of silence that had become obvious.

Jim took a deep breath and remained silent for a few seconds more. "Whatever the outcome," he said eventually and his voice became no more than a whisper and took on a more serious tone, "We've all got to stand back and accept what the evidence tells us. We don't want weaknesses to creep in, no loopholes or uncertainties that smart-alec lawyers could exploit. You understand, don't you?"

"I've already said, I do understand," Lucy responded immediately and this time it was her turn to study Jim's face carefully. She had always believed that she was a good judge of people and her original assessment about Jim was reinforced in that brief moment, but she couldn't resist asking him one further question. "What do you expect to find, is there something specific?"

Jim returned Lucy's steady eye contact and the beginnings of a smile began to form on one side of his mouth "I've been in this game long enough and, you know, there is still nothing that surprises me. There will be something I'm sure of it, you're right there, but what that might be is anyone's guess."

Chapter 29

Ruby got up early the next day. She hadn't slept very well and she felt terrible. She ran the shower, with just a hint of hot water to take the edge off the cold and shivered as she stood under the jet. The initial shock soon left her, and she stood almost motionless as the water pounded onto her head and shoulders. After a while she stood to one side, shook her head and rubbed her face several times with her hands seeking to bring some semblance of alertness back into her life. She felt more awake but it made her head ache.

The sore head didn't leave her for an hour or more. By that time she had completed the rituals of getting up and was sitting drinking her second cup of coffee. She popped two more paracetamols into her mouth and, as she squeezed her eyes tightly closed, she swallowed them with a large gulp of lukewarm coffee. She sat still for a minute or two trying hard not to think too much about the mess Philip was in.

The phone rang and she picked it up thinking that it would be Philip's solicitor, but it was a woman's voice. "Is that Ruby Delacourt?" Ruby did not recognise the voice and she was a little suspicious.

She answered tentatively "Yes. Who is that?" Her surprise was immediately justified.

"Doesn't matter who I am, let's just say a well-wisher with a friendly piece of advice."

As a journalist Ruby was used to having conversations with people who wanted to remain anonymous, but this was different. She felt off-guard and vulnerable but managed to respond authoritatively, "I don't talk to people who won't give their name."

"You'll talk to me because I've got something to say and I know it will interest you."

"Oh, and what might that be?" Ruby said again trying her best to hide how fragile she felt.

"Your friend Philip Cassidy. Do you know anything about his background?"

It was difficult now for Ruby to avoid continuing the conversation, but she had one last go. "I'll answer that when I know who you are. What are you afraid of?"

"I'm not the one who has anything to be afraid of, but it suits my purpose for the moment to keep my name to myself."

Ruby hesitated for a few seconds and that suited the caller. All she was interested in was keeping Ruby on the line. The caller had a message to give and didn't really need Ruby to become actively involved in the conversation. "Let me explain. I bet he hasn't told you about Rachel Black or Karen French has he?" Ruby stayed on the line, her heart beating strongly within her chest making it difficult for her to breath calmly. Her breaths came in short shallow spasms and her hand was shaking so much that she found it difficult to keep the phone to her ear. Still she didn't say anything in response.

"I know you're still there. I can hear you breathing," the caller said confidently. "Rachel was just ten years old and she lived next door to Philip. I've spoken to her and even after 24 years she still remembers. That was in 1995. On its own you might just put it down to a misunderstanding but not when the same thing happened to Karen two years later. The circumstances were almost identical. You don't know what I'm talking about, do you?"

Ruby had been drawn in now and despite her reluctance, she couldn't help herself. "No. I don't know what you're talking about and I'm not sure I want to know."

"You may wish you didn't know, because the truth isn't very pleasant. You probably think Philip is the perfect gentleman, a lot of people do, but there's another side to him. You would have found that out for yourself after a while I'm sure, but I'm giving you the chance to uncover his wickedness now before you get too involved, before it's too late. You should be thanking me."

"Thanking you? I don't even know who you are," Ruby was on the point of ending the conversation there, but the caller got in first.

"Just ask Philip about Rachel and Karen. That won't do any harm will it? I'm not saying anything more now but we've got so much more to tell you. If Philip asked who I am just tell him his daughter sends her regards."

The phone went dead before Ruby could say anything in reply. In truth she was so taken aback that she was speechless. She sat staring into space with the receiver still in her hand. Eventually the buzzing noise coming from the handset made her look down and she felt as if she had just woken from a shallow sleep. Now, fully conscious, but still shaking uncontrollably, she replaced the phone and began to dial Jason Barnaby's number. She needed to talk with someone.

As the ringing tone sounded in her ear Ruby began to drift off again. Her mind returned to the strange telephone conversation and it made her think about her discussion with Philip's father. 'What was it he had said?' she thought to herself. She was brought back to reality when the answerphone switched in and invited her to leave a message. She decided against doing so and instead she replaced the phone, got up and went into the kitchen. She had already put everything from breakfast away or in the dishwasher, although she could not remember doing so. She felt strangely disconnected and was finding it hard to concentrate, but she knew she must shake it off and begin to function effectively. She picked up the phone again and an answerphone message told her that Andy Blackstone had phoned the previous evening and she considered calling him back but decided against it. She needed to speak with someone she knew she could trust. She punched in the number for Graham and much to her relief he answered straight away.

"Hello Graham, Ruby here. Is it ok to talk?"

"Yes of course it is. What can I do for you Ruby?"

"I've just had a very odd telephone call and I'm all chewed up inside. I need to talk. Could you come over do you think?" Ruby didn't realise it but Graham's heart was racing almost as much as her own. It always did when he spoke to her. He wanted to be near her, to help her to do anything he could for her and the chance of meeting up again was a welcome prospect but he knew he needed to be careful. He had loved her so very much and the ending of their affair had caused him so much pain. But she had told him that she loved someone else, so what was the harm? "'I'll be there in 20 to 30 minutes," he said and he heard her say "Thanks" as he put the phone down slowly.

Ruby felt guilty immediately. She was well aware from their previous meeting how he still felt about her, but she also remembered what he had said about her ever needing his help. She managed to convince herself that it was what Graham would have wanted, but she made a mental note to re-establish the way she felt about their relationship when he arrived. Then the doorbell rang.

'It can't be Graham already' she thought to herself as she went to answer the front door. She felt vulnerable following the telephone call and she looked out of the window by the door to see who it was. She was surprised to see Philip's father standing there. His ginger hair was being ruffled by the wind and being short and overweight he looked comical. She opened the door. Her first impression was that he looked almost stern and in fact far from comical. He took a step backwards as if he wanted to run away and he lowered his glance to avoid looking directly into her eyes. "Are you all right?" she asked. "Come on in." He hesitated a moment or two and did not say anything straight away. He knew he would find this conversation difficult and hadn't really thought what he was going to say. He had planned to give Ruby the note he had prepared and allow her time to read it through before they spoke about it. That was still his intention, but he knew he would need to explain briefly what it was all about. He knew he needed to avoid the sort of emotion that had hampered his conversation with his wife the night before but, despite his experience of managing people and facing up to difficult youngsters at his school, he didn't know how to start.

"Well not really," he began. "There's something I didn't tell you yesterday and it's important. It's about Philip when he was young. You need to hear me out before you make any judgements."

Ruby looked startled for a few moments. Her mouth fell open and she had a vacant expression on her face. "I will come in if that's all right," Spencer said feeling that one of them needed to break the silence.

"Yes of course. You just took me by surprise and…" Ruby didn't know what else to say and she let her words hang in the air inconclusively.

"And what?" Spencer asked as he followed her into the hallway.

"Oh, nothing really. I'll tell you later. What do you want?" Ruby hadn't intended to ask the question so bluntly and she realised immediately that it must have sounded somewhat brusque but Spencer hadn't noticed. He was more intent on his own mission and he was thinking to himself as he followed Ruby into the lounge.

"Well, what is it you didn't tell me?" Ruby said helpfully when they were set facing each other. She noticed that Spencer was reluctant to make eye contact and instead he was looking down at his hands which were clasped around some sheets of writing paper. His hands were shaking slightly and the movement appeared more exaggerated at the loose edges of the paper. Spencer noticed this himself and he made a clear effort to stop it but he was only partially successful.

"I've written it all down here," he said nodding down towards the few sheets of paper. "I want you to read it through carefully and then we can talk. Is that ok?" Ruby nodded in response. "I'm sorry about barging in on you like this but we… well I… em… decided that you needed to know."

"You mean that your wife doesn't agree with you. Is that it?"

"Partly," Spencer replied, "but I'll tell you all about that in a minute."

Ruby held out her hand for the note, but Spencer seemed reluctant to release it. "You must know, I'm doing this because I think it's right. It's not that I want to betray Philip. I can't say that I ever loved him as a father should, but I do care about him and want the very best for him. All I ask is that you read what I've written with an open mind. Will you do that?"

"Yes, course I will." Ruby might have sounded reasonably calm and in control but in fact, on the inside, she was quivering like a piece of jelly as Spencer put the papers into her hand. Even then, at the very last moment he thought about changing his mind. There was just a flicker in his eye and a slight hesitancy in his hand, but he remained resolute in his determination that someone else should know the full story. Immediately he felt guilty. Not for an act of betrayal, but for sharing the burden of knowledge with someone else.

"I'll go for a quick walk while you read it through. It's ok I'll let myself out," he said as he got up and started to walk towards the door. By the time he left she had started to read the note and she became so quickly engrossed that she didn't even notice him closing the front door behind him.

It took her about 15 minutes to read the note through. As each section started her heart sank a little further and when she came upon the names... Rachel Black and Karen French, she felt an emptiness that went so deep into the pit of her stomach that it almost made her physically sick. Bile built up in her mouth and she had to go to the kitchen for a glass of cold water to rinse her mouth out but the horrible taste remained with her. She re-read the sections about the young girls who had been near neighbours of the Cassidy family but at different times and locations. There was apparently nothing to connect them other than their friendship with Philip and their complaints about him. Rachel was the first to say that he had tried to drown her when they had been swimming together in a small lake. It was a popular spot and used by local children extensively during the summer months. She and Philip had been the last ones to leave one late August day and there were no witnesses. Philip had been convincing when he said that he had tried to help Rachel when she slipped back into the water from the muddy bank and that she had panicked when he tried to hold her and help her to safety. What was clear was that Philip eventually managed to pull her out of the water and give artificial respiration just in time. Rachel had been adamant that Philip had deliberately held her under the water and only let her go when she had almost drowned. In the end the fact that he had pulled her to safety led most people to believe Philip and to assume that Rachel had been mistaken.

The circumstances with Karen two years later were almost exactly the same, but no one other than Philip's parents were able to connect the two incidents. Each time they moved away from the area severing all ties with old friends and communities. 'If all the details are correct' Ruby thought to herself it would be difficult for an outsider to believe that Philip had been innocent. 'But I'm not an outsider, I know Philip and I just can't believe all this adds up to him being responsible for Helen's disappearance. It's just too scary to comprehend.' All these thoughts were going through Ruby's mind when the doorbell rang. It was Spencer returning from his walk.

Ruby let him in without a word. She looked down at the mat avoiding his eyes. She knew she must tell him about the strange telephone call she had received just a short while ago. What was it the woman had said in closing… "Just tell him his daughter sends her regards." Everything seemed so unreal and disjointed. Ruby didn't know what to think or believe. But she had faith in her own judgement and that had always told her that Philip was reliable, that he was different from some of her other boyfriends. But that made it worse in a way. She had been so wrong in her choice of her husband Ben, could she possibly have made the same mistake? She shook her head partly to clear her mind, but also as a signal to herself that she had not been wrong about Philip. But a seed of doubt had been sown and she could not shake off the dilemma.

Ruby followed Spencer into the lounge where they each took the seats they had occupied earlier. Ruby had the notes in her hand but she was barely conscious of holding them. "Well," Spencer said tentatively "I'm sorry to spring this on you. I just didn't know who else to tell and I knew you would at least be on Philip's side." Spencer was surprised when Ruby didn't respond straight away. He had anticipated a flurry of accusations and denials. In a strange way her silence was even more difficult to deal with and he didn't know whether it would be best for him to say something else or to keep quiet. In the end he chose the latter course but he moved closer to her in an attempt to make up for his lack of communication. Ruby turned towards him as he sat next to her on the settee and she burst into tears. In between her relatively quiet sobs she told him about the phone call she had received earlier. He listened carefully taking in all that she told him and even before she had finished, he had made up his mind.

"I don't think there can be any doubt," he said confidently. "It's her. I bet it's Janet." That thought had already crossed Ruby's mind. Something about the telephone call had made her think about something Spencer had said and she felt a sense of relief that Spencer felt the same way.

"But why? And what's this about being Philip's daughter?"

"I don't think she's referring to herself. This mythical child must be her own daughter, but is it just her imagination or is it real?"

"I suppose it makes sense if she just wants to cause as much distress as possible, but why would she want to do that? Ruby just didn't know what to think and she looked at Spencer for inspiration. He didn't seem any more enlightened than she was.

In fact, Spencer was beginning to be absorbed by his own thoughts. He looked at his watch anxiously knowing that he had an appointment with his solicitor at 11.30 am. It was almost 10.15 and he needed to make a move very soon. He was reluctant to leave Ruby on her own, but they seemed to have reached the end of any productive conversation. "I've got to go soon," he said quietly. Then she remembered that she had asked Graham to come round to see her and she had a warm feeling inside when she thought about him. "I've got a friend coming round soon so I won't be on my own very long."

"I'll give you a ring when I've finished with the solicitors."

When Spencer had gone Ruby returned to the lounge, sat down and started to read the note again. The sections about the two girls, Rachel and Karen, were distressing for her but were relatively straightforward. She tried to assess all the other details in a neutral, less emotional way as if she was not reading about someone she knew and loved. Part of Ruby's formal education had involved psychology and she sought to use these almost forgotten skills in analysing the information. These two mental adjustments helped her a great deal and she was better able to return to two of the incidents Spencer had described with enough detail to bring them almost to life. Spencer had included considerable detail and presented the information with clarity and the wording did not betray any trace of bias. It was a factual account and that helped her.

Just for a moment Ruby wanted to avoid any further analysis of the bleak account Spencer had provided. She had read it all through a number of times, but she needed to re-read those sections she had not studied in detail. She felt a little better in herself now and she knew that putting off the task was not the best idea. Part of her wanted to get it over with and to reach some sort of conclusion in her own mind but the other part had the upper hand at the moment. She thought about this dilemma for a short while, but she knew in her heart that she would wait; wait until she had the chance to talk things through with Philip; when he was better and could give a good account of himself.

Then she remembered Graham. He had said he would only be about 20 minutes, half an hour at most. That must have been over an hour ago. She wondered what had held him up. She was lost in her own world again and her mind strayed from one subject to another. She wasn't really conscious about getting up and going upstairs. In the bathroom she retouched her makeup and put on a small amount of her favourite perfume. As she watched herself in the mirror she was thinking about Rachel Black and Karen French wondering what they were doing now, and what were their memories of those days back in the 1990s that Spencer had described in his note.

Then she went into her bedroom and put on one of her new spring tops and was admiring the effect in the full-length mirror beside her wardrobe. She looked deep into her own eyes. "I can't be so wrong about Philip, can I?" she said out loud but she wasn't able to convince even herself. She had her doubts and they were mounting fast. The evidence gave her little room for hope.

Then the doorbell rang. Ruby hadn't heard a car draw up and the sudden ringing sound made her jump, but at least it brought her back to reality. She looked in the mirror once more and pressed her skirt down across her slender hips, seeking to smooth out any creases. She went down the stairs with almost light-hearted steps as the sun streamed through the window by the door. She glanced out. It was Graham and she felt relieved. Ruby opened the door straight away. She looked as if she was dressed for dinner. Graham, on the other hand, looked like a dog's dinner. "Whatever happened to you?"

"That's a charming reception," Graham replied with a just the beginning of a smile creeping across his face.

"I didn't mean it like that, it's just that you look such a mess. Whatever's happened?" Graham's clothes were muddy. The knees of his trousers were particularly dirty and his hair was all over the place.

"It's the reason I'm late. Some white van ran into the back of mine and the bumper's got tangled together. We've been trying to separate them," Graham was continuing his explanation and Ruby suddenly realised that he was left standing in the doorway.

"Oh, do come in. Sorry," she said.

"I thought you'd never ask," Graham said and Ruby noticed once more the shy almost boyish grin crease his face once more. It made her remember why she had fallen in love with him all those years ago and she thought fondly of the short time they had spent together.

When Graham was settled, and after he had washed his face and hands, Ruby told him about the telephone call and the visit from Philip's father. "What do you make of it all Graham?" she said looking into his eyes as they sat next to each other on the settee.

"I don't think it really matters what I think. The important thing is to do all you can to help Philip, at least until you know what he's got to say about it all."

"I keep saying the same thing to myself, but it's so very difficult, it's just one thing on top of another. It's almost overwhelming."

Graham was uneasy. He got up and walked over to the window. He looked out into the garden and his mind drifted. He was thinking about that lovely summer's day when he had taken the afternoon off work and had driven over to spend a few blissful hours with Ruby. They had a picnic lunch in the garden – omelette and crusty bread – he remembered and then they had gone for a walk along the seafront just a few miles from her home. "I love you Ruby." Those were the words he had written with a piece of driftwood in the sand and she had pulled him towards her and kissed him passionately on the lips as the tide washed around their bare feet. The water had edged its way towards the words he had written and started to blur them. "And I will love you forever," she had said as they watched the words disappear before their eyes.

"What are you thinking about?" Ruby said as she walked over and stood behind him. She put her hand on his shoulder and it took all his strength to avoid turning round and taking her in his arms. Instead he covered her hand with his own "Oh – nothing really," he said "Just trying to clear my mind. I don't feel I'm being much use to you at the moment."

"Don't be silly. It's nice just having you here."

"That's what I mean. I wish I could do something to help. Something more positive," he said and he smiled weakly over his shoulder, before turning and looking out of the window again. He didn't want her looking into his eyes just for the moment.

The phone rang and it was a helpful distraction for both of them. Graham turned and watched Ruby walk over to the table in the hallway. "Hello she said as she put the phone to her ear then she fell silent for what seemed like ages.

Chapter 30

George Baker's mobile phone was ringing on the hall table where he had left it. He thought about leaving it unanswered as he was in a fairly heated discussion with his wife but the temptation to see who was calling proved too much for him – he always needed to know what was going on. "Hello?" he said quietly. He listened in silence for some time as if he was receiving complication information "Thanks Peter, I'll be there straight away."

Peter Lord and Jim Packer were waiting outside George's office when he arrived. It was 8.45 pm and the rest of the outer office was deserted.

George walked through into his office, sat behind his desk and looked up as the others followed him in. "Sit," George said more abruptly than he intended and he gestured towards the two empty chairs. Peter looked around the room, "Sarah looking after you I see."

"What do you mean, oh yes, I've promised to keep it looking like this."

"What did you think I meant?"

"I haven't got time for riddles at this time of night," George said and he looked across at Jim. "Peter told me on the phone… please you've joined us… it's nice to have you back, particularly on this one."

"Yes, the call couldn't have happened at a better time. I would have hated to miss out on the chance to put this one to bed."

"Well what have you got for me then?"

Jim nodded in Peter's direction and he took it as a cue for him to answer George's question. He began to summarise all that they had established at the bypass.

When he had finished all three of them sat in silence for a minute or more each with their own different thoughts. George was the first to speak and he took the others by surprise. He had told Sarah that he had no control over the way in which the authorities would react to his behaviour all those years ago, but at least he could decide when to tell Mowbray about it. Now, he decided, was the right time to make his confession but he needed to let the others know what he intended to do. As he reached this conclusion the words of Andy Blackstone began to ring loudly in his ears. He had never been sure what Andy meant, but he knew it was important and he regretted now that he hadn't sought an explanation at the time. Andy Blackstone had started to point the finger, he was sure of it, but he had held back and George knew instinctively that he needed to be careful, just as Andy had said he should be. He decided to press ahead but he would stay alert and watch closely. "I'm pleased it's the three of us because we need to get one thing out of the way once and for all," he said simply and with no real emphasis in his voice.

"What's that then?" Peter said.

"Your library card. I found it by the millpond at Pashley Park the night Helen went missing."

"You what?"

"Didn't Jim tell you?"

"I've got no idea what you're talking about," Peter said, his eyes moving from one to the other but coming to a rest in Jim's direction.

"He gave it to me," Jim said with no hint of emotion or embarrassment.

"He what... For Christ sake – What's all this about?"

"Look Peter," Jim began to explain "I thought it was for the best. I knew you already had more than enough on your plate."

"Wow, hang on a minute. I can't take this in," Peter's breathing became laboured as he struggled to come to terms with everything that had been thrown at him. It would have been difficult enough on its own, but, coming on top of their gruesome find just a few hours ago, and not just any gruesome find, it all seemed too much for him to take in in one go. He sought to recover his composure looking from one to the other with vacant despair flooding through him. "Why didn't you tell me before?" he said to neither of them in particular.

They both responded at the same time but it was Jim who pushed his voice ahead. "Look, it's difficult – we were all under a lot of stress. I should have. I know that now, but I just made the wrong choice."

Peter sat quietly for a short while not knowing what to think, but it was George who broke the silence. "Just tell me exactly what happened, both of you, and don't leave anything out this time."

"There is not much more to tell," Jim said.

"We need everything out in the open, no more secrets from now on. We will have to come clean, make our confessions and take whatever punishment comes our way. But," and George hesitated a brief moment "But," he continued "We must make sure that we tell the full story this time and not leave anything out. We will have some control over events in the next day or so, but after that it will be out of our hands completely."

Peter was the first to respond and he could see the logic in what George had said "So, what do you want to know exactly?"

"Everything from start to finish," George said abruptly, "Warts and all. What you did that night, 17 March 2003, the date that will stick in our throats till the day we die, who you were with, who you saw, minute by minute and…" George paused for a moment "… I want written statements from both of you before we leave. I will be the one to tell Mowbray about this bloody mess and I want it all recorded in black and white. So let's get cracking."

Chapter 31

Philip had been watching the various working routines around him closely since he had been admitted into hospital. He had been allocated a small single space set back into an alcove at the far end of a ten-bed general ward. The area he was in looked like it had originally been a large store cupboard with the door removed and the gap widened so that it was easier for staff to see into the space from the main room. There was a similar area opposite him which had been converted into a bathroom and toilets and he had already used these facilities more than was necessary during the past 24 hours. He had an ulterior motive for doing so, and his movements in and out did not seem to be restricted or of any special concern to anyone. The nursing staff did not seem to pay him any more attention than they did the other patients. However, a police officer was present continuously, usually on a three-hourly shift basis, and sitting across from him just to the side of the bathroom door. The only entrance to the ward was at the far end, next to a small office which the nurses used day and night and where the police officers exchanged a few words with each other at the beginning and end of their shifts. One of the police officers, a dull looking man named Simon, probably in his early thirties, short and with a developing bald patch to add to his overweight appearance, had been on duty the first day and he obviously felt the whole thing was a waste of time. He seemed more interested in chatting to one of the nurses – who was as equally unattractive as he was – sometimes in hushed secretive tones. Philip concentrated hard and more often than not he got the gist of what they were saying to each other. The previous evening he had heard parts of their conversation about a search of his flat. He already knew that his ski top had been found there and now he wondered whether a second search was about to take place. He decided to make his move sooner than he had anticipated. There had been no secret of the fact that Simon would be on duty again the following morning and Philip made his plans to coincide with his arrival.

Sure enough at 9 am precisely he heard Simon's voice echoing down the ward and he saw the WPC opposite him look towards the sound and make the very first movement out of her chair. At exactly that same time Philip got out of bed dressed only in his pyjamas. "Just going to the loo," he said, but she didn't say anything in response as she stretched her back and shoulders and started walking slowly away from the bathroom door as he went in.

Philip knew already that he could easily get his head and shoulders out of the bathroom window and he wasted no time in reaching up to the top shelf where the spare towels were kept. He had, during his previous visits to the bathroom, brought his outdoor clothes one by one and had hidden them behind the towels. He dressed quickly before pushing his shoes out of the window and then climbed onto the bath and made his exit head first.

He put on his shoes and checked his pockets. He had taken a wallet from the bedside cabinet of the patient nearest to him earlier that morning and now it was safely in his own right-hand trouser pocket alongside some keys and a few loose coins he had also taken for good measure. His own money had been taken from him at the police station and he had no personal belongings at all.

As he walked slowly away from the hospital mingling with workers and visitors, he wondered how long it would be before the alarm was raised. He estimated that he probably had about 15 minutes before Simon became suspicious and a further five to ten before they broke the door down. He would be well away by then he thought as he quickened his step making towards the bus stop he could see in the distance. "Single to Benson Street please," he said as the driver looked up at him with a bored expression. Luckily Philip knew the area around the hospital very well. He had visited an elderly aunt who had spent about six weeks deteriorating slowly in the geriatric wing and he had caught the 28 bus home on many occasions. There were two ten and one twenty pound notes in the wallet and he gave the driver one of the smaller denomination notes. "Sorry I haven't anything smaller," he said expecting the usual protest about the lack of change. Instead seven shiny pound coins and some loose change chugged into the tray before him and he scooped them up trying hard to mimic the driver's apparent disinterest in the financial transaction. The bus moved off before he had taken his seat and he overbalanced slightly before he was able to reach out and grab the back rest of the seat nearest to him to steady himself.

He sat behind a couple, and there were two young women in the seat across the aisle but otherwise the bus was empty. He could see spots of rain hitting and then running down the window beside him making patterns like small saplings in a wood. He watched as one drop started its course downwards trying to visualise where it would meet the bottom sill, but it veered slightly at the last moment and his guess was inaccurate. The couple in front were talking about the holiday they were planning in Spain and the two younger women were whispering conspiratorially in tones so hushed that he couldn't make out a single word above the clatter the bus was making as it weaved its way across town.

He decided to get off at the far end of Benson Street and then walk back to Station Road. That gave him the chance to see if there was anybody about near his block of flats as the bus drove past his address. There were only four semi-detached buildings and the whole area seemed deserted as usual. He rang the bell, got up from his seat and made his way down the aisle as the bus slowed. It stopped suddenly but this time he was expecting it and was not overbalanced. He could not resist looking back at the two young women and he winked at them and pulled an insincere smile across his lips. They were about 17 years old, both with short dark hair and olive complexions. They were not interested in him one little bit but did not seem to be offended in any way. "Thanks mate," he said cheerfully as the door opened and he stepped down onto the pavement just before the bus pulled away again.

The time was just after 9.30 am and very few people were about. Two workmen in bright yellow coats were peering into a hole on the other side of the road exchanging words but they didn't seem to be paying him any attention. They were obviously having a disagreement about what to do next and their voices were raised. Philip was sure that if they were undercover police officers they would not be drawing attention to themselves and it made him feel more confident. He was now only about 20 yards from the front door of the building and he was still undecided. He could either walk past and return later or go in straight away. At the very last moment he made up his mind and he turned to his right, skipped up the two steps and reached out for the door handle. The door opened before him and he closed it quietly. His flat was on the first floor and he went up the stairs two by two pausing at the top briefly, looking around him and listening carefully. He kept a spare key under the carpet at the far end of the corridor under the window. It was well concealed and it took him a few moments to locate and retrieve it. He immediately returned to his front door, put the key in the lock, twisted it a half turn and the door unlocked before him. Again he stepped inside quickly and pushed the door shut behind him. He made straight for the bathroom, opened the door carefully and stood for a moment or two looking at the bath in front of him. Nothing seemed to have been disturbed and he was not surprised. He took the few paces towards the bath and then he noticed a slight mark on the top left-hand side of the panel running the full length across the front of the bath. Tentatively he reached out with the fingers of his left hand and pressed gently. He wasn't sure, but he had the feeling that the panel was slightly loose and he checked the right-hand side to be sure. There was a similar movement that end as well. His heart jumped, momentarily quickening his pulse rate and his breathing became laboured coming in shorter sharper intakes of breath through his half-opened mouth. He shook his head hoping to calm his nerves and clear his mind, but he was only partially successful. Immediately his attention was focussed on the back of the flat tiled area against the wall. There was a wicker basket on the flat surface with a few bits and pieces inside. He reached for the metal comb and immediately he used the thin metal edge to probe between two of the wall tiles just above the flat surface.

very first visit, but the most striking feature was the size and impressiveness of the inside of the flat itself. There was a small entrance area leading into a very large and beautifully furnished lounge with impressive windows along three sides of the room, three good size bedrooms, a kitchen and shower facilities. Philip was standing in the lounge now, plastic bag swinging by his side, having rung the bell and been greeted by a middle-aged man whose well managed and ample grey hair topped the distinguished look that he had obviously been seeking to perfect. "Hello Donald, hope you're keeping well," Philip said but not offering and not expecting a handshake of any sort and knowing that the man's true identity, like his own, had been withheld.

"Yes fine thanks and you?"

"Well you know how it is sometimes."

"Anything I can do for you Mr Denman?" Donald said with what appeared to be genuine concern in his voice.

"I won't be able to make this month's 'do' I'm afraid. Need to keep a low profile for a bit, but I've brought you these," he said as he lifted the plastic bag up to chest height and held it in front of him.

"Tesco's finest baked beans… what a treat."

"Yes… Something like that. You'll need to keep it safely here or wherever, as long as I can collect it again some time. Is that ok?"

"Yes that's fine. I'll have a preview. Is it as good as the last one?" Philip lifted his eyebrows and turned his head so that he was facing Donald directly. "I'd say it's the best yet, especially the first tape."

"I'll look forward to it then. Anything else I can do for you today?"

Philip considered this offer carefully. He knew he could trust Donald, probably in all the circumstances as much as he could trust anyone. He had considered what he would do next on the taxi journey and had come up with a plan of sorts. "Yes, there is actually. I need some slippers and an overcoat, perhaps also a hat. Can you help me with that?"

"Yes, no trouble at all."

"And I need you to ditch these clothes," Philip said pointing vaguely to the shirt and trousers he was wearing.

Donald didn't seem to regard the request as unusual in any way. "I'll just get you a coat and hat," he said.

"Don't forget the slippers."

"No, of course not."

Donald moved gracefully and Philip wasn't really aware of him turning and walking towards one the bedrooms, partly because he was looking out of the window and partly because his mind was concentrating hard on his plans and their execution. He was brought back to reality when Donald called out "Dark- or light-coloured topcoat? There's a choice."

"Dark will be fine," Philip responded as he walked towards the bedroom where Donald's voice had come from. Donald had laid a newish looking coat on the king-size bed and was just about to toss a matching hat next to it.

"What size… slippers I mean, not hat, I've only got one hat."

"How many pairs of slippers have you got?"

"Oh quite a few…. people leave them behind sometimes"

Philip thought this a bit odd but he nodded anyway "Size ten."

"Size ten it is then," Donald said in a matter of fact sort of way as if he had this sort of request every day. "I'll leave you to it."

Philip watched as Donald moved past the end of the bed, his reflection bouncing off the mirrored wall opposite, but he took no notice of that. Philip was left looking at his own reflection and he recalled the occasions when he had enjoyed these surroundings accompanied by some of the young guests who attended Donald's parties there. Quickly he shook those memories from his mind and he started taking off his clothes. He had kept the hospital pyjamas on under his day clothes mainly because it had been quicker that way, but now he was pleased he had kept them. Soon he was standing in the faded pyjamas noticing for the first time the pink stripes running vertically against a cream background. "They sure know how to pick them," he thought with a shrug and he put the size ten slippers on his bare feet. They fitted perfectly. He put on the overcoat and the hat and he saw from his reflection that he was reasonably presentable. The dark brown leather slippers would pass for shoes at a glance and he wasn't expecting to keep the disguise for longer than he needed to. As he walked back into the lounge Donald didn't comment at all on his appearance and did not ask a single question about his motives. Philip was pleased he didn't have to explain.

"Anything else?" Donald asked.

"Just a taxi to the central shopping centre and a ten pound note for the fare."

Donald took his mobile phone from his pocket, punched a few numbers and then put it to his ear. Taxi in ten minutes – on the corner of St. John's Terrace and Winston Place going to the Arndale Centre."

"Ok thanks."

"I've left my clothes on the bed... Oh and my shoes."

Without being asked specifically Donald replied "Yes fine, I'll get them destroyed."

About five minutes later, Philip was standing on the corner at the end of the road watching a taxi moving towards him. He lifted his arm with the palm of his hand outstretched and stared directly at the driver's face. The taxi's nearside indicators began blinking and it drew up at the kerb in front of his slippered feet. "Arndale Centre," Philip called to the driver over his left shoulder as he got in the back seat. "Ok chum," came the immediate reply and they were pulling away just as Philip was settling himself back in his seat.

In less than ten minutes the taxi pulled up in front of the main entrance to the shopping centre. "Keep the change," Philip said even before the cabbie had told him what the fare would be and he handed over the ten pound note Donald had given to him.

"Cheers mate... Thanks."

He made his way to the escalator and began to feel hot in the coat and hat but he resisted the temptation to unbutton it or take the hat off. Philip walked in through the swing doors with H. Samuels jeweller on his left and Clark shoes on his right. He didn't seem to be attracting any attention from the many shoppers walking up, down and across in the wide corridor but he kept looking straight ahead not wanting to catch anyone's eye and making sure he did not bump into anyone. He had been to the centre many times before and he knew there were seats overlooking the central precinct on the floor above just in front of McDonald's and overlooking the larger stores with Debenhams at the far end. Soon he was on the escalator, watching the people going down on his right-hand side but again he chose not to look at anybody in particular. He reached the top, took a careful step forward and followed it with a tentative second before walking off as confidently as he could. He could see the three seats in front and to the right of him and he made directly for the nearest one which was empty. He sat for a minute or two waiting for the right moment. Two or three lone walkers passed in front of him but he was hoping for more cover.

Then he was in luck. A group of friends were walking towards him side by side and about five of them took the diversion between him and the rail overlooking the floor below. It was too narrow for them all to pass together and they bunched up with two particularly large young women right in front of him. At that moment he took off the hat and overcoat quickly, put them into the bin beside him and sat forward with his head in his hands wearing only the hospital issue pyjamas and the slippers.

He couldn't help peeping out from between his fingers to see what people's reaction to him would be. Some took a second look, some ignored him completely and some turned to look again after they had passed, but nobody spoke to him at all. He waited a few minutes and the reactions were similar except for one young boy who tugged at his mother's sleeve and whispered up to her, "What is that man doing mummy?"

Philip decided to add an ingredient and he began making a moaning sound in a low-pitched tone whilst keeping his hands firmly against his mouth. This had the desired effect but it took some time. At last a security guard appeared and sat beside him "You ok mate? Can I help you? What's your name?" The questions were fired off in rapid succession but the man sounded genuine enough. Philip ignored him completely. More words of comfort were given and more questions asked "Looks like hospital pyjamas," he said finally as he reached out and touched the collar.

A small crowd had gathered by now and soon a police officer arrived and asked everyone to move on. "Hello sir. Is there anyone we can call to help you?"

"I don't know. I can't remember. Where am I?"

"Do you know your name? Have you got any identity?"

"It's… it's… I can't remember," Philip said trying to look as lost and forlorn as possible.

"I'll call an ambulance. They can sort it out," the PC said almost to himself as if he was fed up and wanted to get on with something more important.

A few more people had stopped to look at what was going on and as soon as there were three or four in the group it quickly encouraged others to join in and the PC and security guard kept ushering them away. This time the PC stood up, took out his radio and began making a call. Philip couldn't hear everything he said as he kept his voice low but he did hear the words, "Silly old fool."

"Won't be long. Getting an ambulance to come and help. I'll go and meet them at the front entrance," the PC said and he was looking more in the direction of the security guard than he was in Philip's direction. The guard did not reply but he continued to sit next to Philip and offering words of comfort from time to time.

Philip closed his eyes tightly allowing events to unfold around him and it wasn't long before he had been collected by some very patient ambulance staff, walked back to the front entrance and helped into the ambulance which was waiting right outside. He sat on the bed in the back and looked down at his brown slippers, refusing to answer any of their questions.

Chapter 32

Banik was sitting at his desk staring intently at a sheet of white paper. His expression was unconcealed surprise bordering on disbelief, yet there was no doubt. The DNA database had come up with two perfect matches. Banik was undecided what to do next. Normally he would have no hesitation but he had never been faced with the evidence he had before him now. He decided to speak to Mowbray before putting anything down on paper. Instinctively he felt he could trust the Superintendent more than anyone else. "Is that you Superintendent?" Banik said unnecessarily when he recognised Mowbray's voice on the telephone.

"Yes, what is it Banik?"

Banik felt remarkably calm and unruffled. He had decided what to do and it helped to be able to press ahead with a clear plan in his mind despite his general dislike of Mowbray's intimidating manner. "I need to see you straight away."

"What, about the Helen Grant case?"

"Yes."

"Ok then but I need to clear a few things first, make it in about an hour."

"No," said Banik emphatically. "I need to see you now. I'm on my way up."

Mowbray was taken by surprise momentarily. Normally he would have at least established an explanation so that he, rather than the caller, could decide how urgent a matter was in comparison with the half a dozen or so problems that he was wrestling with. "What's it about then?" he barked back but without the bite that he might convey in other circumstances.

"I'll tell you when I get there. I don't want to say anything on the telephone."

Before Mowbray could respond Banik had replaced the handset, got up from his chair and reached for his jacket hanging behind him. He might later reflect on this short conversation and wonder how he had the nerve to speak to the Superintendent so confidently. For now, none of these thoughts crossed his mind. Banik picked up the piece of paper he had been studying so carefully just a few minutes before, folded it in half and put it in the inside jacket pocket next to his wallet.

He was almost in a daze as he walked out of his office without telling anyone where he was going and closing the door carefully behind him. In what seemed like no time at all Banik reached Mowbray's outer office where his PA sat behind an imposing desk like a guard at the Tower of London. "I've arranged to see the Superintendent," he said without waiting for any reply and he squeezed past, knocked confidently on Mowbray's door and opened it almost immediately.

"Take a seat Banik. This had better be good."

Banik looked directly at Mowbray making a final assessment about his decision. The gaze lasted no more than a second or two but Mowbray was aware immediately that he was being scrutinised. Satisfied that his judgement was sound Banik sat down in the chair and took the paper from his jacket pocket. "I'm not sure it's good but it's bloody important."

Mowbray put his pen down in front of him on the desk, sat back in his chair and pushed his bottom lip up towards the strands of his moustache. "Well," he said, "I'm waiting."

Banik wanted to put things into perspective "We've already established that the fingerprints on the note and envelope Helen sent to Philip Cassidy belong to Helen and her twin sister Janet and that Janet was probably the last to handle the envelope. We've also established that DNA evidence shows that Helen sealed the envelope by licking it."

"Yes, yes," Mowbray said irritably. "You've not burst in here to tell me what I already know."

"No, that's not why I'm here, but I needed to start somewhere. Look, out of all the officers who were involved back then in 03, who would you say you trust the most?" Banik expected Mowbray to explode with anger but he wasn't afraid of that now. Instead he was surprised by Mowbray's reaction which was calm and thoughtful.

"If my life depended on it I'd say Andy Blackstone, without a doubt."

"That's what I thought, but I probably asked the wrong question. I should have asked who do you distrust the most."

Again Mowbray did not bite Banik's head off, but it was clear that he'd had enough and wanted Banik to come to the point. "Just tell me what's troubling you Banik, then I'll be able to help."

"I've just got the DNA results. We've got two separate samples, both taken from the same part of Helen's body. One is a match for Spencer Cassidy, the other..." Banik stumbled over his words and he cleared his throat as if he had a dry tickle in his windpipe. "The other is a match for Peter Lord. There's no doubt about it."

"You absolutely sure?"

"Yes," Banik replied almost reluctantly.

Mowbray sat for a few moments without focussing on anything in particular and tapping his thumb and index finger of each hand in a strange relenting rhythm. He looked up at Banik from time to time but, although Banik expected him to say something, he did not speak. At last Mowbray got up out of his chair and walked towards the window at the back of his office. Banik felt sorry for him, a feeling he hadn't ever experienced before.

"What about current serving officers?"

"What about them?" Mowbray replied in dull leaden tones as if the simple act of speaking was almost too much for him.

"I mean you say you trust Andy Blackstone but what about those still in the force?"

"I thought I could trust Peter, but now this, and…" Mowbray stumbled to a halt, thinking about his colleague in a way in which he had not done before. "If I've got to put my trust in anyone it would be George," Mowbray responded. "Yes, George, I've known him since he was a young PC. Mowbray sat staring into space for a moment or two fully absorbed by his own thoughts. His breathing was slow and deliberate, his heartbeat steady and his mind clear and functioning. He knew what he had to do and he would not hesitate in seeing it through. Banik sat quietly watching, not knowing whether he should say anything else and he was a little startled when Mowbray spoke. "Ok Banik you go off now, don't say a word to anyone and stay in the building. Get cracking on your report and make sure you give it to me personally. And Banik… thanks. You're on the list as well you know."

"What list is that?"

"Those I can trust"

Banik stood up for the first time since he came into Mowbray's office and Mowbray turned away again and looked out of the window scratching his forehead gently with his left hand and tapping his thigh with his other hand as if willing himself to press ahead with the unpalatable work ahead of him. Banik decided not to say anything else and he opened the office door and left quietly. Just as the door closed Mowbray walked towards it and opened it again. "Get a message to George Baker. I want to see him as soon as he arrives. Urgent, ok?" he called out to Jennifer, his PA.

Mowbray returned to his chair and sat down wearily. He took a key from the top right-hand drawer of his desk and used it to open the bottom drawer on the opposite side. He took out a blue folder and placed it on the desk in front of him. He had started a chronology of events and now he added a few additional words to the list. Almost before he had finished there was a knock on his door and George walked in. "Ah George, come in, take a seat."

"Thank you, Sir," George responded but his voice had a quiver and he felt uncomfortable. He knew he needed to explain everything and he was close to the point when he would do so but he wasn't sure that the time was right.

"I've got some bad news I'm afraid," Mowbray began and he paused briefly flicking the tip of his moustache with his lower lip. "Just heard from Banik, he's got the DNA results. There's no doubt I'm afraid, Peter Lord's DNA was on Helen's body. It's positive I'm, afraid. There's also another match — it's Spencer Cassidy."

"Philip's father — the schoolteacher? I've always had my doubts about him. Did seem a bit creepy."

George didn't respond immediately. He was momentarily caught up with his own thoughts and analysis and his brain was stumbling about almost aimlessly trying to make sense of it all. He blinked a few times trying to clear his head, trying to see the connections and desperately wanting to find a solution. He knew in that instant that he would have to explain everything to Mowbray now, everything that happened sixteen years ago, he could not delay any longer but it saddened him. "There is something else you need to know," he said simply and then he began to unburden himself. He stumbled over the first few words but then he settled and felt relief more than anything else. Mowbray listened in silence and a deep weariness was creeping up on him making it difficult for him to concentrate. He let out a huge sigh "Look George," he said and he shook his head from side to side. "What a mess and so many of you compromised. I've got absolutely no choice now."

"No, I can see that but…"

Mowbray cut him short abruptly. "I might, just might mind you, be able to spare you at least from immediate suspension. But not Peter Lord or Jim Packer. I need to see the ACC at once."

George sat quietly for a while just nodding his head.

Chapter 33

Mowbray's meeting with the ACC did not last long but that didn't make it any less distressing. It was the part of his job that he disliked the most and it never got any easier. Most aspects had now been taken out of his hands and would be dealt with by the IOPC. Decisions had already been made that Peter Lord, George Baker and Jim Packer would be served misconduct notices and suspended from duty pending investigations. Mowbray had been given 24 hours to hand over all aspects of the criminal investigations in regard to Helen Grant's death and the other charges facing Philip Cassidy. He knew that he needed to use that time wisely and he had a plan. A plan he hoped would give him some control at least for the time being.

When Mowbray got back to his office from his meeting with the ACC he sat quietly for a moment and the silence around him seemed to close in and engulf him. Part of him wanted to be swallowed up by it and transported somewhere far away, somewhere, anywhere as long as he could avoid the dreadful mess in front of him. He knew the officer who would be taking over the case and he trusted and respected her. He believed that she would do a thorough job, but she did not know the people involved like he did. The ACC had told him that that was an advantage and he could see the logic in that view. However he owed it to his colleagues to make sure that all the paperwork was in order and more particularly that their individual indiscretions were put into perspective. Whatever influence he had over that was minimal, but he had argued that there needed to be some continuity and it had been agreed that DC Lucy Atkinson would be seconded to work with the new team. He was pleased about that.

"Get Lucy Atkinson on the phone right now – tell her to meet me in Committee Room 2 in an hour. And… and… get Banik to join us as well." Jennifer received this demand with a look of displeasure on her face, but that didn't register in her voice when she said she would contact them straight away. As she was reaching out to pick up the phone it rang again and it startled her. "Tell Banik to come straight away," Mowbray said without any introduction and ending the call as abruptly as he started it.

Mowbray looked around him again and sniffed as he flicked at his moustache with the index finger of his left hand. He put a blue file under his arm and as he passed Jennifer's desk he called back "Committee Room 2. Have you spoken to Banik yet?" and without waiting for a reply he continued striding off down the corridor and didn't hear Jennifer say "Up yours" in a sweet sickly voice.

The committee room was impressive with wood panelled walls, ornate ceiling and a large oval table in dark oak. Mowbray sat in the middle chair facing the window placing the blue file carefully in front of him. There was a knock and Banik came into the room almost reluctantly. He knew that the committee room was often used when staff were given a bollocking. From Jennifer's tone he thought he might be heading for trouble. "Come, come," Mowbray said when he looked up and saw Banik's face and his anxiety began to lift.

"We need to sort this out once and for all, and we're going to sit here until we've got some answers," Mowbray said and he sat back in his chair, lifted his chin slightly, clenched his teeth and let out a burst of air through his nose. "I'm seeing DC Atkinson soon – but we need to clear up a few things first."

"I'll do what I can," Banik said calmly, but I've already told you everything I've established – it's confirmed in my report."

"Report – I've not seen that yet."

"Just finished it. Was going to bring it up but this sounded urgent."

"But nothing new?" Mowbray said with a questioning tone. "You will have to pass it on to the new DI. I'll let you know who that will be, ok."

"Just one thing I haven't explained properly that is."

"And what's that?" Mowbray shot back accusingly.

"I've told you about the DNA?"

"Yes, yes – Peter and Spencer Cassidy, yes."

"And that both samples were found on the same part of Helen Grant's body?"

"Yes, yes."

"What I didn't say explicitly is that it was definitely around and inside her vagina."

Mowbray let out a deep sigh as if fighting against evidence he wanted to dispute, but finding it difficult to pinpoint where he could begin. "Well that is a body blow I must admit. Unless…" Mowbray's mind circled around the theory he was beginning to build up and he just about clung on to its feasibility.

Banik wondered if Mowbray wanted him to say anything else as the silence extended for what seemed like ages. Then Mowbray brought it to an end. "Ok Banik, I get the implication – I just don't believe it."

They looked at each other across the table as if they were both seeking explanations and hoping the other would come up with a solution. It was Banik who spoke first. "I deal in facts – for me it's either yes or no. So it's hard. You've not heard me say this before but I'm with you. I don't believe it either."

"That makes it very simple then," Mowbray said smiling. "Someone must have set them up, but who, when, why, how?"

"Let's start with the how," Mowbray continued. "And let's start at the beginning. What's the name of the person who dealt with the forensics at the time?"

"That was Pauline Brinkstead– I've worked with her before, very good. Still about I believe."

"And have you got everything still kept safely downstairs?"

"Of course," Banik replied. "It's an open case – I'm sure we've got everything."

"I know it's a huge ask, but could you check through it all again. See if there is anything they might have missed – get this… What was her name?"

"Pauline Brinkstead."

"Yes, this Pauline woman – get her to help if you can."

Banik got up and walked towards the door. He felt weary all of a sudden, not just a tired weariness, but more a feeling of helplessness because he wasn't sure he could see this through on his own.

"I'll see what I can do," he called back without much conviction.

The first thing Banik did when he had returned to his office was to look through his contact address book. Sure enough, the name of Pauline Brinkstead, was listed with contact details and he noted that she was still working just a short drive away.

Pauline answered his call almost before he was ready to talk to her and he was pleasantly surprised when she agreed straight away to do all she could to help. It wasn't long before Banik was amongst the boxes of evidence. They were stored at just the right temperature in row upon row stretching up and beyond. Banik had decided that he already had enough of an overview of the Helen Grant evidence and that he needed to look more towards areas that, for one reason or another, had been categorised as unconnected, inconclusive or lacking authenticity. It wasn't long before he was fully immersed in his work and he was initially unaware that Pauline Brinkstead had arrived and was being accompanied towards him by one of his assistants. Banik noticed that she looked tired and the colour seemed to have drained from her face which took on darker shade of grey as it creased around, what once might have been high cheekbones. Banik quickly explained what he needed to do and it wasn't long before they agreed how the search would best be undertaken between them.

It was slow going and neither of them wanted to take any unnecessary shortcuts. After about two hours Banik decided to let Mowbray know how they were doing and he phoned him. Jennifer answered in her best professional voice "He's still in the committee room," she said, "but I could put you through there if you want."

"Don't worry, I'll talk with him later – just let him know that I called."

At almost that exact moment Mowbray was coming to an end of his meeting with Lucy Atkinson. Mowbray had informed her about the DNA evidence Banik had told him about earlier and she now knew that she was to be seconded to work with the new team. She was looking forward to it.

Chapter 34

Mowbray arrived early the next morning, but Banik and Pauline Brinkstead were waiting for him. "Just give me a minute to settle in, then we can get on," he said as he passed by but they were not sure whether or not to follow him into his office. They looked across at Jennifer but she was occupied painting her nails.

"Well, what have you got for me?" he said as he ushered them into his office ending their uncertainty. Mowbray sat at his desk and moved some pens to one side almost aimlessly. In almost one movement he looked up, raised his eyebrows and took a small sniff of air through his nostrils. "Well?"

"As you know," Banik continued "It's all been reviewed at least twice before and we would both say that they did a thorough job both times." Banik looked at Pauline at this point as if to establish whether she wanted to add anything, but she was deep in thought and didn't notice. Her mind, as it had on numerous occasions before, had transported her back to that day in March 2003. It had been the first case where she had headed up the forensic team and she wondered whether or not she had led the process with the thoroughness it deserved. Now she thought she had the chance to recheck everything and she had no qualms about doing so even if it meant uncovering any mistakes she might have made.

Getting no indication from Pauline that she wanted to add anything Banik continued "The main bulk of the evidence is straightforward – all correctly logged, initialled and dated – where everything was done by the book and evidence followed up and outcome documented. That's the bulk of it. Then there is a substantial number of items that were categorised as being unconnected. You can imagine the whole park was searched, so there is a lot to go through, but again all recorded properly and in many cases with photographs showing the items in situ. We found nothing new, nothing to help us and no surprises. So that does not help us at all."

Banik had taken a chair opposite Mowbray and Pauline sat next to him. They both felt uncomfortable but Mowbray, even if he had noticed, did not change the mood in any way. "Is there anything positive at all?" he said abruptly.

"Well…. perhaps," Banik replied before he continued "There was a black bin bag with the collection of evidence. We don't know why it was there, whether it's connected to the case or not. At first glance it looks like a collection of rubbish, nothing logged or recorded."

"Well," Mowbray replied shaking his head from side to side as if he could see everything slipping away from him. "What's the significance then?"

"We found a cardboard box amongst the rubbish, just screwed up, didn't think much of it at first."

"And?" Mowbray said with a hint of temper attached to the word.

Pauline moved as if she was going to reply this time but she paused slightly. She had woken in the night more than once worrying mostly about the box and its contents. 'Had I made a mistake?' she had thought over and over again. She reached the point where she knew that any further sleep was impossible. When she had first uncovered the item that Banik had referred to and examined it closely a realisation had hit the dark recesses of her mind like a lightning bolt crashing across a night sky. She knew in that blinding flash that she had made a crucial mistake and she felt pain in the pit of her stomach. She forced herself to recall all the minor details that jumped up at her haphazardly until the overall picture was as near to complete as possible. In her mind she could see her colleague, Eddie Short, standing by a bench seat just after they had finished searching a workman's hut near the bypass just a few miles from the park. Eddie had not applied himself diligently enough that day she recalled and it troubled her. She wondered now whether she had done enough about it. At this point Pauline looked directly at Mowbray who up to then had not acknowledged her at all or asked her how she was connected with the case. He had assumed that she was one of Banik's assistants. "I'm Pauline Brinkstead by the way, I was the senior forensic officer at the scene that day back in 2003."

"Ok, ok," Mowbray snorted.

"The items that really interest us were in the box…" and she paused slightly "… a used condom together with regulation issue police protective gloves. As Banik has said we don't know where they were found, why they were amongst the evidence, they just looked part of a rubbish collection."

"Not much use then?" Mowbray said with more than a hint of desperation in his voice.

"Well maybe not unless we can link them to the case and we are in the process of trying to do that."

"We've not done any DNA tests yet," Banik added. "But I'm sure we will be able to process that without any difficulty and very quickly."

"Well, what are you waiting for?" Mowbray said and his voice took on a squeaky almost excited tone.

Banik and Pauline walked side by side, each with their own separate thoughts and it wasn't long before they were back downstairs in their own research area. "What's the matter?" Banik said almost immediately as they sat down.

"I just get the feeling that if we find something useful, and I hope we do, it will come back to haunt me for the rest of my life."

Chapter 35

Ruby had difficulty separating fact from fiction in her mind as she drifted into and out of sleep throughout the night. The point at which her waking thoughts ended and her dreams began was blurred and a thought kept pushing its way to the front of her mind but she could not make any sense of it. She blinked a few times and she began to uncurl from the foetal position she had assumed in the latter stages of sleep. Almost immediately she was fully awake.

She started to analyse in her mind all the details she had discovered over the previous days but she wasn't ready to make any more sense of it than she had the day before. She made up her mind quickly and it wasn't long before she was looking at the reflection of her naked body in the full-length bathroom mirror waiting for the shower to warm up. Soon she was standing under the powerful warmth of the water gushing from the shower head, allowing it to flatten her short dark hair and follow the contours of her body before hitting the shower basin around her feet which she kicked from side to side in rhythm with the flowing water. She brushed her fingers through her wet hair and then turned towards the jet of water allowing it to strike her full in the face. She stood like that hoping for inspiration.

She switched the shower off, stepped out onto the bathmat and reached for her towelling gown behind the bathroom door, pulling it around her like a cocoon and dabbing her hair and face with the high soft collar. And it was then that she remembered. Her chin lifted and her eyes opened wide looking back at their reflection in the mirror. She had remembered the small white envelope she had picked up off the mat the previous evening. It had gone out of her mind completely at the time, but throughout the night it had for some reason begun to gnaw away at her. Now it seemed important and hurriedly she made her way downstairs not worrying about the wet footprints she left behind or the fact that her dressing gown hung open revealingly on her slender frame.

Ruby took the small white envelope from the table beside the front door and looked closely for the first time at the handwriting on it. Her name and address were written in a neat and tidy hand in blue ink. There was no stamp or any other markings. She took the envelope into the lounge and slumped back onto the two-seater settee under the window next to the television. She studied the envelope again for a few seconds but then hurriedly, with her index finger tore the envelope open and removed the single sheet of folded white writing paper.

"I need to see you please. I won't take up much of your time but I don't know where else to turn to. My name is Becky and my mother is Janet Grant. I have only recently found out that Philip Cassidy is my father and what terrible things he has done. You won't like what I've got to tell you but you must listen to me. Please." The note was signed Becky Grant and there was a mobile number for Ruby to contact.

Ruby uncrossed her legs and sat back in the settee as she looked ahead into the space in front of her but without focussing on anything in particular, her eyes darting from side to side and rapidly blinking in the daylight coming from the window behind her.

It seemed to Ruby that at every turn she uncovered something about Philip that was disagreeable and she was certain she was about to establish another unpleasant side to his background and personality. Yet at the beginning of their relationship he had appeared to be sensitive and considerate, the exact opposite of her ex-husband, but now it seemed that they were very alike in so many unpleasant ways. Ruby shrugged this thought aside and looked down at her bare feet. She was beginning to feel cold.

She quickly re-read the note then put it on the seat beside her next to the envelope. She sat for a few minutes thinking about everything she had found out about Philip in the past few days and then she shook these thoughts from her head. The motion caused the dressing gown she was wearing to gape open even more, so she stood up, pulled the edges of the fabric around her and reached behind her for the towelling belt which hung from the one remaining strap at the back. She fastened the belt with a single loop bow and almost in the same movement made her way upstairs to dress but her thoughts continued to be centred on her growing uncertainty about Philip.

When Ruby was dressed she sat on the bed and reached for the phone on the side table. Soon she was listening to the ringing tone, her heart beginning to race as she contemplated the conversation she was about to begin.

"Hello?" a voice answered cautiously.

"It's Ruby Delacourt. I've got your note. You said you wanted to talk," Ruby's own words sounded more confident, but that was a disguise concealing her fragile emotions which she managed to keep just below the surface.

After a few seconds delay the quiet voice continued "You will meet me, won't you? I really need to talk to you."

"Yes… yes don't worry we can meet up, no problem. When do you want…?" Ruby's words were interrupted.

"Can we make it right now? I can come over straight away."

"Yes, that's fine," Ruby replied quickly but the final word was delivered slowly and her voice trailed away as she considered how she should make her request without making it sound too defensive. "I wonder, do you mind if I ask a friend to join us. He knows all about…" again Ruby struggled to find the words which would be least unsettling or emotive "… about your father," she finally added hoping that she had hit the right note.

"I really wanted to see you on your own, can you trust him?"

"Yes absolutely, don't worry, I'm sure Graham will be helpful to both of us,"

"Who is he then… this Graham?"

"He's an old friend of mine, a journalist, but I would trust him with my life."

There was silence for a short while as Becky struggled to decide what to say next. In her heart she had visualised a meeting when she would feel confident and able to say what she had to say without restraint, but that vision had been about a meeting with one other person, with a woman who she believed would want to know everything and would not be looking for excuses or to put up barriers. Now she wasn't so sure and her confidence was beginning to evaporate. "I… I…" she began "I'm not sure."

Ruby could sense the unease and uncertainty, but was determined to press ahead. "You've said you want to talk with me and I want that too. I want to hear what you have to say and from what you said in your note I won't like it. I've gone through a lot recently and now there's something else that I suspect might be even worse for me. I need the support of a friend, you can understand that, can't you?"

There was silence again but this time Ruby had the feeling that Becky was coming to terms with her request. "Ok then," she said at last. "If you must you must."

Ruby pushed the final note of reservation to one side and instead picked up on the agreement. "Thanks, that's settled then," she said quickly. "I'll call Graham straight away. What time will you get here?"

"About half an hour, three quarters at the most, is that ok?"

"Yes, that's fine. You know the address."

"Yes," Becky said with what Ruby took to be a sarcastic edge to the word, but she shrugged it aside thinking perhaps that she was being too sensitive. "I'll see you at about 10.30 then. Ok?"

"Yes, see you then," Becky said in response.

Ruby replaced the telephone handset in the cradle and then picked it up again immediately. She punched in Graham's telephone number which she had committed to memory without really trying.

"Graham is that you?" Ruby said in response to a few mumbled words that were impossible for her to decipher. Graham recognised Ruby's voice immediately and it helped to push aside the muzziness that sat like a grey mist inside his head. He had drunk far too much alcohol the previous evening and had slept badly as a result, the early hours of the morning being the only really restful part of the night.

"Graham, are you alright?"

"Nothing that a glass of water and some Alka-Seltzer won't put right," he said at last as the daylight around him and the need to concentrate began to bring him back to reality. "Sorry Ruby, what is it?"

"I was hoping you could come over, but if you're not feeling well,"

"I'm well enough, don't worry. What's the problem?"

"It's complicated, could I explain when you get here? I've got someone coming over in about half an hour. I just wanted you to be with me but…"

"No buts… I'll be there," Graham said curtly and put the phone down before Ruby could object.

Ruby was left to wander about the house in a daze. For some reason she thought about her ex-husband Ben and at the same time cupped her left breast with her right hand remembering the pain so vividly that she could almost feel it. One evening Ben had punched her hard and brutally. It was the last time he had hit her. Physical pain was immediate and real and because of that she felt she could cope with it more effectively than she could the many mental scars he had left with her. One of these scars made her feel that she could never trust another man again, at least not the absolute trust that needed to exist between lovers. Now that particular scar was beginning to push itself to the surface of her mind and tears began to fall and follow the lines around her mouth until they were about to fall from her chin, as she brushed them aside with the back of her hand. "I will never trust Philip again," she thought to herself, but if that meant she could never trust anyone, Ben would have won. It would mean that Ben would always be with her and she was determined that he would never have that sort of hold over her ever again.

At that very point the doorbell rang and she was glad to have the interruption. It was Graham, she greeted him with the sort of smile he hadn't seen on her face for a long time. "I'm so pleased you could come," Ruby said as she reached out for his embrace plunging her face into the warmth of his neck and allowing the tears to fall again but this time unrestrained.

After a while Graham edged back from her embrace and looked her full in the face. "Ok, then what's all this about?" Ruby returned Graham's searching gaze, took a deep breath and told him as much as she knew about Becky. Then the doorbell rang again and it startled them both. "That will be her," Ruby said as she stood up and made her way to the front door. Becky was about five feet five inches, slim with short dark hair.

"Is he here?" she said in the same quiet voice Ruby had noticed when they spoke on the telephone.

"Yes," Ruby responded simply and without any further explanation. "Please come in."

It wasn't long before the three of them were seated facing each other. Becky was more confident than Ruby had expected and she got the impression that she wanted to make a start. "Ok then," Ruby said, "what is it you've got to tell me?"

"Mum never told me who my dad was, said it wasn't important and that she would make it up to me, which she did in many ways, but I always wanted to know and I think she was aware of that." Ruby noticed that as she spoke Becky grew in confidence and her voice became stronger. "I was brought up in the north east, a little village just a few miles from the sea, mum met this nice bloke, Ted Grant, and they got married, he's been a good father to me. Then when I was about 11, we moved south, near Gravesend.

"Why was that? Do you know?"

"No, not really. Mum said something about wanting to be closer to family and friends, but I'm not so sure. It wasn't really close to where she was brought up."

"What about your mum, what happened to her?"

"Look, I don't really want to talk about that. It's got nothing to do with it as far as I'm concerned."

Ruby realised that her questions had unsettled Becky and she needed to take a step back, to let Becky tell her story with as little interruption as possible. "Sorry," she said simply.

After a brief pause, Becky looked into space and took a deep sigh as if she was collecting her thoughts and deciding where to start. "I hate him," she said at last "I hate everything about him, my real dad I mean." Tears started to well up in her eyes and she wiped them away with the back of her hand. "Haven't cried for ages, not about him at any rate."

"It's ok, it's alright, you cry if you want to," Ruby said but she could see a steely determination in Becky's eyes and sat back waiting for her to continue.

"He's not worth my tears, not after what he's done to Natalia, not after what he's done to so many young girls. It's unbelievable that he's got away with it for so long."

"You've not mentioned Natalia before… Tell us about her," Ruby said.

"I met her a few years ago and she became my best friend… She still is. But her life… for the most part that's been destroyed and my father, he is the man responsible." Becky looked up at Ruby "You don't know what he's capable of, what he's like, you've just got no idea."

"You need to tell me. I'm not expecting it to be pleasant, but I think I'm prepared for that."

"We were such good friends, Natalia and me. We went everywhere together. She came to England with a group of young friends from Romania. I don't know the full details but she was living in London at first and then she came down to Gravesend…to start a new life she told me, and that's where we met, in a coffee bar one Sunday afternoon." There was silence for a few moments and Becky looked across at Ruby and Graham as if she was seeking some sort of approval to continue but they both looked back at her with unchanged expressions on their faces.

"We often spoke about my dad, and me not knowing anything about him. Then one day when mum was well out of the way we decided to have a good look around. I knew my mum kept all of her personal bits and pieces in a drawer under her bed. I had never had the nerve to look though the papers before but Natalia sort of egged me on, made me feel more confident. The first things we found were news cuttings about Helen's disappearance. I knew all about that, or at least I thought I did. There were two boxes of stuff. Some of it wasn't very interesting and we were beginning to get a bit bored when we found the envelope. It was addressed to Philip Cassidy and inside was a note written by Helen asking to meet up in Pashley Park. I knew enough to know that it was important. It was dated 16 March, the day before Helen disappeared!"

"Did you find anything else? Anything important that is?"

"There was a photograph of a youth, a boy of about 16 I'd say, and my mum had written something on the back but it was all crossed out. We couldn't make out what it said. Then we found another picture, this time the same man we thought, but older. My mum had written on the back of that one as well, it said 'Philip Cassidy' and then 'One day I will get my own back'. Natalia said I should ask my mum what it meant but I knew she would only fob me off as she had so many times before. For some reason I knew straight away that he was my father."

Whilst Becky had been talking she kept her head lowered, her eyes focussing on the floor in front of her, but she seemed confident. She paused briefly, and as the seconds ticked away she became aware of the silence. She took one deep sigh, raised her eyes in their direction but did not appear to look at them directly.

Instead she seemed to look right thorough them as if they weren't even there. Ruby shivered at the thought that she was watching and listening to a ghost.

"So we had his name and we knew what he looked like. It seemed that he was only a few years older than me. Mid-thirties at the most and very good looking with kind eyes, big blue eyes and at that very moment I felt really chuffed."

Again Becky paused for a few seconds but this time she looked directly at Ruby with a half-smile forming across her mouth. "Stupid wasn't I, just like you, but I had the guts to do something about it. My only regret is that I left it too late, too late for Natalia that is and now I think I hate myself almost as much as I hate him."

The smile was gone now and in its place Becky's face took on a much darker, more intense expression. Ruby watched closely and saw herself in Becky's face and she shivered at the thought and her own recollections of being humiliated and betrayed. Becky returned Ruby's piercing eye contact not challenging her to look away first, but seeking to understand what thoughts were going through her head and wondering if she had guessed correctly. Almost at the same time she thought about something completely different. She thought about Natalia and the last time they had met. "Natalia says she is getting over it, but I'm not so sure."

"Just tell us what happened."

Becky looked at Ruby again. "We had the photograph and we had a name so we had something to go on. We found something straight away on the internet. But that didn't help a great deal. Well not at first anyway. It was coincidence really."

"What was?"

"The fact that I knew Natalia. It wasn't easy for any of them. They got the odd job here and there but it was all a struggle. I met up with some of them, the ones from Romania, and knew that there were blokes around who tried to get them involved…. in dodgy work, I mean."

"Yes, I can understand that," Ruby responded simply.

"But I don't want to go into too much detail, it's all too distressing, sorry."

This time it was Graham who responded. "Ok, we don't need the detail, just take your time and tell us what you want to, ok?"

"It's just that one day Natalia was messing about, it was soon after we found the photograph."

"And…?"

"And one of Natalia's friends said she recognised him – my dad that is."

"That was one hell of a coincidence wasn't it?" Graham said.

"If you don't believe me just say so, but I'm telling you the truth."

"It's not that we don't believe you," Ruby replied.

"Well it sounds like it," Becky shot back with more than a hint of venom in her voice.

"Sorry, ok, just tell us what happened."

"Well, not much, they didn't talk about it again. But a few weeks later Natalia seemed distant, much quiet than usual. I asked her a few times what the matter was."

"And what did she say?"

"'You don't want to know.' That's what she said and of course I was even more curious then. It took me a while to get anything out of her."

"But she told you in the end?"

"Bits and pieces. And then she just vanished. None of her friends seemed to know where she was and it was some time before I heard from her."

Ruby and Graham, sitting side by side, looked across at Becky sitting alone on the other settee. She seemed small and frail and she was fidgeting with her hair. They both nodded encouragement for her to continue.

"They were making videos – not just porn ones, more than that. Natalia had found out she could make good money and had gone along thinking it wouldn't do any harm, but it got out of hand apparently and my father was right in the middle of it, the most sadistic one."

Ruby moved over and sat next to Becky on the other settee, putting a comforting arm around her shoulder. "It's ok Becky," she said. "Almost there."

"But it's your boyfriend we're talking about. It's all because of him, the sick bastard."

"Just tell us what you have to. That's all. Don't worry about us."

"I'm not worrying about you, you've still got your looks, that's more than Natalia has. You should see what they did to her."

Ruby was beginning to tremble and Becky noticed straight away. They were sitting close, side by side, and Becky turned her head very deliberately so that she could look directly into Ruby's eyes. "You must have realised something?"

Ruby did not respond immediately, she just sat, head bowed. "I've been wrong about people before," she said eventually in a whisper so quiet that Graham didn't hear what she said.

"I've not seen Natalia for a while, but me and mum will visit her again soon. She is back in Romania, still trying to get over it."

Becky looked weary, but she obviously wanted to finish all of her explanations and then get out of Ruby's life. "Mum told me that I had been conceived the very same evening Helen went missing. They had sex just the once apparently and never got together again. What with everything going on, the search for Helen, the police and all that, no one seemed to live a normal life for the next few months and then when she told her mum and dad that she was pregnant they just wanted to get away from it all and it was then that the family moved up north. She didn't even tell Philip that she was pregnant."

Ruby fidgeted on the settee, trying to get more comfortable. She had a stiff neck from looking at Becky next to her but she didn't want to do anything to distract Becky from completing her story.

"Mum always had her doubts about Philip – wondered whether he knew more about Helen's disappearance than he let on. Maybe that he was actually involved in some way. At least that's what she told me. And then this business with Natalia. That just made me…" Becky sat with a glazed look on her face and paused for a moment. "I just wanted to kill him," she said eventually in a cold calculating voice. "Then me and mum came up with this plan. I thought it would kill two birds with one stone, you know what I meant. We decided to stitch him up, you see," Becky went on. "I'm the girl who went missing in Méribel. I'm Amanda."

Chapter 36

He sat on the park bench looking out towards the millpond. It was overgrown now, with patches of stinging nettles and brambles fighting for the space to thrive – neither was winning and it was the ones that grew there before that were struggling now for footholds.

It was mid-afternoon and it had been a reasonably warm and sunny day for the time of year but now a slight chill began to creep up on him as he decided what to do next. He was relatively calm, especially in the knowledge that one decision, the final decision, the most important one, had already been made. His plans had been developed over a considerable period of time and he had been meticulous in his preparations. The financial side had been the most problematic as he wrestled with ways to generate as much capital as possible without raising too much suspicion. It often meant that he needed to deal with people who themselves had something to hide but none perhaps more than he had, and they were the ones he could trust the least. Yet it had to be done. Over a number of months he had accumulated a not insignificant sum through the sale of his bungalow, the liquidation of his drawdown pension pot and the transfer of his current account, now held safely in an off-shore bank account and all under his new identity. It would keep him in relative luxury for the rest of his life and all he had to do was to make his final move.

Before these financial plans could be finalised he needed a new identity. He often sat in front of the fire at night with a glass of whisky in his hand, thinking, planning, scheming. He had noticed that a film *Day of the Jackal* was in the TV programme and he recalled the way in which the Edward Fox character took the identity of someone whose name and details he got from a gravestone. But almost immediately that idea was cast aside. 'Keep it simple' he thought to himself but at that stage he wasn't sure what his approach would be. In the end he had decided on the name Jason Truelove. That was his second cousin's name and he began undertaking the process of collecting all the important documents. His second cousin lived alone in a fairly remote area and everything about him and his living arrangements made the tasks easier. Birth certificate, income tax references, credit and debit card details and finally the treasured passport. He even managed to get utility bills and NHS identity details to complete the picture.

Peter Lord had asked him once what his strategy was for survival. Without a second thought he had replied "I always have a plan, mostly about keeping my enemies in sight, in front of me. That way they can't stab me in the back and if I know where they are, I can blame them if something goes wrong."

"Is it just your enemies you want to keep close, what about your friends?" Peter had asked casually and without any particular implication.

Jim Packer had a clear memory of this brief conversation as he sat thinking about his future and his good fortune. It was ironic, he thought, that it should have been Peter who asked the question because it was almost a prophesy come true.

His gaze now fell upon one of the other benches in the clearing. A bench that had a particular place in his memory. There was nothing about it that made it stand out in any particular way and a casual observer would not have given it a further glance. But for Jim Packer it held special memories – the memory of good fortune and foresight. He remembered following Peter and Spencer that night to this very spot, keeping just the right distance behind them and using his police surveillance training to good effect. In fact he was particularly gifted in his ability to melt into the background and he had used that ability, not just professionally.

He was aware that Peter and Spencer didn't usually spend long periods of time together in these secluded places and just before he left he saw them move apart, with Peter throwing down the condom he had worn and then clumsily and with embarrassment pulling up his trousers and adjusting his zip. Jim watched as Peter and Spencer drove out of the car park and round the corner one in front of the other. He assumed they were heading for the Blacksmith's Arms, a country pub not too far away where he had followed them on previous occasions. Tonight, however, he would leave them to their own devices and he knew that he had a couple of hours before Peter would meet up with him later in the evening.

Jim had seen Helen Grant from a distance many times and she was just the sort of girl he absolutely loved to watch. He had been especially lucky on two occasions when she had been with one of the boys who were always hanging about. On the first occasion when he had watched his view had been partly obscured and he felt somewhat frustrated. However, he had seen glimpses of Helen kissing the boy and then she sat back on the bench just a few yards away with her arms outstretched and her eyes closed. The boy had unbuttoned Helen's blouse and moved his hand inside to cup her breast. Jim's excitement and his own arousal grew in anticipation of what might happen next, but all of a sudden Helen and the boy moved position and were then mainly out of his view. On the second occasion Jim was sure that a different boy was involved, and that time he could hear, see and enjoyed everything that had taken place.

Jim's main pleasure was in watching from afar, but just occasionally he could not resist seeking a more active role. He knew he needed to select such opportunities very carefully and there had been only one other occasion when he had taken matters further.

There had been other times when he had planned everything in advance and then waited for the right moment to put those preparations into effect, but everything that needed to fall into place had eluded him in some minor detail. He was not someone who would act on impulse or to deviate from a planned course of action. That was asking for trouble he thought. He smiled to himself again and recalled that the psychological profile provided by the so-called expert referred to the likelihood that the suspect in Helen Grant's abduction would act on the spur of the moment and would take risks. Jim Parker wasn't like that at all.

He had targeted Helen and began his plans even before his observations of her most private sexual experiences but that had been the icing on the cake. He decided where he would strike, the time, the process and most importantly the place where he would take her. There could be only small windows of opportunity when everything would fall into place, but he was prepared to wait or to cancel everything completely if necessary. Then on 17th March 2003 everything came together. He had followed Peter and Spencer that evening and had watched them together for a short while. He did not get any personal sexual pleasure from watching their intimate moments or in fact from seeing adult men and women together. His sole sexual pleasure came from watching the sexual experiments of young teenagers, as if he was reliving his own first clumsy adventures into his very early conquests.

Jim was about to follow the same path he had taken a few times before in the hope of seeing Helen on her own and just for once he felt lucky. That made him stop and think for a while and all of a sudden he remembered the discarded condom. His thought processes moved up a gear and he became more focussed. The possibility became highlighted in his mind and a plan of action formed quickly. He knew immediately what he needed to do and he set about the process in a calm and efficient manner. He knew exactly where the discarded condom was located and despite the poor light he was able to find it without any difficulty. He put on the protective gloves and took out one of the evidence bags he kept in his jacket pocket when he was on duty. The area was completely deserted and in no time at all Jim was walking away with the evidence placed carefully in his inside jacket pocket. It was too good an opportunity to miss and it wasn't as if he had a particular choice, the opportunity was there and he had taken it. It wasn't long before everything else fell into his lap.

His thoughts turned to a quotation which came forward in his memory from time to time. 'Oh what a tangled web we weave when first we practise to deceive' and he mouthed the words almost inaudibly, over and over. He was in no doubt now that he had spun a web that could only trap and deceive those who might be looking or asking questions about him. He also felt confident that he would not be the one who would end up being trapped in the middle of the web, but he was about to place someone else in that unenviable position.

And then he saw her in exactly the right place. Helen was clearly on her own and was walking towards him along the narrow path just a short distance from the car park. Despite the cool weather she wore a short black skirt and a little jacket over what appeared to be a light-coloured blouse with a high neck. He noticed the slim pink shapely legs as they passed and she looked at him in a slightly hesitant way and he nodded briefly in response. Soon after they had passed each other he stopped, took out a white coloured cloth and tipped a small amount of liquid on it from a bottle he had in his jacket bottle. Then in one action he turned and moved towards her retreating figure, grabbing her from behind and placing the white cloth firmly across her mouth and nose. Almost immediately her legs began to buckle and the brief cry she made sat on the wind sounding no more than a bird call. All he then had to do was to scoop her up, carry her to his car parked just a few yards away and place her in the boot – legs bent, arms folded and her pretty hair all over the place. In a flash he was in his car and driving away.

He drove well within the speed limit down Buckhurst Avenue, heading the short distance out of town towards the new bypass under construction. Then all his other careful planning began to pay dividends. He knew the way – every twist and turn – and he knew exactly where he was going and what he would find when he got there. Parts of the by-pass were busy during the day, but usually there was no one around after about 5.30 pm except the main site office at the far end. Even so, he had selected a location that he had observed was not currently used at all and was very out of the way. An old workman's hut, brought to the site at the very beginning and not used at all for a very long time. It was perfect for his purposes.

He didn't want to leave any trace at all on the rough pathway and had found out on his previous visits – some on foot – that the ground was well impacted, rocky and, even when wet, did not leave hardly a trace of car tyre marks. None-the-less he decided to stop from time to time on his way back to brush away what little evidence he might have left. He also did the same at the point when he stopped outside the dingy hut.

Helen was beginning to moan slightly as he opened the boot and he wafted the white cloth around her mouth and nose again sending her back into the trance – like state she had been in before. He carried her to the hut and through the door he had opened earlier and placed her carefully on a large blanket on a raised area at the back of the room. He took out some duct tape he had put in a bin beside the blanket, tore off a strip, and covered her mouth just as she was beginning to come round again. He liked it when she began to whimper and he delayed covering her mouth for a few seconds so that he could hear the short panting sighs she made – similar to those he had seen and heard her make when she had been with the boy in the summerhouse.

But even when his mind was occupied about conquest and his own sexual satisfaction, the other part of him was never switched of completely – the part securing his safety – the rational logical side that protected him. He had placed a large plastic sheet in the boot of his car and had wrapped this around her when he had lifted her up and out of the boot of his car. That same plastic sheet was now between her and the blanket.

Helen was closer now to being fully conscious and the terror was mounting in her eyes. Jim quickly tied her arms behind her back and moved her just a little so that she was propped up against some old sacks filled with what looked like sand or gravel, but still with the plastic and blanket beneath and behind her. He sat on a few pallets just a few feet away and watched, sensing how frightened and vulnerable she was. That pleased him. "Just do everything I say and you will be ok," he said and she shook her head, craned her neck and mumbled the only guttural sounds she could make against the gag across her mouth. All of a sudden he moved towards her as she tried to stand up. He didn't need to use much force to push her back and as he knelt in front of her, just short of arm's length away, he reached out and placed his hand on her left breast gently and deliberately almost as though he was watching someone else touch her in that way. Helen took a sharp intake of breath and shivered slightly, squinting her eyes shut as if to make herself believe that this wasn't happening to her. She struggled even more as he reached out with both hands this time and began unbuttoning the high-necked blouse she was wearing until it gaped open revealing a white bra with pretty pink stitching around the cup. "I'll take off the gag," he said, "if you promise not to make a noise," but she didn't respond in any way. "Up to you." Helen was struggling to breath and she was beginning to panic. Her need for air increased as her body reacted to his touch and her fear mounted. She nodded slightly and to her surprise he moved away from her again, sat on the pallets silently for a short while and then said, "Say please," in a mocking tone with his teeth clenched in a forced grin. Helen bowed her head – she didn't want to look into his eyes – short jagged breathes spluttered from her nose. Panic was mounting within her as she felt she was about to suffocate and a tiny movement of her head turned into a nod. Jim moved forward again, this time placing a restraining hand just above her bare knee and below the hem of her short skirt that had risen up revealing her underwear. He watched his own hand as he moved it slowly up her leg but then almost immediately he took it away and in the same movement moved it up towards the tape on her mouth. "If you make any noise you will definitely regret it. You know what I mean don't you?" The words were not delivered harshly and were no more than a whisper as his face came close to her own. He ripped off the tape in one short deliberate pull and Helen took a deep breath through her mouth and then started to sob.

"It's ok, it's ok," he said.

"Please, please," she whispered back "Please let me go – I won't say anything I promise."

"I'll leave the tape off. Just do as I tell you, that's all," he said. "Then I'll let you go – I promise."

It wasn't long before Jim had done everything he wanted. He sat back on the pallets from time to time just to watch her as she was forced to repeat the words he asked her to say. He hadn't undressed himself at all except for taking off his jacket. He just wanted to touch and watch himself touching her. But more importantly he didn't want to leave any evidence of intimacy behind. He looked at his watch and realised that he didn't have much time left. He wanted to ensure that he didn't have to rush at all and that he could get back before Peter was likely to arrive at their meeting point.

He was sorry that his fun was coming to an end but he knew he had to put in motion the stages he had planned so carefully. He sat back and took one more look, one more long gaze taking in every detail. Helen had done everything he had asked, just occasionally pleading with him to let her go and making small whimpering sounds from time to time. "Ok, you can go now," he said eventually and she believed him. "I think I can hear someone coming outside," he said.

"Just pull the blanket over your head and hide for a minute in case they look in." Helen wasn't sure at first, but then she quickly pulled the plastic and blanket around her and ducked her head inside. "That's a good girl," he said. "Won't be long now."

Jim knew that he could not let her go, but he didn't want to look into her eyes when he made his final move. The whole of his body weight crashed onto her small frame preventing her from struggling at all and knocking the breath from her lungs. As she made the small efforts she could to breathe his powerful hands prevented her from inflating them again and soon it was all over.

Jim stood up briefly, took some items from his jacket pocket and then knelt down in front of her. With just his thumb and index finger he took hold of the corner of the blanket and moved it away slightly. He saw her hair first and not much else. Then he put on the protective gloves he had placed on the floor in front of him before moving more of the blanket and revealing the lower part of her body. He carefully located the used condom he had placed next to the gloves and then squeezed some of the contents around her pubic hairs and down inside her. He picked up her panties and placed then next to the area he had contaminated with DNA. Then he covered her very carefully again and prepared to move on to the next stage of his plan.

Later that evening after he had completed all of his tasks, he made sure that he was involved in the search that he knew would begin that night. But, more importantly, it was early next morning that he made sure that his allocated task was the one he had already mapped out for himself. "I'll take the area down towards Buckhurst Avenue," he called out as the proposals for a wider search away from the park were discussed. Peter Lord and another officer were also allocated areas on the northern side. "Best drive out and then swing back so we cover the area twice," Jim called out to Peter as he left the car park and took exactly the same route he had followed the night before. As he was leaving the car park he saw the forensic team arrive in their van.

Jim made straight for the old workman's hut and stopped as close as possible to the place he had parked his car before. He got out, sniffed the air and looked around with exaggerated emphasis. After waiting a short while he took out his mobile phone and called Pauline Brinkstead. "Hi Pauline – could you come down straight away and do a forensic search down here?" and he gave her the directions. "It looks just the sort of place where Helen might have been taken."

Jim didn't have to wait long before Pauline and one of her colleagues arrived. "I've only had a quick look inside. Thought it best to leave everything else to you. I know what you're like," he called out. "I'll have a look over there."

"Ok, but don't go stamping about with your big boots." Pauline and Eddie Short began their painstaking work inside the hut. They had not been allocated any other areas to comb and were happy to have something tangible to do. "Thanks Jim – leave it all to us now," Pauline called out to him.

Although Jim was satisfied that not one small trace of Helen would be found either inside or outside the hut, he knew that there had to be a risk and his heart drummed within his chest until the tension began to lift.

"I think we've done all we can here now Pauline said as she walked over to him. She was wearing an all-white, head-to-toe protective garment. Even her shoes were covered with what looked like plastic bags and they were pulled tight around her ankles by an elasticated drawstring. Jim smiled as he saw her plod over towards him.

"We need to be certain. Are you absolutely sure?"

"Yes, positive," Pauline replied.

"I've been thinking," Jim said. "This is just the right sort of place. If someone took her it couldn't be more perfect."

"It's clear I tell you," Pauline shot back.

"But we need to be sure, absolutely sure before we sign it off," Jim looked around, kicking a few lose stones with the toe of his shoe which he noticed were already covered in dirt. The ground was just a little damp, typical of early spring, but the area they had parked on was hard packed and relatively dry. Jim wanted to draw attention to a particular area and he walked a few paces towards it, kicking a few more lose stones as he went being careful not to scuff the shiny toe cap. "Let's just think this through. If I'm right, he'd have to bring her by car."

"Yes, I agree."

Jim lifted his chin just a bit and looked around him as Pauline followed the direction of his gaze and she began picking up on his enthusiasm. "Just a tad older than my oldest," she said as she looked directly into Jim's eyes. "You got any kids then?" she said.

"No, but if I had I certainly wouldn't want them ending up in a place like this."

"Yeh, I know what you mean. Come on then let's get this done."

Pauline called over to Eddie who was standing by a small wooden bench table. He had brought the cardboard box they had taken to the workman's hut and placed the lid carefully on top. Eddie was just about to say something but his intended words were interrupted. "I know it's your last day, but stop daydreaming. This is important. It's always important."

Eddie was getting used to this now. He hadn't wanted to serve out all of his month's notice and was longing to set off on his new adventure. "Ok. What do you want me to do?"

"Just be diligent, pay attention and record everything properly and carefully," Pauline had told him, almost in a motherly way, which Eddie took exception to.

Almost an hour later they had done all they could. An evidence box contained the few samples they had found. Eddie had played his part. He had taken photographs, collected and recorded a few items and generally he had looked busy. In fact he was bored and keen to get away. He saw Pauline and Jim standing by the bench seat and Jim picked up his coat before they moved away as he approached. Eddie stood for a moment or two watching their retreating figures "I'll make my own way back," he had called out and he saw Jim raise his arm in response. Then something on the bench caught his eye and he picked it up. "Is this part of our collection?" he called out as they walked away but his words were lost in the wind. "Please yourself," he called out but with no real strength to his voice and by that stage he didn't really care. He picked up the item and tossed it casually into an otherwise empty box, squashed the box flat with his foot and put it in a black bin liner which contained some other rubbish.

Jim was remembering all of the details of his time with Helen as he sat on the bench now. Although he felt confident that he had thought of everything at the time there was still one thing he recalled that unsettled him. Just one thing he wasn't certain about, it was that uncertainty which contributed to his decision to disappear. He might still have made that choice if he had no doubts at all, because that was the safest choice and he was a very careful man. Each of his carefully planned stages all these years ago now raced through his mind. He had hidden Helen's body well and knew that concrete would be poured in the area of the drainage shaft within hours, the false number plates he had used on his car that night had been carefully disposed of, he had taken the blanket and plastic sheet to a safe place and seen them burned before his eyes, alongside all the clothes he had worn and he had sold the car long ago to someone in Scotland. He felt relaxed about everything, but he knew how easy it was to make a mistake. But there was one thing he couldn't remember, he couldn't recall checking that the evidence bag containing the used condom and protective gloves he had worn had been in the jacket pocket before it was consumed by flames. He could remember taking his jacket off and leaving it on the bench seat near the workman's hut and then putting the used and unused duct tape in the pocket when he returned from disposing of Helen's body. He just wondered now whether or not the evidence bag had fallen out when he did so. Still too late to do anything about it now, and he was comforted to some extent by the fact that nothing had been said about it at all either at the time or subsequently.

Before Jim moved from the bench overlooking the millpond he had one more decision to make – the last important one of the day. Everything else had been decided and lodged clearly in his mind. He had to decide whether or not to go to his preferred spot near the summerhouse and take up his hidden viewing position. He had seen two young girls and two boys heading that way and he was sure he had watched them there before. All of a sudden he stood up, lifted his chin up slightly as if sniffing the air around him and his decision had been made. 'Riding his luck' was one thing he thought 'Pushing it' was something completely different. Without a second thought or backward glance he walked back to his car and started his journey to Stansted Airport.

Chapter 37

Andy Blackstone was feeling calm and relaxed, a welcome break from the usual problems he faced and he wanted to take full advantage of it while he could. The pain distracted him and it was a relief to be free from its clutches. George Baker had visited and told him about the misconduct notices they had all received and it saddened him. Now he wanted to see an end to it all, to be there when the killer was finally identified and brought to justice. That would give him special satisfaction and it would be an added bonus if he could be part of that process. George had told him about DC Lucy Atkinson being seconded to work with the new team. He did not know much about her but George had said that she was good. They were all on the outside now, not privy to information, not receiving every scrap of evidence as it came in and that put them at a disadvantage. Andy was hopeful that Lucy could help fill that gap. He decided to contact her.

"Is that DC Atkinson?" Andy said when he heard a female voice answer his telephone call. Andy explained who he was and that he had information that might be useful to the investigation team. "Could you pop over to see me do you think, I'm not so good getting out these days." That wasn't entirely true of course, but he wanted to meet Lucy in familiar surroundings, a place where he felt comfortable and relaxed.

"I'll have to check with my DI but I don't expect any problems," Lucy responded "But can you tell me what sort of information you have?"

"Not happy talking on the phone. Need to see you face to face. Sure you understand," Andy replied, not giving Lucy any real alternative.

It was just over an hour later when Lucy phoned back and she told Andy that she would see him straight away. Now Andy was watching out for her arrival, standing by the window and trying not to make it too obvious. He felt strangely excited and more alive than usual and his heartrate quickened as he saw Lucy's petite figure get out of her car and walk almost timidly up towards his front door.

Andy wasn't sure exactly what Lucy would look like and how she would behave, but she was nothing like any of the pictures he had formed in his mind. She was pretty, petite and friendly, but he could tell straight away that she had an inner strength and he warmed to her immediately.

"Well, what have you got for me?" Lucy said when the introduction had been completed and they were sitting facing each other.

"It's more a question of what we can do for each other. I only know what I've been told and there are probably lots of details you can add, particularly anything recent."

"Perhaps we will come to that in a minute or two. I thought you said you had something specific to say."

Andy thought for a while, mulling over all of the details and particularly the issues he had discussed with George Baker just over a week ago now. "It's probably nothing really," and he paused slightly, "but I've had this feeling for some time. You know everything, about us I mean, the secrets we've all kept these past sixteen years."

"Yes. I know everything, I know all about that."

Andy looked directly into Lucy's eyes. He thought he detected a slight hesitancy, just a flicker, nothing more, but it encouraged him. He wanted to find out what she knew and, in that split second, he believed that there was something. It hadn't been an obvious signal but he was still good at reading people and now he decided to trust his instincts. He let out one huge sigh and then another.

"I've always though one of us, one of us coppers I mean, knew a lot more than they wanted everyone to believe."

"Yes," Lucy prompted simply.

Andy was reluctant to say the name. He had no real proof, just a hunch, but he had bottled it up long enough. "Jim Packer," he said eventually. "He was the only one who knew about everyone else. All the little secrets. I'm not saying he did it, kill Helen I mean, but he knows something, I'm sure of it."

"We are coming to the same conclusion, but not for the same reasons," Lucy said.

"So, what other reasons are there? Do you have something definite?"

Lucy had been told to be careful and not to give too much away. The DI had been most insistent and she thought about that now. "I can't go into the details, but Banik's come up with some new DNA evidence. We think we have enough but we are not sure yet."

"If it's him, or if he is shielding someone else, he could be one step ahead. We can't hold back now."

"It's out of my hands I'm afraid," Lucy said and her voice was tinged with regret.

"It needs someone to rattle his cage. See what reaction we get. Why not knock on his door? That might prompt a response."

"We can't do that unless we are ready to arrest him. You know that as well as I do."

"But I could," Andy said.

Chapter 38

Andy Blackstone was sitting in his car waiting for the schoolchildren to cross in front of him. He had ignored Lucy's suggestion that he should leave everything to the police and now he was heading in the direction of Morton Avenue where Jim Packer lived. When the road was clear he moved off and he began rehearsing in his mind what he intended saying to Jim when he opened the door. It had been a long journey he thought but now it was coming to an end; he just hoped that it wouldn't be too late.

He soon passed a pub on his right and continued up the hill. He hoped that Jim Packer would be in but he had decided not to telephone in advance believing that a personal visit would have more impact if it was unannounced. Although the evidence now seemed to point more directly at Jim there was still the feeling within him that there might be other possibilities and he didn't rule them out completely. The forensic evidence against Peter Lord and Spencer Cassidy could not be overlooked just yet and the lies they told about their whereabouts was another incriminating factor. Andy was therefore hoping for a reaction from Jim Packer when he knocked on his door.

Andy had by this stage moved further up the hill, past a children's play area to his right and was now outside number 57. He stopped, looked over his shoulder to see if there was anyone about, got out of his car and walked as confidently as she could up to the front door and knocked.

The man answering the door was nothing like Jim Packer. He was younger, thicker set and considerably shorter. Andy was taken by surprise for a moment. "Is Jim Packer in by any chance?" he eventually said. "Too late mate. He moved out over a week ago."

Chapter 39

Jim Packer looked up at the large display sign. There was just over an hour to go before his flight time and he saw that his boarding gate was displayed. He only had hand luggage and he had kept that to a minimum. This small holdall now swung easily from side to side as he made his way casually down towards the boarding gates. He stopped at the gents' toilet briefly mainly to see if anyone followed him in. He wasn't expecting to be followed but he just wanted to be sure. He had a pee, washed and dried his hands, all the time being aware of people around him. There weren't many people about and everyone was intent on their own business, either rushing in and out, or taking their time and gossiping with friends.

Jim had chosen Stansted Airport carefully. He had never used it before and that was his first consideration. Depart from somewhere unfamiliar and head to a destination never previously visited. That was the plan and his flight to Ljubljana was perfect he thought, as was the series of bus and tube journeys he took to get to the airport. He even wore a hat and scarf pulled up high around his neck. As he approached the gate for his flight he took off his hat and scarf and looked around for somewhere to sit. There were plenty of seats and he chose one directly opposite two young women waiting for the 13.05 EasyJet flight that would whisk them off to Slovenia. "Might as well have something nice to look at," he thought and he began to concentrate on the taller one of the two. A single pearl earring sat neatly in the lobe of her ear and the sweep of her neck flowed towards a delicate mole just above the swell of her right breast. She caught his eye briefly and he looked away towards the EasyJet boarding gate which had just started to come to life. He decided to sit and wait until most of the other passengers had queued and boarded. He had booked an aisle seat in row 11, so taking his seat on the plane and finding a space for his small holdall wouldn't be a problem.

The two young women were long gone by the time he made a move, leaving behind them just a hint of perfume and he followed their scent until it disappeared in the walkway. Jim Packer wasn't anxious, but he was aware. He didn't expect to be missed until he was well on his way and even then he was sure they wouldn't even begin to consider the real motive behind his disappearance. All his planning assumed, however, that either sooner or later, his colleagues would begin tracking him down.

The woman in the seat next to him had a strong Irish accent and he had listened to her chatting away to her son in the window seat. The boy, who was well behaved, was mixed race, about ten years old and was wearing a white football shirt. "Probably a Spurs supporter," Jim thought, although his own knowledge of Premier League football was limited.

"You going skiing?" the woman said and it was a second or two before Jim realised that she was talking to him.

"No, just meeting some friends," he replied reluctantly. He didn't really want to get into any conversations, preferring to remain as anonymous as possible.

But the woman didn't notice his reluctance "We're visiting family."

"That's nice," he replied and he turned slightly to look at her properly for the first time. She had a pretty face he noticed but her blonde hair was swept back from her forehead almost too harshly. Her Irish accent seemed even more pronounced, but it didn't seem too harsh for Jim's ear. Any other time he would have been more than happy to chat away aimlessly but now he just wished to be left alone. "Hope it goes well though," Jim said eventually and with that he got up, stretched and made his way down the aisle to the toilets. He took his time hoping that the woman's attention would be diverted in his absence and he was in luck as she was preoccupied with the in-flight magazine when he got back to his seat. The cabin crew came around with drinks and he ordered a coffee with milk and a chocolate bar. He had had a good meal at the airport and now he was happy with just a snack. He finished his coffee and then sat in silence for a while. His thoughts were only interrupted by the announcement by the captain that they had begun their descent into Ljubljana Airport and would be landing in about 20 minutes. Jim had already decided that he would catch the free shuttle bus from the airport to the main bus station in Ljubljana and then take the local service bus to Bohinjska Bela, a small village just north of Lake Bled. He had selected the village partly because of its pretty name but mainly because it was out of the way and had a number of small properties for short-term rent. They arrived at Lake Bled after numerous local stops and then headed to the top end of the lake and past a large imposing villa. They continued heading north for a few miles along narrow roads which gave way to a short stretch of dual carriageway. At that point there was a delay and they slowed to a walking pace. There had been a landslide covering at least half of the road and a taxi was parked by the rubble and the driver was directing the traffic through the area, which was made even more difficult as a bulldozer was positioned across the road ready to push the debris down the slope on the right hand side. As they approached he looked directly at Jim and gave a thumbs-up sign and Jim smiled weakly in response. Jim wasn't sure exactly where his stop was and he started to move to the front hoping to catch the driver's eye. He had given his destination to the driver when he got on at the bus station and now he heard the name Bohinjska Bela called out over the driver's shoulder in his direction.

That night he retired early having had a lovely mixed grill dinner enough for four people he thought as he struggled to finish it, and a bottle of red wine that had just the right amount of acidity to cut through the rendered fat of the meat. The early stages of sleep soon descended on him and there were moments when he felt he had some control of his thoughts but that control soon melted away pleasantly. It wasn't long however before seeds of doubt started to flicker across his subconscious mind. He awoke suddenly and concentrated hard, seeking to recall details of the dream he had just experienced and a cold uncomfortable sweat crept up on him. He saw Helen's face now wet with tears and terror, only partly obscured by the untidy mess of hair hanging and clinging to her cheeks, nose and mouth. He didn't feel remorse exactly but he wished there could have been another way.

He got up and went to the toilet, had a drink of water and then returned to the pleasure of his big warm bed. He pulled the covers up and around his chin seeking comfort against the chill of the night. It was a while before he got to sleep again and then he endured a very fitful night.

The room was a blaze of light when he awoke the next morning as the sun rose just above the mountain across the valley. He felt a chill in the air and noticed straight away that something wasn't right. He wasn't sure what it was at first.

He could focus clearly and hear voices coming from the room next door and he could just about lift his head off the pillow. But otherwise he couldn't move and he began to panic. He tried to move his arms and legs but they wouldn't budge, and then the voices became louder and he was aware of a face moving close to his own and the stale warm breath hit his nostrils. He made an attempt to shout out, to scream, to call for help, but not one sound formed within him.

"Hello pussycat," the face close to him said and a thick heavy finger prodded the side of his nose. "Been waiting for you to wake up."

Jim made another huge effort to shout, he called on all his resources to begin forming the sounds deep within his chest, straining every sinew and willing his body to produce the screams he could now hear only in his head. A tear formed in the corner of his eye and started to roll down his cheek. He had always been the one in control, the one calling all the shots, and this lack of control had a particular impact on him. His head began to throb, his eyes hurt and the tears now coming one upon the other seemed like splashes of boiling water against his face.

"You gave him too much of that stuff," the one with the face called over his shoulder and Jim was just able to make out the response as it hung in the air. "No odds really. He's not going to complain." They both laughed loudly and the one with the face tapped Jim's nose again. "Hear that mate – he don't give a damn."

The feeling of having no control continued to overwhelm him. He wanted to call out "Why? How?"

but not even the slightest of sounds formed within him. He was fully conscious, aware what was going on around him, but unable to participate or do anything about it. His inner struggles intensified making him feel that the blood vessels in his temples and forehead would explode with the unreleased pressure. But he just lay there unmoving, eyes bulging and at their complete mercy.

He heard their voices again. "Just get cleared up here and then on our way." "Make sure we've got everything – all the paperwork."

Jim Packer became aware that the one who spoke to him before was coming closer again.

"Thought you were so very clever didn't you?" and this time the chubby finger tapped him on the cheek rhythmically in time with his words. "But all you've done is make it so very easy for us. What a prat."

"Leave him alone," the other one called out but it had no effect.

"Followed you easily enough. Didn't even have to work hard really," and then the face got right up next to his and was almost touching. "Put it in the sole of your shoe – knew you always wore them. Best tracker device on the market."

Jim tried hard to move again but he soon gave up the attempt and the man whose face was close didn't even know that he had made that attempt.

"They'll empty your new bank account – more than enough I'd say. Got to pay our wages as well and we don't come cheap. You should have known there would be consequences. You made too many enemies in Birmingham." Then almost abruptly the face moved away slightly and Jim could see a clenched fist raised as if to strike him, but he could not even blink or flinch in response. "You're not much fun," the man said as he moved further away.

Jim wanted to call back "Another time mate, you wouldn't have got away with any of that," but he could not conjure up the words.

Jim could hear the two men moving about the room and occasionally he caught sight of one of them as he took items from the bedside table and dropped them in a black bin bag.

"I've found the passport, bank card, driving licence and some other papers all in Jason Truelove's name. Anything else?"

"Look in that end pocket in his holdall. Tear out the lining if necessary."

"No, nothing else."

"We only need the stuff to get the money out and that's all in Jason Truelove's name. That's what the boss said."

After a short while the movements around him stopped and he heard a car door slam outside. He had rented a small ski lodge located at the top of a steep slope on the outskirts of the village. It had parking for two cars in the front and a small wooden building to one side which acted as a wood store but which could also house at least one large car. He had returned from the restaurant the previous night by taxi, and he remembered the steep twisting climb and the smell of the car's clutch burning as it took the climb hesitantly. Now he could smell wood smoke and he wondered what they were burning outside.

The two men were chatting away as they returned to his room but he could only hear the end of the conversation. "Let's get him into the car now before the drug wears off."

"Don't worry, he'll be quiet for a couple of hours yet."

"Just do what I tell you."

"No need to make such a fuss – we've got plenty of time."

"We move him now, ok? No messing about," the second man said with steely determination in his voice and there was no further response or objection.

Jim sensed that they were moving closer to him and he could smell their body odour – rancid, pungent and filling his nostrils. He could see, he could smell and he could hear but he couldn't move or make a sound.

"Ready, lift," he heard one of them call out, and he felt himself floating in the air as they each took hold of the sheet under him and half lifted, half dragged him across the bedroom and outside to the area where the cars were parked. He was swaying from side to side as if he was in a hammock. They lifted again and dumped him in the boot of one of the cars. He still couldn't move, but he could see flashes of light and a bright blue sky above him and then the sun's rays hit him fully in the face blinding him temporarily and it was then that he saw her face again – Helen's face, but this time she was smiling in her very special way and the sparkle in her eyes lit up the whole of her face. That vision disappeared in an instant as the boot was slammed shut, popping his ears and plunging him into complete blackness. Now his other senses were obliterated – he couldn't see or hear anything above the sound of the engine as the car started up and moved slowly down the steep slope rocking him from side to side. All he had left was his imagination and that began to play the most agonising trick on him. Then he saw it again, but this time the vision of Helen's face was right up against his own and she was laughing. It seemed so very real to him, so real in fact that he could feel her hot breath on his face and the spit coming from her lips as she goaded him.

The road became less bumpy and it didn't seem long before the car came to a stop. And then he felt hands grabbing at him as the bright light hit his eyes again. Then he was rolling, falling slithering down and dust and debris began filling his nose and mouth. He came to an abrupt stop against some rocks knocking his head and snapping it roughly to one side but the numbness of his body didn't register any pain yet panic was in his mind. His face had been the last one Helen had seen and now she was looking into his eyes again and he knew that her face would be the last he would ever see. Just for a split second he felt movement in his arm and, with all the strength he could muster he reached out to push her away and to scratch out the burning eyes he could see and which stared deep into his own. But as he reached out, all that he began pushing aside were the rocks and dirt raining down on him from the dual carriageway above. He was being buried alive in dust and dirt and he was fully aware of the irony of it all. He was guilty of a brutal and humiliating violation of a perfectly innocent girl and the punishment now being inflicted on him mirrored the torment she must have suffered at the very end – in the darkness, alone, afraid and utterly helpless. But the irony was that he wasn't being punished for his brutality towards Helen. That thought consumed him now and was the very last thing he remembered as he took the last few breaths of his life before utter darkness descended upon him.

Chapter 40

Ruby's appointment with Jason Barnaby was for 11.00 am and she arrived promptly. Her journey had not been without problems, but she had left home early enough to avoid most of the heavy traffic and she was thankful for that. She felt relatively calm, mainly because she felt that she was reaching the end of a journey and that all the uncertainty was behind her now.

"Have a seat. Do you want a coffee or anything?" Jason said as she entered his office and she shook her head in response. Jason sat back in his chair, exhaled and tapped his teeth gently with his left hand. He was wearing a smart grey suit, pink shirt and silver tie. "Quite the professional package," Ruby thought.

"Can't say I'm pleased about the outcome but at least everything's clear now," Jason said at last and this time Ruby nodded in response. She felt strangely detached from it all, almost as though she was watching a play from a position on the stage but taking no part in the proceedings. Relief, acceptance, pleasure even – these were the emotions she was feeling but they were private and she didn't feel the need to share them.

She had met Philip just a few times since she had visited him in hospital and each time it felt she was stepping further away from him. In her mind she envisaged that she was wrapping a parcel with layers of brown paper until the package was so tightly bound that it could never escape and plague her again. It was as if it was now firmly consigned to history.

She knew now that Philip had not been involved in Helen's disappearance but that was no real relief. The police were now pursuing other lines of enquiry and the charge sheet was mounting. It seemed that Philip was likely to go down for a good many years.

Jason Barnaby was now summarising all of that. He did this in his usual efficient way, stopping at various stages to establish that Ruby had understood and then progress to the next point. Finally Jason explained all he knew about the international police search for Jim Packer which, despite considerable efforts, had not been able to establish his whereabouts. "Just seems to have disappeared into thin air," he said at last. Ruby made every effort to convince Jason that she was paying full attention, but to be honest, her mind was elsewhere. She had examined her conscience so many times over the previous week or so, not quite believing that she had been so mistaken about the people she had loved.

"You're going away on a long holiday now I understand – best thing," Jason said and he stood up signifying that the meeting was coming to an end.

For Ruby it was the end of another difficult stage in her life and she had to decide whether to face the future alone. She felt betrayed, vulnerable and reluctant to put her trust in anyone else ever again. The text message she had received from Graham almost a week ago had remained unanswered. He had said that he would always be there for her and she knew that she only had to say the word.

Usually Ruby felt confident about making decisions and sticking with the consequences, but on this occasion she was frightened and hesitant. Her father's death had been traumatic and she desperately missed the opportunity of talking over her problems with him. He had never made decisions for her but always seemed to steer her in the right direction. What she needed now she thought was to get as close as possible to an environment filled with his memories and she knew the ideal place. With that thought in mind and somewhat abruptly she thanked Jason for all of his help, shook his outstretched hand almost absentmindedly and with a clear purpose in mind, turned and walked confidently out of his office, down the corridor and out of the building via the reception area, leaving the clicking of her heels and a hint of perfume behind her.

It wasn't long before she was in her car and heading south. She came to the roundabout she knew well in about ten minutes, hardly noticing the passing of time. She took the slip road and turned left passing the white chalk cliff to her right, she soon reached the tunnel which took her towards the centre of town. She turned left again at the next roundabout passing a large Tudor style house and along into South Street heading towards the river walk. It was a place she knew well and soon she had parked the car at the far end and was walking towards a bench seat looking out over the river. She had often sat there with her father, talking about life, politics and everything else under the sun. She noticed, possibly for the first time, that the seat was dedicated to the memory of Gladys Raward and she wondered if Gladys had ever sat at a spot close by and looked at the view across the pretty town up towards the castle on the hill. Ruby closed her eyes trying to picture her father's face hoping for inspiration. When she opened them again she had her answer. She took out her mobile phone, went to the messages section scrolled down and with just a hint of regret selected the 'delete all' option and watched as the messages disappeared before her. Ruby sat and thought for a while and then she looked down at the phone in her hand. Almost immediately she got up and, with all her might, she threw the phone high into the air and heard it land in the river with a loud plop. She watched as the ripples pushed their way out from the centre and then, one-by-one they faded away into the distance as if they had never existed. She would face the future alone and she sat for a long time wondering what that future might hold for her.

Keith Newman

You have done me a great honour by reading my story and I thank you. I hope you have enjoyed the journey through all the pages. I do want to hear your view – good and bad, so please send me an email with your comments.

Email: keithnewmank850@gmail.com

Keith Newman was born and raised in Lewes, East Sussex and has lived in the area all his life. He attended the Secondary Modern School for boys in the town and he left there a few days after his fifteenth birthday. Keith has a wife, three children and five grandchildren all living in Sussex.